A man on the run
A city on the watch
Magic on the loose

The Lanternlight Chronicles

"You were *meant* for this magic, my dear Whitsun. You have been an instrument in the hands of some higher power."

"The gods, you mean?" Whitsun's tone was scornful.

"If you like. Though personally I prefer to put my faith in men."

Whitsun nodded. "What did I tell you?" he asked Glustred.

Slowly the man turned and stared at him, his blue eyes boring into Glustred's brown ones.

"We are the future."

THE LANTERNLIGHT FILES

THE LEFT HAND OF DEATH

WHEN NIGHT FALLS

DEATH COMES EASY

BY PARKER DEWOLF

EBERRON

THE LANTERNLIGHT FILES

BOOK 1

THE LEFT HAND OF DEATH

PARKER DeWOLF

THE LEFT HAND OF DEATH
The Lanternlight Files · Book 1

©2007 Wizards of the Coast, Inc.

Cover art by Cyril Van Der Haegen
First Printing: July 2007

9 8 7 6 5 4 3 2 1

ISBN: 978-0-7869-4713-3
620-21532740-001-EN

U.S., CANADA,
ASIA, PACIFIC, & LATIN AMERICA
Wizards of the Coast, Inc.
P.O. Box 707
Renton, WA 98057-0707
+1-800-324-6496

EUROPEAN HEADQUARTERS
Hasbro UK Ltd
Caswell Way
Newport, Gwent NP9 0YH
GREAT BRITAIN
Save this address for your records.

Visit our web site at www.wizards.com

DEDICATION

For my mother
1921 - 2006

ACKNOWLEDGMENTS

To Mark Sehestedt, my editor, I owe a debt for clean, conscientious editing that made the story better in every respect. There are many others for whose support and friendship I am grateful.

To Calye, I owe a debt for much good advice and good sense, both about this book and about everything else.

CHAPTER 1

The young man's hands beat out a nervous rhythm on the rail. From time to time he passed a silken handkerchief over his forehead or touched it to his face as if breathing in its perfume. His eyes flickered from one side to the other.

Above him came a rosy light that suffused him in its glow, turning his face and hands a dark scarlet. Shadows passed over and beside him, and several times he started at one, staring around him until he detected its source. The air was filled with a low, ominous rumble that occasionally quickened to a roar then died away into a sullen growl as if some great beast were bearing the weight of the city on its shoulders and protesting its ill-fated role at carrying the strain of millions upon millions of tons of soil, masonry, and flesh—human and less than human.

He turned and stared out over the rail. Before him was an inferno of fiery metal that poured in an unceasing waterfall a quarter-mile wide. Great sheets and chunks of iron, twisting and whirling in the currents, hung for a moment on the brink

1

of infinity then crashed over the edge, disappearing into an unknown depth from which came the distant roar of the mighty furnaces of the Cogs. The young man put the scrap of silk before his face and breathed again, straining out fumes that were potent enough to make almost anyone stagger. From where he stood, he could only dimly glimpse the other side of the chasm: a rocky wall that ascended to a distant ledge from which unseen observers controlled the great flow of metal in the foundry at the heart of Sharn.

Bridges here and there spanned the chasm—slender threads of metal, magically inured against the heat. In several places these turned into long flights of stairs ascending or descending above the flow. Figures passed along these bridges and up and down the stairs, most too far away for the young man to discern anything about them. Now and again one would come close enough for him to see a few details, but for the most part the area of the cavern in which he stood was deserted.

The man wiped his forehead again. Sweat drenched his thin frame. Elegantly clothed, he was unaccustomed to such conditions. For the twentieth time he pulled a small device from his waistcoat pocket and checked it. The result dissatisfied him, for he shook his head, replaced the device, and started with a half cry as a voice spoke from behind him.

"Master d'Cannith?"

The young man nodded. "Rranstrewth! You startled me!"

The other made no response. The young man examined his features closely. The newcomer stood, weight balanced on both feet, resting on his heels, hands by his sides. His dark thinning hair swept back from a high forehead that bore no traces of sweat despite the overwhelming heat of the Cogs.

"You're Ulther Whitsun!" the young man exclaimed with an air of triumph at an unexpected discovery. "I met you last year at the *lovely* ball to celebrate the opening of the Karrnathi Embassy."

Whitsun gave no acknowledgment, but his companion's features immediately grew more relaxed.

"My House has hired you before," he observed. "In the matter of Lady Showaya's necklace. And, if I recall, we asked you to take care of that *most* unpleasant fellow who was causing us so much trouble about trade regulations with Droaam. Capital! Your reputation *precedes* you, my dear fellow!" He giggled. "And now you're working in the interests of House Vadalis. I suppose you need to pick up money where you can find it, but don't you think you're *slumming* a bit?"

Whitsun reached into the recesses of his cloak. The other exhibited a certain tension that dissipated when Whitsun produced a leather bag. He shook it, and it jingled. For the first time he spoke.

"This is the full amount. As requested." He bit off each word.

D'Cannith took the bag and weighed it in his hand. His other took his handkerchief and again wiped his forehead.

"My dear fellow," he observed, "if we *must* do this sort of business, why not do it somewhere *civilized?* I mean, *the Cogs?* Really! I realize one sees few people down here—few one would *know* at any rate—but still . . ."

"It's all there," Whitsun said. His expression did not change.

The man delved into his waistcoat and produced several sheets of parchment. He handed them with a flourish to Whitsun, still holding the money bag. *"Really,"* he observed. "There was no need to bring *gold*. I can't imagine where I shall secret this tribute, and one hesitates to walk today through the streets of Sharn openly *displaying* this kind of money. Even airships aren't safe."

Whitsun ignored him. He was studying the parchment. He

rubbed the pages between his fingers, sniffed them, and pronounced, "Good." He tucked them in a pouch he carried at his waist.

The other sniffed. "Of *course* it's good. You didn't think we'd try to cheat you, did you? Even our House, low as it has sunk in the postwar era, hasn't sunk *that* low."

Whitsun did not answer. His face had turned pale, and for the first time there was sweat on his brow. He wiped it away with an unsteady hand.

"What's wrong with you?" d'Cannith asked. "This place? Well, my dear fellow, *you're* the one who set this ridiculous site for the exchange. Not my choice, I can tell you." He gestured with the money bag, still clutched in his hand. "Come now, my dear fellow. Straighten up. Let's get out of here to some less beknighted place."

Whitsun bent almost double and retched. His hands clutched the rail. His companion put out his free hand to steady him.

Whitsun came up with startling speed. One hand darted for the money bag, while the other gripped the young man's embroidered sleeve, swinging him around against the rail.

"*Here!*" shouted the young man. "What do you think—?"

Whitsun's other hand twisted d'Cannith's wrist. The latter, with a howl, let go the money bag, which dropped to the ground with a metallic *ching!* The young man ducked and pulled both arms back, leaving Whitsun with his waistcoat. He dropped to a fighter's crouch and from behind his back pulled a dagger.

Whitsun drew no weapon, but he tossed the useless garment over the rail where it disappeared into the blackness and heat. His eyes watched each move by his opponent, searching for an opening.

"You *bastard!*" gasped d'Cannith. "I see what your game is. But if you think you can take one of the dragonmarked—"

He lunged, and Whitsun dodged. D'Cannith went sprawling and slid, headfirst, toward the rail. He dropped his dagger and reached out to grasp Whitsun's leg, pulling him off balance. The two crashed together. Whitsun stamped down at the man's hand. The latter, with no other weapon in his grasp, clutched the bag of coins and swung it at Whitsun. It struck with a dull thud, and Whitsun grunted in pain. D'Cannith raised the bag to strike again, and Whitsun slashed with his dagger while at the same time reaching for the coins.

The coin bag blocked the blow, and from the torn cloth a stream of gold poured over the stone slabs, sliding over the edge into the abyss. Whitsun and d'Cannith both cursed.

D'Cannith grabbed the remains of the bag just as it was about to disappear over the edge forever. His yell of triumph was cut off as he looked up to see Whitsun's boot heel descending on his face. It struck true, propelling him backward. With a shriek, d'Cannith vanished, still clutching the coin bag. Whitsun, on his stomach, thrust his face over the precipice in time to see the dark shape of d'Cannith's body vanish just above the molten metal, as the water in his body turned to steam and exploded him from within.

Whitsun pushed back from the edge and sat up. A few coins still lay on the ground, and he picked these up and stowed them away in a pocket. Then, getting to his feet, he limped off into the darkness without a glance behind.

Along a narrow street in Boldrei's Hearth in the lower central plateau of Sharn, a stream of dirty water trickled down the narrow gutter in the center of the cobblestones. A scrawny cat sniffed at it, decided it wasn't thirsty enough, and turned away. It dodged a pair of hobnailed boots that plodded along the street and with a yowl darted into a nearby alley.

The stream continued, fed by the contents of chamber pots thrown from upper windows of the district and washed along by the steady drip, drip, drip of water falling from far above. Here in the lower parts of Sharn the rain never ceased.

Whitsun turned up his collar and tried to walk as close as possible to the walls where there was some promise of shelter. Flaring torches illuminated a maze of dangling signs: The Blind Orc, The Goblin's Head, The Two Dragons. Groups of ragged men lounged in the doorways of some of the dingier establishments and called in cracked voices to the hoards of passersby, offering goods of doubtful provenance and legality.

Whitsun ignored all such solicitations. He turned in at a doorway with a silver ball dangling over it. The room was bare save for a single scarred wooden desk and a young man sitting behind it with a pale face and hair so blond it was almost white. Behind him a tattered curtain concealed another archway leading to the back.

"Hello, Targon." Whitsun's tone was pleasant and unhurried.

The youth rose slowly, his face, if possible, even paler. "Ulther Whitsun."

"The same." Whitsun looked about the office. "You seem to have kept everything nice and comfortable."

Targon swallowed twice. "I heard you were dead."

"Sorry to disappoint you." Whitsun sat down on a corner of the desk and traced one of the gashes in the wood with a finger. "I know you did your best." There was no animosity in his voice.

The youth's words came in a rush. "It was Dashmiell, Whitsun. Him and the others. I swear. I was only—"

Whitsun lifted a hand. "It's all right, Targon. I'm not really interested." He looked curiously at the curtain. "There wouldn't be anyone back there, would there, Targon?"

The white-haired boy shook his head.

The older man casually walked over and flipped back the curtain. Satisfied, he returned to the desk. "I need to send a message."

Targon nodded and produced a pen and parchment. Whitsun thought for a moment, then wrote swiftly. He signed it and handed it to Targon, who skimmed it with a professional air.

"Right. I'll get this out right away." He cleared his throat. "That's, uh, five galifars."

"Surely not." Whitsun looked at him reproachfully. "Surely you have a discount for old friends?" He stood.

Targon looked up at him then down at the desk. "You're right. Three."

Whitsun reached in his pocket and produced two of the gold galifars from the bag that had been cut in the fight. He laid them side by side on the table. Targon contemplated them for a moment then swept them out of sight.

"That's all then, is it?" He stood with an air of relief.

"Not quite." Whitsun produced from his inner pocket the papers d'Cannith had given him. "I need these kept safe."

Targon backed away hastily. "No! Absolutely not! I know what kinds of papers you carry around. You're not leaving them here!"

"Relax." Whitsun smiled. "I like you too well, Targon, to burden you with something like these." He folded the papers into a packet. From the desktop he took a candle and dripped some wax over the papers' edge. Then, with the speed of a striking snake, he snatched Targon's wrist. The youth gave a yelp, but Whitsun forced his hand down, imprinting the large ring Targon wore into the wax. He released the youth, who backed away. Whitsun drew a quill from a handy inkwell, scribbled an address on the front and laid the completed packet in the precise center of the desk.

"See that gets delivered to me at my office, Targon. It should take a few days to get there. Ten or twelve, if I know the kind of service you and your kind provide. That'll keep it safe and it'll keep me happy. And when I'm happy, you should be happy."

He rose and moved to the door. "Oh, and Targon . . ."

The youth paused in the act of lifting the packet.

"You haven't seen me. And you haven't seen that packet."

Targon nodded, his face still devoid of color. He massaged his wrist slowly.

Out the door, Whitsun dodged a mule train as it rambled through the streets, a sedan chair floating behind it. Some nobleman seeing how the other half lived in the City of Towers. Whitsun's mouth curved in a mirthless smile.

He made his way along the narrow streets. If anyone had been watching him, they would have been hard pressed to follow his figure, though he was not thin and made no apparent effort to conceal his movements. Rather, observers would have found they had an urge to look away, a sudden interest in something else. If any had defied the urge and had followed Whitsun's shadow as it glided along the busy streets, they would have been plagued with a headache and sweaty palms, accompanied shortly thereafter by feelings of nausea that grew steadily stronger until they collapsed wheezing on the curbstones.

Whitsun's strides led him to a dank stone doorway sur-mounted by a crudely carved sculpture that might have been taken by an astute observer for the head of a howling turkey. Above it, a signboard proclaimed, The Bone and Bristle. Below in smaller letters was the legend, "Urmas Glustred, Prop." A sign to the left of the stone archway leading into the inn's common room, penned crudely in chalk, declared, "We dont serv goblins—This means yoo."

To the left of the inn, a stone railing marked the edge of one of the shafts that were characteristic of the geography of the City of Towers. Looking out over it, an observer could see that the Bone and Bristle was actually cantilevered out over the drop. Below it, large wooden beams supported its bulk, thrust into great stone sockets in the cliff wall below. Space in the city was valuable, and over the centuries of its existence enterprising architects had found ways to build practically anywhere. The shaft plunged sixty or seventy feet before coming to a stop on paved flagstones—though these were usually covered with a layer of garbage tossed from the inn's windows as well as the windows of other buildings that overlooked the shaft. The consequent stench rising from the shaft encouraged the inn's patrons to keep shut those windows that overlooked it.

Whitsun made his way through the Common Room, mostly deserted at this time of day save for a few sodden figures huddled around a table, greasy mugs in front of them, shoulders hunched forward. Glustred, standing behind the bar, nodded shortly to Whitsun and resumed his polishing of a long club, a spike thrust out of either side of its swollen end. His dark hair was pulled back into a ponytail and tied off with a leather thong that ended in a silver catch, the one piece of ornament around his person. His chins wobbled and flapped when he moved his arms. He was a big man, standing a full head and a half above Whitsun, and though his skin was flabby and pale, as of someone who had not seen the sun for a long time, there was muscle and bone beneath. His shoulders coiled when he lifted glasses from the bar and polished them with a filthy cloth. He looked, in short, like a man who had once been formidable but had let himself sink slowly into a sedentary middle age.

At one end of the room was a small green door. Whitsun unlocked this and mounted a steep set of stairs that rose in three abrupt turns. They ended in another door that bore the legend, "Guest." There was nothing more.

He unlocked this door and entered a long, narrow room. Originally conceived as a storeroom, it spanned the entire breadth of the inn. At present it contained nothing more than a table, a chair behind it, two more in front of it, and in the corner two iron-bound chests. In one corner of the room, set at an angle, was a fireplace, whose stones climbed to the low, raftered ceiling. Two windows cut through opposite walls. Both of them were shuttered. Near one was Whitsun's bed—no more than a simple mattress rolled in a bundle and set against the wall until needed. Whitsun barred the door, unlocked one of the chests and from it drew an opaque flask and a glass—probably the only clean one in the Bone and Bristle. He poured himself a short drink, tossed it back, and poured another one. Relocking the flask in the chest, he opened the shutters of the small, leaded window that looked over the street up which he'd just come and contemplated the crowds that swirled and eddied outside.

The rain-slicked paving stones shone in the light of everbright lanterns that dangled from iron rods thrusting out into the street from the buildings that lined it. They illuminated the faces below them, some thin and fine boned, others tusked and hairy. From them a babble of speech floated up to Whitsun's ears. Every accent in Eberron seemed to mix in that cauldron and rose from it in a grating growl of language from which no clear word could be distinguished. Whitsun's mouth twisted.

Seen at close distance, Whitsun was closer to fifty than forty. Silver flecked his hair, and deep crevices lined his face. A pair of thick eyebrows beetled over his eyes, which were dark and remarkably sharp and cold. His hands were slender and calloused, as if he were of good family but accustomed to hard labor, and across the back of one was a single long scar that shone a dirty white in the dim light. At times he unconsciously stroked the scar, running his fingers over its ridge. His face rarely expressed emotion, but when he was angry, his brows drew together in a V, and the tips of his ears turned scarlet.

He sipped his drink carefully in neat, economical motions. His eyes passed over the crowd once again, and then he turned from the window. Snapping his fingers, he lit an everbright lantern that hung from the wall. He sat at the table, pulled a piece of parchment toward himself, dipped a goose quill in a nearby inkwell, and began to write, the pen scratching over the parchment.

A small speaker tube next to the door coughed.

"Someone. Up. See you." Glustred's voice sounded distorted, as if he were speaking from under water.

A moment later, there was a pounding on the door. Whitsun set down his pen, gave a deep sigh, and rose. He lifted the bar from the door and opened it.

A man staggered into the room in a rush, his body carrying him against his will to fall against Whitsun. He was rail thin, dressed in a ragged cloak, stained and torn, patched clumsily in places. His hair stood out from his scalp in thin patches. He hunched over, nearly doubled, hands wrapped around his belly, face tucked down. Whitsun caught him and swung him around before he could upset both of them. One of his hands swung shut the door, dropping the bar across it.

Smoke rose from the man's clothes. In the yellow light from the lantern, it eddied and clouded. The room smelled of burned flesh.

A hollow groan burst from the man's lips. His legs gave way beneath him, and he sprawled on the floorboards. His arms were still clasped before him, but Whitsun could now see his clothing beneath the cloak was in tatters. In several places it had been burned away, and the skin beneath bubbled black and charred. Blood trickled onto the floor from a deep cut across his forehead.

One hand reached up to grasp Whitsun's. The flesh was like paper. There was strength in the arm, though. It pulled Whitsun's face close to the burned, bleeding caricature of a visage.

"Left . . ." a harsh voice whispered. "Your . . . left . . . hand."

The man's hand moved with surprising speed to grip Whitsun's left wrist. He pulled the limb down and against his chest, against a bundle his other hand clasped firmly against his chest. There was a small flash, as if a spark leaped. Whitsun gave a sharp, low exclamation and jerked his left hand back. His body snaked away from the man lying on the floor, his right hand massaging his left while his cold eyes appraised the sight before him.

"Norn?" he said. "Norn Maresun! Who did this to you?"

The figure on the floor writhed in agony. "I . . . didn't know," the lips moaned. "It wants . . . you."

"Who? What? Who wants me?"

The man's body stiffened and elongated as if all his limbs were being pulled on an invisible rack. A strangled scream erupted from his mouth. His back arched, lifting his torso from the floor. Then it all collapsed. His head fell sideways, and there was a brief rattle in his throat, ending in an exhalation of air—and nothing.

Whitsun stared at the corpse.

A clenched fist smashed into the door, nearly shivering the wooden panels.

"Open! In the name of the Watch!"

olurrh!"

Whitsun's eyes flicked back and forth from the body resting on his floor to the door. He rose and glanced about the room.

In two steps, he crossed to the other window, opposite that which looked upon the street, and opened it. A long, dark space lay beyond, stretching down into nothingness.

Whitsun reached for the bundle the man had held to his chest then hesitated for a moment. Gritting his teeth, he picked it up. Nothing happened, and his face cleared. He pulled it free of Maresun's corpse, then lifted the body easily, carried it to the window, and pushed it out. A whistle of displaced air marked its fall. Without bothering to mark its progress, Whitsun closed and locked the shutters, doing his best to ignore the pounding and shouts that were growing louder from the other side of the door.

He picked up the bundle, which he now saw was wrapped in a greasy cloth, and looked about the room. Rejecting the chests as hiding places, he crossed to the fireplace and, bending, pushed it up as far as it would go. To one side of the flue was a small shelf. The bundle sat, propped against the wall of the chimney. Whitsun hastily wiped soot from his hands. From a pouch at his side, he drew a bit of powder and tossed it at the hearth with a muttered word. Flames sprang up, filling the room with heat and light.

He looked at the spot on the floor where Maresun's blood had stained the boards. Drawing a knife from his pocket he cut a quick slash in his right hand. Drops splattered on the floor and table, marking the parchment he'd been at work on before the interruption. He wrapped a clean cloth about his hand and walked slowly to the door. Raising the bar, he stood back.

The men who erupted through the doorway were all large. None were below six feet, and the leader, whose coarse features and jutting lower teeth proclaimed him a half-orc, was nearly seven feet. He stooped to avoid striking his head on the rafters. Together, the three, wearing the uniform of the City Watch, filled the room. Whitsun moved back against the wall near the fireplace and waited.

"Whitsun!"

The leader's voice was a harsh growl that banged the syllables together like rocks.

"Captain Talvun." Whitsun's voice bore nothing but contempt. "What's the matter? Things going slow down in Firelight? Still looking for the Lucky Nines? Or are you just looking for boozes to roll? If so, talk to Glustred. I'm sure he can oblige you with a few customers."

Talvun's small, pig-like eyes took in the room.

"Don' fool wit' me, Whitsun." He bent and opened one of the chests, a thick hairy finger poking over the contents. "We know what you been doin'."

"Really? What have I been doing?"

One of the other Watchmen stood by the door. The other wandered over to the table, picked up the parchment, and stared at it with blank incomprehension.

"Laren d'Cannith," Talvun snarled.

"Yes?"

"Know him?"

"I've heard of him."

"Ah!"

Whitsun smiled wearily. "Don't be an idiot, Talvun. Well, more of an idiot, anyway. Who hasn't heard of Laren d'Cannith?"

"Whatchoo know 'bout him?"

"Enough to know he's good to stay away from."

Talvun brought down a meaty fist on the table. "Stop stallin', curse you!"

"Oh, very well." Whitsun put his hands behind his back, like a schoolboy giving a recitation. "Laren d'Cannith. One of the younger generation of House Cannith. Like a lot of that generation, not enough to do since the end of the War. Word has it that he's been working up some lines of enterprise for himself on the side."

"What kind of lines?"

"Blackmail's the most common. And prostitution. I've heard d'Cannith owns several bawdy houses in parts of the city. He pays a hefty amount to you fellows to keep them open. The two feed into each other. D'Cannith lures prominent nobles to the houses with promises of discretion then asks for hush money." Whitsun stretched. "This going anywhere?"

Talvun grunted. "He don' pay not'in' to nobody no more. He's dead!"

"Really?" Whitsun's eyebrows raised. "How do you know?"

"We got people seen him goin' into Cogs las' night. He never

15

come out. Dis mornin' we find dis." He held out a crumpled silk handkerchief. "His. By Forgefall. Stuck in railin'."

Whitsun shrugged. "You've got a long way to go between him going to the Cogs and him being dead. An even longer way to me having anything to do with it."

"Yeah? He tol' some'un he was goin' to meet some'un in the Cogs. Some'un seen you der, 'round when he go der." Talvun grinned, showing a rotten fang protruding above his upper lip. "Whachoo gotta say to dat?"

"All you've got to go on is some people who think they saw him. And me. They could be wrong. You don't even know if he's still in Sharn. Maybe he decided he needed a vacation."

"T'ink you smart?"

"I think I'm smarter than you, but that's not saying much."

Talvun's arm seemed to extend from its socket several joints as his fist slammed into Whitsun's chest. The blow lifted the smaller man from his feet and drove him against the wall. He sank down to the floor, coughing.

The Watch Captain looked at him, eyes gleaming. "No more funny. You smart? Jus' answer. Where you go las' night?"

"Out."

Whitsun's voice was strained, and he breathed heavily. He got to his feet slowly.

"Out where?"

"Opera."

Talvun's face was a blank. "Got ticket?"

Whitsun fumbled in an inner pocket. The guards tensed, but he brought out a neatly folded slip of paper. Talvun looked at it, turned it round several ways, smelled it, then snorted and threw it on the floor.

"I don' b'lieve you!"

Whitsun shrugged again. "Doesn't matter to me. You're

looking for Laren d'Cannith. I haven't seen him. Where do we go from here?"

"Captain!"

One of the Watchmen was staring at the floorboards. "Blood!"

Talvun stalked over to examine the stain, then wheeled on Whitsun. "Well?"

"I cut myself." Whitsun exhibited his bandaged hand.

"How?"

"I slipped over a drunken Watchman."

Talvun's muscles bulged, and Whitsun braced himself for another punch, but it never came.

"C'mon. We go to Watchtower."

The bigger of the two Watchmen gripped Whitsun's arms tightly and half-dragged, half-walked him across the room and down the stairs. Talvun followed, growling at the remaining Watchman, "Toss it." He included the entire room in his parting gesture.

Erix Javashi smelled. The commander of the Watch was human, but he'd associated with half-orcs for so long that he had taken on some of that race's characteristics. One of which was a distinct lack of personal hygiene.

He lounged in his leather chair behind a table whose scarred and battered surface bespoke long use. A door behind him led to the cells, from which occasionally a scream would drift into the room, hanging in the air like smoke.

Whitsun sat across from him on a hard chair, hands fastened securely to the chair's arms on either side of him. Blood dripped from a cut on his lip, and one of his eyes was beginning to swell.

Javashi put his feet on the table, leaned back, and closed his eyes. He spoke to the ceiling.

"I'm going to ask you once again. After that I won't be so nice. What have you done with Laren d'Cannith?"

Whitsun shook his head. "Nothing. Never met him. Never want to."

Javashi brought both feet to the ground with a crash and leaned forward across the table.

"You're being an idiot, Whitsun. Whoever's paying you, it's not worth it. Why hold out for them?"

Whitsun made no reply. Javashi watched him, a nasty smile creeping across his face.

"I know all about you, Whitsun. Maybe you've wondered why I even allow you to operate in my territory. You're a killer. And a thief. And everything else. If someone has a problem they want taken care of and they're not particular about the solution, you're the man they go to. Need a bit of blackmail? You're the man. A paper stolen? Someone disappeared? When there's something underhanded and a sleazy bit of business, who do people think of? Ulther Whitsun."

Whitsun was still silent. From a jar on the table Javashi selected a small dottle of crushed leaves packed into a tight ball. He popped it into his mouth, chewed slowly, then spat into a bucket in a corner of the room.

"So I ask myself, if Laren d'Cannith was causing trouble for some people—and word on the street is that he was—who are those people going to go to? Who's going to solve their problem?" His voice sank. "Look, Whitsun, personally, I don't give a goblin's arse if d'Cannith's dead or out of Khorvaire or whatever. How you do your business is your business—just provided it doesn't interfere with *my* business. But now I've got House Cannith leaning on my neck like a Karrnathi bloodhunter. I don't like that.

They're looking for their bad little boy, and I want to give them an answer. So I'm asking you again. Where is he?"

"If you're that up on the dragonmarked houses," Whitsun retorted after a short silence, "why not ask some of them? It's no secret that members of House Cannith have been spitting and clawing at each other since the War's end. If this Laren d'Cannith is really missing, it might well have been another member of his own house that shoved a dagger into him."

"Or someone paid to do it." Javashi came around the table and perched on it in front of Whitsun. "Where'd the blood come from that was on the floor in your room?"

"I told you. I cut myself."

Javashi reached down and tore off the bandage from Whitsun's hand. He squeezed the hand hard, and Whitsun winced.

"Talvun tells me there was a lot of blood on the floor."

"Talvun is an idiot."

Javashi backhanded Whitsun casually. "I wonder," he remarked, slipping off the table and strolling around the room, "whether you'd be missed if something happened to you. Suppose you resisted arrest and the Watch was forced to put a bolt between your shoulders. Think anyone would notice?"

Whitsun did not reply.

"Maybe I'll—" Javashi broke off at a knock on the door. "What?"

A half-orc stuck his snout around the jamb. "Message. From headquarters."

"Well, hand it over!" Javashi snatched the slip of paper from the officer and lifted his hand. The half-orc, easily a foot taller, winced as if at a blow and hastily closed the door.

The commander perused the message and pursed his lips. He looked at Whitsun. "So that's who you're working for."

Whitsun raised an eyebrow, as much as he was able to over his swollen eye. "Who? Why don't you tell me so I can bill them?"

Javashi sat back on his table and tapped the paper against his hand. "Do you know who's here?"

"Sorry. I'm a stranger in these parts myself."

"Your councillor. From House Vadalis. A—" he consulted the slip "—Soonam Mirkor. Friend of yours?"

"Never heard of him."

"Well, he's here to talk to you. So it looks as if you'll be sticking around in the land of the living a bit longer. Too bad." Javashi paused. "I was looking forward to helping you out a window." He stood and rapped sharply on the door. The half-orc stuck his face in.

"Yeah, boss?"

"Take Whitsun down to the cells. He's got a visitor."

The councillor Soonam Mirkor moved through the corridor cautiously, holding his robe as if he feared contact with the floor or walls. He was a slight man who had a peculiar trick of making his surroundings appear smaller. As he entered Whitsun's cell, he seemed to draw it together around him.

"Ulther Whitsun?" His voice was dry and rasping, dry as old papers rattling together at the bottom of an empty chest.

Whitsun's mouth curled. "The same. Not that there are a lot to choose from."

Mirkor showed no signs of smiling. He seated himself after carefully brushing off the stool in front of the table that filled the cell. He carried a black leather case under one arm, the sides worn smooth with use. He placed this on the table between them and took out a piece of parchment. He examined this and placed his fingertips on it.

"Commander Javashi says you're here on suspicion of murder."

Whitsun snorted. "I'm here because Javashi and Captain Talvun have fewer brains than cabbage."

"One takes it then," Mirkor said, clearing his throat slightly, "that you are . . . ah . . . innocent? Innocent of any crime?"

The man across the table looked at him. "What crime would I be guilty of?"

"Ah, quite. Quite. This young fellow, d'Cannith, now. You had nothing to do with him?"

"Quite." Despite his injuries, Whitsun was more relaxed than his interrogator. He crossed his legs and rested his elbows on the table.

"And the commission you undertook for our house? It has been . . . ah . . . fulfilled?"

"Quite."

There was a silence that gradually grew larger than the room. Mirkor was the first to break it.

"Excellent. And the . . . ah . . . papers?"

"Will be in your hands shortly."

"Excellent."

"As soon as I receive my payment."

Another silence.

"One thinks," the councillor observed, at last, staring at the ceiling, "One thinks those whom one represents should prefer to see what they are paying for first. After all, one has only your word that the problem has been . . . ah . . . disposed of."

Whitsun spread his hands. "No payment, no goods."

Mirkor studied the parchment before him some more. "This attitude is disturbing, Whitsun." He put the parchment back into the case and stood. "One thinks you might become more reasonable in a few more days."

Whitsun glanced around to ensure no guards were listening, then leaned forward and spoke quickly. His ear tips glowed.

"Now you listen to me. Your house hired me to take care of something. I held up my end of the bargain. It's not my fault if the City Watch, for once in their lives, decided to pay attention to what goes on under their noses. We agreed that if there was any sort of trouble in this job, you'd make sure none of it came to me. I held up my end of the bargain, and I expect you to hold up yours."

Mirkor looked at him. His eyes, half hooded, made him look reptilian. His voice lost nothing of its calm.

"You're hot property just now, Master Whitsun. A few days in here won't hurt you. Look on it as a vacation. A chance to get away from it all."

Whitsun came around the table with a speed surprising for one of his build. He bounced into the solid figure of a guard who materialized in front of the councillor. Mirkor vanished through the doorway, his voice floating back down the corridor.

"In a few days' time, Master Whitsun."

Prison life had its own routines and rhythms. On the outside, the sun rose and set, and folk governed their lives by its cycle. In the upper reaches of the city, nobles attended balls and funerals at which bargains were struck that would affect the lives of thousands. In the bowels of the city, folk came and went, pulling, pushing, hauling, building—all the things that made life in the great city continue.

In prison, with no windows and nothing save the body's own patterns to tell the prisoner the hour, time stretched out into a uniform line. Meals were the only break in the monotony. Whitsun counted each meal with a small stroke on the wall. At two per day, he had reached number eight when there was a clatter in the corridor outside his door.

The half-orc guard, who had delivered food to him, gave no explanation and no apology. Instead, he shoved his prisoner along the corridor. Whitsun passed through several chambers and at last was pushed through a heavily barred and studded doorway onto a rough cobbled street. A steady drizzle was falling, drops splashing on the stones and forming oily puddles and streams that ran down the sloping way. Whitsun, his belly growling—prison food had been barely edible, and he'd consumed little of it—made his way down the street. The guards had relieved him of the coins he'd had in his pocket when he was arrested, but Glustred could be relied upon to supply something hearty and filling and tasty if one didn't look at the ingredients too closely.

He looked about him, as one who has spent four days in the confines of a prison cell, reveling in the open air, the feel of rain dripping on his face and a breeze that carried familiar scents of rotting food and human waste. The Watch Station in which he'd been imprisoned was several miles from the Bone and Bristle, but the way was mostly downhill. As usual, the streets were full of bustling crowds—men, orcs, elves, gnomes, dwarves, and others shuffling along, jostling one another, dodging out of the way of others wheeling carts or hauling loads from above or below. The sounds and smells of 200,000 beings living together in the same confined space filled the air.

Whitsun pushed his way through the throng, using his bulk freely, ignoring the curses of those whom he bumped. He gave scarcely a glance to those on either side of him, but every now and again he stopped by a shop window, apparently studying his reflection in the glass. At times, a keen-eyed observer might have seen his eyes flitting back and forth along the way he had come.

He arrived at the Bone and Bristle in time for the evening drinking to begin and shoved through the doorway, already filled with revelers. The barmen were passing along mugs of ale and other spirits to a clamoring crowd from which the smoke of a hundred pipes mingled in a low, dark cloud that hung in the center of the room. In one corner of the room, a small group of men and dwarves sat close round a table, voices pitched low. Every now and again, one would half rise and survey the rest of the room to make certain they were not overheard—though no one in the crowd showed the slightest interest in their obvious conspiratorial discussions.

Glustred was not working but was leaning against a post at the side of the common room, watching all that was going on before him. Whitsun sidled up to him, and the innkeeper took his pipe from his mouth and spat.

"You're out then." It was a statement, not a question.

"Aye." Whitsun stood passively, looking at a group of dwarves who were downing enormous pitchers of ale as fast as the barkeepers could serve them.

"What'd they charge you with?"

"Nothing. As it turns out, they didn't really want me." Whitsun's eyes were dreamy. He slipped a hand behind the innkeeper's stout back. His hand snapped around Glustred's left wrist as it supported the innkeeper's not inconsiderable weight against the pillar. He jerked it down, around, and up. Glustred rose on his tiptoes, his right hand groping in his breeches pocket.

"Ah. Ah. None of that please." Whitsun jerked harder on the arm, and the innkeeper groaned. "You know, it's curious," the smaller man continued. "I pay you a considerable sum every month for the use of that room. And I seem to remember that part of the bargain was that you'd keep an eye out for the Watch and let me know the instant any came into the inn." He jerked again.

Glustred's lips moved, but no sound came out of them except a kind of whine an animal might make if it were in deadly pain.

"So why, when Talvun's men banged on my door, didn't I know about it?"

A dribble of saliva worked its way out of Glustred's mouth and down his chin, but he still said nothing.

"What's that?" Whitsun continued. "You say Talvun paid you a bribe? But I'm already paying you a bribe, Glustred. How much did Talvun pay you?"

He jerked upward on the arm, and Glustred moaned loudly enough to attract the attention of an elf sitting at a nearby table. The elf looked at Whitsun, then looked quickly away again.

"Two galifars. Genuine."

Glustred's voice was forced between his teeth and his tongue.

Whitsun reached into the barkeeper's pocket. Something jingled. He pulled out the coins and looked at them thoughtfully. Then he put one of them back and slipped the other into his breeches. He released Glustred's arm and stood back.

The innkeeper massaged the injured limb and glared at Whitsun. He turned his back on him and deliberately walked behind the bar. He faced the crowd and placed both hands on the counter, palms down.

Whitsun's mouth curved upward. He walked through the doorway to his room.

Inside, he shut his door behind him, barred it, and leaned back against it. For the first time, he allowed his face to crease into a scowl as he regarded his chamber.

Talvun's troops had been thorough. The tops of both chests were torn from their hinges. The table was scarred with knives to make sure it contained no hidden compartments. The bed was torn to pieces, and bits of straw from the mattress were strewn about the floor, several boards of which had been wrenched up in the search. The walls were gouged in places, and the back window—that through which Whitsun had tossed Maresun's body—swung open.

Whitsun closed it against the rain, which had begun to fall harder now, and carefully stirred some of the straw with his foot. He examined the chests and satisfied himself that though their contents had been rifled nothing had been taken. He searched the room thoroughly and then disappeared down the stairs. He returned after with a mug and a bottle. Pouring himself a drink, he sipped it, standing by the window looking out over the street. He drained the mug and set it on the table next to the bottle. Then, with a sigh, he went to the fireplace—the glamour showing the illusion of fire had, of course, long since faded—and thrust a hand up the flue.

The expression on his face changed from resignation to surprise. He reached up further then drew down a rag-wrapped packet. He looked puzzled and troubled. He laid the packet carefully on the table and, rather than make any immediate attempt at opening it, sank down in his chair and contemplated it for a time, chin in his hand. From the bar, a long, low hum of conversation and drinking floated up the stairs, but it did not disturb Whitsun. He stared at the bundle as his right hand mechanically caressed his left in ceaseless motion. At last he rubbed his eyes. Without any attempt to investigate the bundle further, he unrolled his mattress, stuffed it with what straw he could find, and rolled himself in a blanket to sleep.

CHAPTER 3

Whitsun awoke several hours later. He stretched, sat up, looked about as if surprised at his surroundings, and arose. After making his ablutions and taking a quick drink he sat at the table for a time, arms folded, staring at the bundle. The rag, which appeared to be surprisingly free of soot from the fireplace flue, shone with grease—or something else—in a few places. It was a dirty gray with ragged edges. There was no clue as to whether Maresun had wrapped the object in a cloth of his own or had taken the bundle intact.

At last Whitsun stood, walked slowly around the table, and, using a charred stick he pulled from the hearth, pried apart the swaddling. A glint of metal beneath the rags stopped him for a moment before he continued, without hurry, to unwrap his prize.

When the wrappings were pulled apart, Whitsun contemplated the object.

It was a ring about twelve inches in diameter, made of a

dull silver metal. In places the metal seemed tarnished black. It reflected little light, which made it curiously difficult to see. Whitsun rose and with a wave of his hand lit an everbright lantern, but even so the object remained partly in shadow. Whitsun's brows drew together as he stared at it.

The ring was broken on one side by a gap of two or three inches. One surface was covered with embossed script, the letters flowing and seeming to shift in the lantern light. Three slender struts extended toward the center of the ring where they held a rough-cut green stone, translucent and dimly glowing.

Whitsun carefully examined the ring. He passed a hand above it, being careful not to touch it. At last he went to the door, opened it a crack, and whistled.

There was a scrabble of clawed feet in the corridor, and a long, slender mink, its body undulating across the floor, slipped into the room. Whitsun chirruped to it.

"Hullo, Maggie. Here, girl!"

Maggie submitted to being picked up and stroked. Her muzzle explored his pockets, searching for food. Whitsun ran his fingers over her whiskers, and she vibrated with pleasure. Finally, he placed her on the table next to the ring. She sniffed the rag and scuttled across it, nosing the ring, her eyes bright. She rubbed her fur against it, nudged it with her nose, and showing every sign of enjoyment, rolled onto her back and wriggled against the metal.

At last Whitsun murmured, "Good girl," and picked her up. She strained toward the ring, but he carried her to the door, thrust her into the corridor, and shut the door against her. Her claws scrabbled against the wood for a few moments then disappeared down the stairs.

The man resumed his silent examination of the ring. At last he muttered, "Oh, well," reached out, and grasped the metal.

No reaction. Whitsun shifted it to his other hand then held it in both hands. He rubbed it, stroking it, running his fingers along the embossed characters as if trying to read them by touch. After a time he rose and rummaged through the chest until he found a piece of parchment. Further search discovered a quill and bottle of ink. With these he made a copy of the peculiar characters that covered the ring, tracing their outlines as exactly as he was able. He also made a rough sketch of the object, with notes indicating what the various parts of it were made of. He sat, fingers absently caressing the artifact, while he examined his drawing.

A long, phlegmy cough, like a carcass crab clearing its throat, came from a corner of the room. Glustred's voice, magically amplified, floated in the air.

"Visitors on the way up."

A smile touched Whitsun's lips, and he answered, "Thank you." He rewrapped the ring in its covering and thrust it into one of the chests whose lid he shut. He folded the parchment and slipped it into his jacket out of sight just as the knock came at the door.

"Come!"

Whitsun seated himself behind the table, facing the door. It opened abruptly, spilling his visitor into the room.

The room was small, and the man who entered made it considerably smaller. He was well over six feet, muscular, with a broad chest that threatened to burst the lacings of his leather jerkin. His hair was coarse and black, growing thickly down his forehead, which was framed by a bristling brow surmounting deep-set black eyes.

He moved into the room with a liquid grace and stood before the table. A large hand, hair growing on the back of it, rested on the scarred wooden surface. His pointed nails drummed impatiently.

"Master Whitsun?"

"You found him."

"I want to talk to you about a business matter."

Whitsun gestured to the chair, and the other sank onto it.

"I don't usually see shifters in this neighborhood," Whitsun observed.

His visitor nodded coolly. "We are not welcome," he acknowledged. "Do you have a problem acting for one of my race?"

"Your gold's the same color as anyone else's." Whitsun looked the shifter over in a penetrating way that bordered on impudence.

"And you are not particular about its source?" The shifter bared his long, sharp teeth in a mirthless smile.

"What's the job?"

The shifter leaned forward across the table, crossing his hands in front of him. "My name is Assat Maru. I am recently arrived in Sharn, and I am new to the ways of your city."

Whitsun nodded. "By your accent, Master Freylaut, I'd say you are a Karrn."

His visitor glared. "I said my name is—"

"Yes, I heard you. I'm not deaf, Freylaut. Or feeble minded. If I decide to do business with you, it might as well be under your right name as under an alias."

Freylaut leaned back, fingers working slowly. "How," he asked, his voice softening to a rasp, "did you find out my real name, Master Whitsun?"

"Oh, for the sake of the Host!" Now it was Whitsun's turn to be irritated. "I just told you we don't get many shifters down here. You think every agent worth anything in this area hasn't marked you down already?" He half turned in his chair. "Tell your friend to come in. She's missing half of it, listening at the keyhole."

The door opened, and a woman came into the room. Whitsun rose and pulled another chair out for her.

She was clad in dark blue, the color of still water on a quiet night. Her dress covered her like a sheath of fine silk. Her red hair spilled down her back in a series of curls, and two long, slender plaits, tied with ribbons edged with gold, hung from either side of her face. Her almond-shaped eyes were pale violet, like the first intimations of sunrise, and they stared at Whitsun in a mixture of amusement and curiosity.

"How did you know I was there?" Her accent, somewhat heavier than her companion's, was charming.

Whitsun shrugged. "Word out is there's a shifter in the area and that he's got a human female for a companion."

Freylaut scowled. "Never mind. You know who we are. That doesn't matter. What matters is what we want from you."

Whitsun ran his eyes slowly down the woman's figure. There was almost something predatory in his gaze. He ignored the shifter. "What's your name?"

Freylaut growled, a low, menacing sound in the back of his throat that echoed through the small room. The woman placed a slender hand on his arm and did not take her eyes from Whitsun's face.

"Delru. Delru Abaressena."

He nodded. "What's the problem?"

Freylaut leaned forward and lowered his voice.

"Very well, Whitsun. As you guess, we are from Karrnath. We arrived a week ago by lightning rail on a delicate diplomatic mission, the details of which don't concern you. We were careless at the station, and a thief stole something from us."

Whitsun lifted an eyebrow. "At a lightning rail station? How . . . shocking. What was it?"

There was silence for a minute, then Delru answered. "An artifact. I have had it for some time, and it is very dear to me. I am sure it would be of no value to anyone, but it is precious to me. It holds many memories. The thief does not know what he possesses."

"If that's the case, the thief probably got rid of it at the first opportunity."

She shook her head. "I have reason to think that this is not so. We have tracked the thief to this district, but now he has vanished. We wish you to find him and recover my possession."

Whitsun shook his head. "Sounds like a problem for the Watch. You'll have to pay them a bribe, of course, but with the right amount of incentive, they're good at catching thieves—especially the kind of lowlifes who hang out at the lightning rail, dipping the pouches of newps."

"Dipping the . . . please?" Her brow creased in a tiny frown.

"Picking pockets of newcomers in the city." Whitsun leaned back in his chair. "An experienced dip can cut your purse, drain it of coin, and have it back in your pocket before you turn around. Never mind that. You still haven't told me why you've come to me."

Freylaut growled. During Whitsun's dialogue with the woman his face had grown blacker and blacker. Now he moved behind her and stood with his hands on her shoulders, his sharp nails denting the soft flesh.

"We need you to recover what we lost," he told Whitsun. "It is not for you to know why or how we chose you."

Whitsun shook his head, keeping his face fixed on Delru Abaressena. "I don't work like that. If I work for you, you tell me the truth. And you answer any of my questions truthfully. If I use a truth spell and find out you've been lying, our contract's broken. It's as simple as that."

"You are a hard man," she told him.

"I'm a *live* man—which is more than can be said for some others I know."

He rose and walked to the window, where he gazed at the crowded street, his back to his visitors. He spoke again.

"If I agree to work for you, our agreement is exclusive. That is, I agree to work for you and only you. That way you can be sure I'm not playing off someone else's interests against yours. But I have to be sure I understand just what those interests are. And for that I need the truth. It's confidential, but I *need* it. If you can't promise that, let's end this right here."

There was silence behind him for a moment. Then came the sound of the shifter's footsteps moving to the door. They passed through it. Whitsun waited until his alert ear caught a creak from a stair halfway down the flight. Then he turned to face the woman again. "Well?"

She sat, hands resting easily on the table in front of her. "There are . . . certain difficulties . . . in going to the Watch."

"Such as?"

"The artifact is mine." She spoke swiftly and with a sense of entitlement, her breath tightening around each word. "It is mine by right and mine by possession. Nevertheless, there are some who might dispute that right. They will have already approached your Watch and offered them a substantial sum for this item. I cannot possibly match their offer. So I turn to one such as you who is—how would I put it—*unrestrained* about retrieving such an item."

Whitsun grunted. "You want me to go up against the Watch?"

"Surely there is no need of that." She leaned toward him, her voice pitched low and musical. "You need merely to search where they do not. To recover this item from the thief who took it and silence him. Surely this cannot be too difficult a task for one deserving of your reputation?" She smiled. "The reward for success would be considerable."

Whitsun looked at her in silence for a few minutes. Then he strode to one of the chests—the one opposite to that in which he had earlier placed the mysterious ring—and pulled out a fresh piece of parchment. He wrote in silence, ignoring the woman seated before him. The pen scratched over the parchment. From below faint sounds from the common room of the Bone and Bristle drifted up and hung in the air like faint smoke from a wood fire burned low.

At last Whitsun finished and passed the parchment across to the woman. She read it without comment and retuned it to him with a nod.

He took out a knife and pricked his finger, letting a few drops of blood spill on the parchment. He passed the knife to Delru, who followed suit. Both of them placed their left hands on the document, and Whitsun muttered a word. The parchment glowed briefly. Whitsun folded it and stowed it carefully in the chest.

"There," he observed. "Now I've agreed to find the thief and recover your property."

Delru frowned. "It will be necessary to dispose of the pickpocket."

"Let me worry about that. There may be some other ways to deal with the problem." He looked at her. "I assume you're prepared to cover all expenses?"

She extended a hand and with an odd gesture casually plucked a leather bag from the air. "This should be enough for the present."

Whitsun glanced in the pouch and nodded. "Give me a description of the man who stole this thing from you."

"May Freylaut rejoin us? He saw the man more clearly than I."

Whitsun walked to the corner of the room and tapped the speaking tube. "Glustred? Ask the shifter to come up."

Freylaut entered forcefully, striding up to Delru. "Is all well? Has he insulted you?"

She patted his hand. "All is fine, dearheart. We have come to an arrangement. He will help us."

Whitsun pushed over a chair with one foot. The shifter ignored it.

"Sit, please," said Whitsun. "I don't like getting a crick in my neck when I'm talking."

Freylaut turned to Delru, who nodded. The shifter took a seat, and Whitsun's lip curled.

"The thief. What did he look like?"

"Small. Thin. Like a sewer rat."

"Shifter?"

"No. Smell was wrong. Human."

"Clothes?"

"Dark green jerkin. Black trousers. Tattered cloak."

"Hair?"

"Black but patchy. Small scar on the right cheek."

Whitsun's hand moved slightly, but his voice continued in the same tone.

"This was at a lightning rail station. Which one?"

Freylaut looked at Delru, who answered. "Cogsgate. At . . . Tavick's Landing it is called, I think."

Whitsun nodded. "Who knew you were coming to Sharn?"

"No one," the woman replied. "That is to say, none knew when and where we would arrive."

"But someone was expecting you?"

Delru answered with an appearance of reluctance. "Yes. We are here to meet certain representatives of the council. The Karrnathi government has empowered certain informal embassies that may be able to resolve a few of the issues outstanding since the end of the War. We are one such embassy." She smiled. "You see, Master Whitsun, I am being very frank with you. Such is our agreement."

"Wise choice. Why bring this thing with you? Does it have a name, by the way?"

"It is called the Orerry of Tal Esk."

Whitsun wrinkled his brow. "Tal Esk. Where's that?"

"Xen'drik. Far to the south. Few who live in Khorvaire have ever seen it."

"And the artifact?"

"In shape it is a silver ring with a gold sphere inside. They are so attached that the gold will spin within the silver."

"How big?"

Her slender hands described a circle of nine or ten inches.

"Any writing on it?"

"Writing? Yes. In an ancient language, but that is of no concern, since no one is now alive who can read it. But there are jewels set within it—rubies in the silver ring, emeralds in the gold sphere. Doubtless, that is why the thief took it."

Freylaut, who had been exhibiting growing symptoms of impatience, rose abruptly. "You do not need to know any of this! All you must do is recover our property." He said something to Delru in a language Whitsun did not recognize, though his pronunciation of some of the words seemed to indicate it was spoken in the Eldeen Reaches. She replied sharply in the same language, and her small hand made a cutting gesture. The shifter fell silent.

Whitsun watched. Then he rose and said, "I think that's enough to start with."

Delru also rose. "Wait below, Freylaut, please," she said sweetly.

The shifter went out, sending Whitsun a teeth-baring snarl as a parting gift.

The red-haired woman placed a white hand on Whitsun's shoulder.

"I rely on you, Master Whitsun," she said. "I believe I can trust you. In my country, that is a rare thing and so is valued."

She bent forward and kissed his cheek. Then she vanished through the door, leaving a fragrance of nightberries in her wake.

Whitsun remained standing for a while after his visitors departed. One hand absently stroked his cheek. After a time he retrieved the object brought to him by Norn Maresun. He unwrapped it and ran his fingers over it.

"Norn, Norn," he murmured to himself. "What did you get yourself into?" He shook his hand, rewrapped the ring, and put it in his closet. Then he crossed to the corner and tapped the speaking tube.

Glustred's voice responded, "What?"

"A few moments of your time. Unless you want me to come down there."

There was a scramble of feet on the stairs, and the big innkeeper burst through the door, his face red. "What now?"

Whitsun reseated himself at his table. "Norn Maresun."

"Never heard of him."

Whitsun said nothing, and the big man wilted.

"Dipper. Works Cogsgate. Lone wolf, though I heard he used to run with Tarkanan. Ain't seen him around in a couple of weeks."

Whitsun rose and opened the back shutter.

"Look."

Glustred looked down. "Balls! What's that?"

"The late Norn Maresun. He came through that door a few

days ago when you were busy not watching, courtesy of Talvun."

"And you did him?" Glustred backed hastily away from the window.

"No." Whitsun shook his head. "He was already dead when he hit the ground. I was just keeping him out of sight."

Glustred exploded. "Balls! What were you going to do? Just bloody leave him down there? Wait for the drudges to find him next week when they collect the garbage? What about me? How am I supposed to bloody explain another bloody body? You know what happened after the last one. How——?"

Whitsun lifted a hand, and Glustred's flow of speech ceased.

"The point, my friend," he observed, "is that Maresun brought me something. A mysterious something. And now I find out that he stole another mysterious something from someone else. I wonder if the two somethings are connected."

He paused. His companion obviously wanted to speak but didn't.

"Well," Whitsun said finally, "I suppose we may as well start with Maresun's lodgings. Things may become clearer after that."

Glustred found his voice. "We?"

"Yes. I think I'd like you along on this little expedition. You don't seem to be much use as a guard over my place of business, so I'll try you as a guard over my person."

Glustred opened his mouth and, catching Whitsun's eye, shut it very quickly.

Cogsgate in Lower Tavick's Landing was a district of warehouses, where goods were trundled to and fro on handcarts or on magically floating platforms. Massive gateways loomed, some with the sign of House Deneith cut into their stone, others incised with the insignia of House Kundarak. In places, buildings leaned across the way toward one another as if about to embrace. Narrow alleys opened into unexpectedly wide courtyards, and broad avenues shrank in the blink of an eye to emaciated lanes.

Through all this surged a frothing sea of people, its waves beating against the buildings that lined the streets. Street vendors called out their wares, beggars held forth battered cups, beseeching help in cracked voices. One elf, whose leg ended above the knee in a soiled bandage, intercepted Whitsun and Glustred, pulling at Glustred's sleeve.

"Crown, sirs? For a war veteran? Missing a leg in the service of Breland."

Glustred shook off the elf, but Whitsun stopped. "Veteran? Which front?"

The beggar seemed taken aback at the question. "Why . . . uh . . . Thrane, sir. Sword Keep."

"Ah," Whitsun said genially. "Then you'll have been in a few battles indeed. Well done, soldier. For keeping us free, my thanks." He embraced the startled elf and dropped two crowns into his cup. He and Glustred walked on, leaving the elf staring at their wake.

Glustred waited until they were out of earshot then said, "What in the name of Dolurrh's depths did you do that for?"

Whitsun reached into his pocket. "You lost something."

"That's my purse, curse it! How did you get hold of it?"

"I took it out of the pocket of our friend back there."

Glustred whirled. "A dip! Bloody Dolurrh! And I didn't recognize him!"

"No. He's a bit new to these parts I should imagine."

Glustred stared in vain through the crowded street behind them. "No. He's gone." He turned back to his companion. "Why'd you let him get away? Why not just grab him and shout for the Watch?"

Blandly, Whitsun reached into his pocket and displayed three other purses. "I thought it better to handle it my own way," he said and strode on.

Ahead the crowds grew thicker, and their pace slowed at times to a shuffle. Whitsun followed in the bigger man's wake, while Glustred relied on his arms and his considerable bulk to clear a path. They arrived at a square along one side of which ran a line of market stalls.

The two inquirers walked to the foremost stall, which displayed an array of rugs and richly woven blankets. Whitsun tapped the owner on the shoulder.

"Hey, friend. I'm looking for—"

An explosion of shouting and cursing broke out at the next stall. A tall, thin man dressed in better clothes than were usually seen in Cogsgate had a hand on the collar of an equally thin boy.

"Street rat! Stole my purse!"

He whipped out a rapier, its jeweled handle glinting in the lantern light. The boy, wriggling like an eel, escaped from his grip and produced a knife. Spectators skittered backward, forming a cheering ring around the two.

Whitsun ignored the ruckus. He watched the outskirts of the crowd carefully and with a sudden lunge seized a young woman in a dirty cloak whose hand was darting toward one of the onlooker's purse strings. She yelped and twisted away, but Whitsun retained his grip on her wrist. She drew a knife, but Glustred, looming up on her other side, plucked it from her hand and slapped her. She staggered and went limp. The two men pulled her back into the dark recesses of the stall, whose owner was among those cheering the knife fight outside.

Whitsun pushed up an eyelid of the body before them, examined what lay beneath, and looked reproachfully at his companion.

"Can't you learn subtlety, Glustred? How long before she's conscious?"

The innkeeper picked up a bucket of dirty water that stood to hand and tossed it over the recumbent figure, who sputtered and sat up, clutching her head.

"Now," the big man announced.

The girl made a feeble effort to rise. Whitsun pushed her back.

"Not so fast. A few questions first."

Her black eyes looked unspeakable things at him.

"Norn Maresun. Where's he lodge?"

She spat. Glustred slapped her again, lighter, and her head jerked. She wiped a trickle of blood from her nose.

"Where?" Whitsun repeated.

She was silent. Glustred lifted his hand.

"Tumbledown."

"Where in Tumbledown?"

"Merkle Close. Second right. Third door." The words came through swollen, bruised lips.

"Excellent. Thank you. That'll be all."

The girl rose, staggered momentarily, and clutched at Glustred's massive frame, then was gone in a flash of dirty legs.

Well, let's see if our late friend can give us any help." Whitsun rose and started out of the stall. Glustred followed then slapped his pocket with a curse.

"Balls! Cursed dipper twerked my bag."

"That's what you get for standing too near her." Whitsun was unsympathetic. "You do seem to have trouble holding onto that purse. How much?"

"A sovereign. A few coppers."

"Probably more than she's seen in a month, working these parts. Come on."

Whitsun led the way out of the square along a twisting alley, their way marked by a foul stream running along a cobbled gutter.

"After we find—"

A black form shot out of the shadows before Whitsun. At the same time two more figures closed on Glustred from the rear.

CHAPTER 4

The two men who attacked from the rear were smaller than Glustred and evidently looked on the innkeeper as a two-man task. For the time being, at least, this left Whitsun free to deal with only one enemy.

The attacker, carrying a short sword, the hilt of which was muddy, though the blade was sharp and bright, feinted to the left. Whitsun remained poised on the balls of his feet, hands empty.

His opponent, who had evidently expected him to draw a weapon of some kind, hesitated then lunged. Whitsun dodged and kicked out low and hard, smashing the man's knee. The ruffian fell with a curse, cut off when Whitsun's boot heel struck his forehead.

To the rear Glustred was engaging his two attackers, wielding a wicked-looking knife. One of the men was bleeding from a slash across the biceps, the cloth of his shirt hanging down in a tattered rag. The other was hanging back, looking for a way to disengage.

A movement to Whitsun's front drew his attention. A thin man with streaked hair and slightly pointed ears landed on the pavement. Whitsun could not tell from where he had jumped; he had been that quick. He darted in and cut at Whitsun with two sharp blades attached to his knuckles. In the lantern light they looked like claws. He leaped back, forward with another slash, then back.

Whitsun followed, aiming a savage kick, but the shifter—so he plainly was from the cast of his face and the more-than-human sleekness of his movements—flitted out of the way. Their combat progressed steadily down the alleyway, the shifter daring in a step then retreating two backward. Whitsun stalked him grimly.

The building walls on either side fell away as they emerged on to one of the countless bridges that spanned the City of Towers. For the first time Whitsun glanced about. The bridge was deserted. On either side, shafts fell away to an unknown depth, while above them walls pierced with glowing windows soared endlessly upward.

The shifter continued to retreat, drawing the fight onto the bridge itself. Whitsun watched every move his opponent made, waiting for an opening. He struck less than before, conserving his strength. Of Glustred's fight he no longer heard anything.

The shifter's eyes flicked, looking for a fraction of a second behind Whitsun. The man spun, cursing. A second shifter had dropped behind him, leaping from a ledge at the edge of the bridge. Now the two faced him, one to either side.

He backed until the cold touch of the stone balustrade was against the small of his back. The shifters were cautious. Having brought him to the bridge, clearly their strategy from the beginning, they were in no hurry.

A shout came from the area of the alley, a shout of Glustred's voice proclaiming triumph in his combat. As if it were a signal, the shifters moved. One struck high, aiming at Whitsun's neck. The other hung back a fraction of a second, and when Whitsun parried the first blow, the second fighter rolled and struck against his knees.

Clawed hands gripped Whitsun's calves, and the shifter tipped him over the side of the bridge.

In a city crisscrossed by bridges, accidents happen. That needs no saying. It would be going too far to say the inhabitants of Sharn were used to falling off bridges, but it was not an unusual occurrence.

Therefore, they prepared.

Even as Whitsun's legs went up and over the railing, one hand was groping in his pocket. His fingers closed around a small feather, and his lips moved in a spell.

The walls rushed by him, then slowed. He began to drift as if the air itself were slowing his fall. He was moving at a pace at which he could look through the windows he was passing, those not blocked by wooden shutters. Many were darkened, the panes dusty, but in a few rooms there were figures moving about. In one a group of men sat at a table. One had just stabbed a dagger into the board before him, and Whitsun watched it quiver as he drifted past. In another scene, a man and a woman were locked in a close embrace. It was only after he'd passed it that Whitsun realized that although the woman's arms had been around the man's waist, his hands had been at her throat.

A sudden jerk brought him out of his thoughts. Instead of drifting, he was falling faster. Three hundred feet below him, the stones of a courtyard rushed up to meet him.

He cursed and snatched at a rocky window sill. His fingers

slipped off, and he struck against a projecting stone. His leg went numb. He reached out and grabbed as an iron bar went by. His arms jerked painfully as he caught it and held. He was dangling a hundred feet above the courtyard.

He hung for a moment, catching his breath. His fingers ached with the strain of holding his 250 pounds. He looked about, seeking a better hold. His eyes brightened, and hand over hand, he pulled himself closer to the wall. A long pipe snaked down the side of it, designed to carry rainwater from some site far above. Whitsun reached out and tugged it. It creaked but held.

He eased his bulk onto it and slid down. Ten feet from the courtyard the pipe stopped, and Whitsun dropped. He stood on the cobbles, looking up at the long shaft. Then he muttered something inaudible and turned to go.

A shout from above drew his attention. Glustred, looking in the gloom like a captive airship, floated down and alit next to him. Whitsun raised an eyebrow.

The big man glowered at him. "Saw you go over," he grunted. "Thought I'd better come too. That was my last damned featherfall spell." He shook himself like a dog shaking off rain water. "What happened to you?"

"The spell failed." Whitsun's tone was calm, but tiny worry lines creased at the corners of his eyes. "Or rather, it stopped working. I don't know why." He put the problem from him with a gesture. "Did you recognize any of our friends up there?"

Glustred shook his head. "Probably thumpers looking to roll a few newps for their bags."

Whitsun considered. "I don't think so. We don't look like newps. And thumpers aren't usually that organized. Also, the ones who came for me didn't try for gilt; they just wanted to tip me over the rail. If they were after our bags they would have tried to keep it quieter."

"So who were they?"

"Don't know yet. I don't like it." Whitsun shrugged. "Well, they seem to have sent us where we were going anyway."

"This is Tumbledown?" Glustred looked around. "Never been here."

"You surprise me. I would have thought this was just your kind of place. Come."

Three narrow stone archways offered exits from the courtyard. Each had letters above it, deeply incised into the keystones but so worn that they could barely be made out. Whitsun led the way through one of these archways and down a wide, twisting passage with many wooden doors opening off it. The passage spilled them into another street, largely deserted, though a few shifty figures flitted back and forth in the gloom. Everbright lanterns burned here, as they did everywhere in Sharn, but many had been smashed, and their twisted metal frames protruded from their sockets like strange sculptures. Twenty feet from where they stood, a fire was burning in the middle of the street. A small group of figures gathered round it, holding out hands to its warmth.

Whitsun led the way confidently, walking away from the fire and its silent circle of watchers, dodging piles of refuse that lay rotting in the narrow way. Glustred hesitated. His companion looked back.

"Come along! What's the matter with you?"

"Are there any rats there?"

Whitsun kicked one of the heaps of garbage. A muffled squeak came from beneath.

"Yes, I'd say so. Why?"

Without answering, Glustred picked his way cautiously down the street. A shadow scuttled in front of him along the cobbles, and he jumped back with a curse.

"Come along, come along!" Whitsun's tone was amused. "That I should see an innkeeper who's afraid of a few rats!"

Glustred abruptly changed the subject. "What happened to you up there?" he asked, making a vague gesture up and back in the direction from which they'd come.

Whitsun's lips compressed. "I don't know. But I'm going to find out before I fall off another bridge."

Their path took them through several more archways and passages and down two flights of broad steps, slick with water. Whitsun never hesitated and seemed thoroughly familiar with the narrow ways. They emerged at last onto a broad avenue. Doors pierced the sides of buildings that lined the street so close to one another that they seemed to open upon the same dwelling. Many were broken or ajar. The buildings themselves were fantastic piles of crumbling masonry; it was easy to see the source of the district's name.

One dark alley seemed especially noisome with smells. An everbright lantern—one of the few that remained intact—illuminated the words "Merkle Close" cut into the stone. Beneath it someone had scrawled some rude words and a crude illustration. Whitsun turned down the alley and took the second doorway to the right, which led to a hallway so narrow he and Glustred could only pass along it in single file. Whitsun stopped in front of another door and pushed it with two fingers. It creaked crazily, and Glustred glanced up and down the hall, but nothing stirred. The two men stepped through the crack and stood in Norn Maresun's room.

It was narrow and extended back some fifteen feet, ending in a whitewashed wall that was broken by a small leaded window high up. To one side was a mattress spread on the floor with a cup and a plate next to it that indicated Maresun dined on the floor. The only furniture in the room was a chair and a rickety table next to the back wall. The bottom of the chair was cracked, and Whitsun tested it before sitting and looking around him.

The room was crowded with an extraordinary collection of objects. It was as if a magpie had taken up residence and was furnishing a large and more than usually messy nest. There were piles of clothing, some of it fine and some mere rags. Boxes, bags, and bundles all lay scattered or heaped on one another, spilling out their contents. A gauntlet, metal gleaming in the light that filtered through the filthy windowpane, lay curled around a dagger whose blade was rusted away. On another pile a child's rag doll surveyed the scene disconsolately out of one cracked button eye.

Glustred looked about. "What a way to live!" He shook his head in disgust.

Whitsun stirred a pile with his foot. "Our late friend doesn't seem to have found dipping to be a very profitable career."

"So what are we looking for?" the big man inquired. "You said a something. That's not much to go on."

"I know." Whitsun rose and sauntered over to the window. He opened it, letting fresh air—or what passed for fresh air in Tumbledown—wash over the room. "All the same, I'd rather not say just yet. You'll know it if you see it. You take this side."

The two began to search the room. Glustred tossed objects over his shoulder, looking like a large, shaggy dog searching for a bone. Whitsun was more restrained and methodical, placing objects to one side, working the room from back to front.

They had been at it for about a half hour and were coming to the end of the search when a sound from the doorway made them both spin around.

An old man was standing watching them, so bent he was doubled over. He supported himself with a stick and was clad in an assortment of rags. A hood covered part of his face.

"Looking for something?"

The voice was cracked, punctuated by a cough that sought to clear phlegm from deep within his chest.

Whitsun straightened. "Yes. Maresun has something that belongs to me." From one side Glustred began to circle cautiously toward the old man.

The visitor laughed. It sounded like gravel falling on glass.

"Maresun has lots of things that belonged to others. Now they belong to him. But he still can't pay rent." The old man's face screwed itself into an excess of fury. "Gods rot his hide! Four sovereigns he owes me! But have I seen a crown? May the gods rot the skin from his—"

"Four sovereigns? For all this?" Whitsun glanced at the narrow confines of the room. "When did you see him last?"

"Are you inquisitives?" The old man's mouth took on a cunning twist. He coughed again, wheezing and leaning on his stick. Glustred took the opportunity to move a bit nearer to him.

Whitsun shook his head. "No. Just interested parties."

"I've not seen him in a week. And who's going to pay me? That's what I want to know."

Glustred moved fast, but the old man was faster. As the big innkeeper made a dart at him, the ancient one let his stick clatter to the floor. In his hand was two feet of shining steel. He stood straight, the rapier's tip touching Glustred's throat. His voice and stance was now that of a young man.

"Just who are you people, anyway?"

Whitsun stood very still, keeping his hands in the open.

"Whitsun's my name. I was hired to find something Maresun stole."

The young man's glance flicked over him. "Ulther Whitsun?"

"That's right."

"A little on the down market side, aren't you?"

Whitsun sat down on the cracked chair and spread his hands. "I'm just looking for something."

"What?"

"Sorry."

The young man looked at Glustred. "What about you?"

The innkeeper's voice was slow in coming. "I don't know. He hasn't told me either."

Slowly the point of the rapier lowered, and Glustred let out a breath. "Who're you?" he asked.

"A neighbor."

"Close neighborhood."

The young man's bright eyes stared at him without blinking. "We look out for each other."

"As long as it pays," observed Whitsun.

The other jerked his head in agreement. "Would it pay me to help you?"

"It might. For example, if you help me I might forget I saw Lassar Redhand living in Tumbledown."

The rapier came up in an instant, and Glustred, who had moved around to be closer to Whitsun, flinched.

"Lassar! Balls!"

"I don't like hearing that name." The rapier was pointed at Whitsun.

"I imagine the Watch would, though. Twenty murders in two months. That made even them sit up and take notice. Still, my memory's a bit faulty." Whitsun tapped his forehead. "I might forget this whole thing."

The cold, unblinking eyes stared at him. "You might not have a chance to forget."

Whitsun smiled. "You don't think I'd come down here without backup, do you?"

There was silence for a time before the rapier lowered again.

"What do you want?"

Whitsun stood. "If Maresun stole something and found it was worth a lot more than he thought, who would he tell?"

The young man thought.

"Sharessa. She lives two doors down. I don't think you'll get much from her, though."

"Why not?"

Very white teeth gleamed. "That's as much as I'll say. You never saw me."

"Saw who?" Whitsun asked blandly. The teeth flashed again, and the young man was gone.

Glustred looked at his companion with respect. "How'd you know who it was?" he asked.

"I transacted a little business with House Lyrandar about the time the heir to the house disappeared."

Glustred snorted. "If I recall, they found him cut into pieces and stuffed into a garderobe."

"We all have hobbies. Come." Whitsun walked out of the room without a backward glance.

Sharessa's rooms, upon inquiry, were found down a sloping passageway opposite the one that led to Maresun's chamber. The two searchers halted outside the door, and Whitsun applied an ear to it. He rose and nodded to Glustred.

"Go ahead."

The innkeeper hit the door with his shoulder, bursting it inward. The two entered a room that was, in its essentials, a duplicate of the one they had just left.

From a pile of rags in a corner came the sound of raw sobbing, like fingernails scraped over slate. Glustred crossed the room and plucked forth the figure of an emaciated female whose pointed ears and sharp features proclaimed her elf blood.

Her sobs continued, and she twitched and shivered uncontrollably. Whitsun looked disgusted.

"This is what Lassar meant. She's a lilyweed head."

"Lilyweed?"

"Something new. From what I understand, it's only been on the streets a few months. Concentrated essence of dreamlily juice. It's mixed with lilyweed. The heads shove it into their veins." For the first time, Whitsun's voice sounded disturbed.

The innkeeper sniffed. "Someone's been burning something around here."

"That's the smell of the drug. It's stronger than dreamlily. More expensive, though, from what I understand. If she's hooked on it, it must run to money."

Glustred shook the woman. "Snap out of it! You hear?"

"That won't work," said Whitsun. "You'll just scare her or send her into a fit."

Glustred looked at her, marveling. "An elf hooked on dreamlily. Who'd have thought? I always imagined they were above that kind of thing."

"Most are. Or at least they think they are." Whitsun's tone was dispassionate. "But that makes it all the harder for one who becomes addicted to get away from the habit. For our young friend here, there's nothing much the future holds but a slow death. If she gets enough money to keep her supplied with weed, she might last another few weeks, but not much more than that." He leaned down and pushed the hair away from her face. "She was beautiful once."

Glustred looked at his companion in some surprise.

Whitsun stood abruptly. "What we need is water. Go see if you can find some. Two buckets, at least, and it's got to be drinkable."

During his companion's absence, he laid Sharessa down and searched the room. He found nothing of interest and stood for a time looking down at the elf woman, who shivered and wept unceasingly.

Glustred returned, carrying two buckets. He glared at his companion.

"Next time *you* try finding drinking water around here!"

"Hard time?"

Glustred snorted. "If you lived here, would you drink *water?* Everyone laughed at me."

"Well," Whitsun said calmly, "at least you got it. Come. Hold her."

They propped up the elf between them, and Whitsun began to pour water down her throat. At first she coughed and choked and spat out more than she consumed, but at last some consciousness returned to her eyes, and she began to drink thirstily. When the first bucket was emptied, they went on to the second. At last she sat up on her own and looked at the two men.

"Who're you?"

"Friends of Norn." Whitsun's tone was light and friendly.

"Yeah? Where is he? He was s'posed to get me more weed."

"When was that?"

"I dunno. A while ago. Is there more water?"

Whitsun and Glustred exchanged glances.

"No. Maybe later." Whitsun smiled. "Sharessa, where did you get the money for lilyweed?"

She shook her head roguishly at him. It was a grotesque gesture. "Secret. That's a secret." Already her eyes were beginning to dull.

"But I'm a friend of Norn's." Whitsun's voice remained light and cheerful, but his fist, hanging by his side, clenched. "I'm sure he'd want you to tell me."

"I needed more weed." The woman's face grew long. "I didn't have any. An' I *needed* it. Tha's why I had to sell it."

"What? What did you sell?"

Whitsun waved Glustred back. His face was tense.

"Sold it, eh?"

"Yeah. To Paaltova. He ga' me two sov'reigns for it."

"I see. And then you bought weed with that?"

"Where's Norn?" The elf woman began to cry, her body shaking with dry, racking sobs. "I wan' Norn. Why doesn' he come back?"

Whitsun let her sag back onto the floor, where she curled up and promptly went to sleep. "That's it," he said. "We've got to find this Paaltova."

Glustred sighed. "How do you know she was even talking about the thing you're looking for? Whatever it is."

"Look around. Can you see anything here anyone would pay two sovereigns for?" Whitsun got to his feet. "It must be something they got recently, so chances are it's what I'm after. At least now we know where all Norn's profits went. He must have been dipping half the pockets at the lightning rail to keep her in supply."

Glustred looked thoughtful. "Funny. I never would have thought he was a weedie."

"I doubt he was. But he seems to have paid for his girlfriend's enjoyment. Come on."

Finding Paaltova proved easier than they hoped. A derelict war veteran begging at a corner—Glustred examined him closely—directed them to a shop located in the lower floor of a building that soared up into the darkness.

Whitsun pushed at the door, which creaked open a few inches

then stopped. He pushed harder. Glustred came to his aid, and between them they forced an opening.

Inside was chaos. Paaltova's stock lay, for the most part, scattered on the floor—boxes flung open, jars and pots smashed, bundles torn apart and their contents flung around the room.

Glustred looked about. "Someone got here before us."

Whitsun ignored him and moved to the back of the shop where a set of shelves had been pulled over. "Give me a hand."

They moved the shelves to one side, revealing the figure of a man sprawled facedown on the floor. He was middle-aged, but his skin was leathery and seamed with lines. His body was short, and he had long, sharp fingernails that had dug into the wooden floor during his death throes. A shock of bright red hair stood up from his head, and to one side were the smashed and twisted ruin of a pair of spectacles.

Where the back of his head should be was a pulpy mess of bone and brain.

"Paaltova," Glustred said gloomily.

Whitsun nodded. Part goblin from the looks of him, I'd say. He had turned the body over and was examining a series of shallow cuts on the corpse's hands and face.

"It appears he didn't want to tell his visitors something. So they tried to persuade him. They had him tied up *here*—" he pointed to an overturned chair with a few bits of rope still attached to it—"then he either escaped or they let him go, and he walked or ran over *here*." He pointed to the position of the corpse. "He was facing away from them when they decided he'd outlived his usefulness, and someone got to work on his head from behind. I should think that he offered to show them what they wanted. As soon as he got it for them, they took care of him." He looked around. "Let's see if they found what they were looking for."

More searching was enough to convince both men that their object was no longer in the shop. Glustred straightened and cracked the muscles in his back.

"Where now?"

Whitsun considered. "I suppose back to the girlfriend. She might have some idea of who did this, though I doubt it."

The big man nodded. "What about all this?"

"Oh, I imagine the Watch might get around to it in a month or so." Whitsun's tone was scornful. "In any case, we shouldn't get caught here."

They retraced their steps to Sharessa's room. As they approached, Whitsun laid a cautionary hand on his companion's arm.

"Watch out!"

The door was ajar. Glustred, quietly for so large a man, approached it and hit it with the flat of his foot. It crashed open, meeting no resistance. The searchers entered and stared at the object dangling from a rope affixed to a hook in the wooden ceiling.

Whitsun was first to act, seizing Sharessa around the waist. "Cut her down!" he snapped at his companion.

From somewhere Glustred drew a knife and slashed the running noose around the elf woman's neck. Together they laid her on the floor, and Whitsun placed a hand against her neck, feeling for a pulse.

"Dolurrh!" Glustred muttered. He stepped back.

Whitsun forced her mouth open and pressed down a few times on her chest, then felt the vein at her neck again. He shook his head. In death, Sharessa's face had gained a peace it had not held in life, and it was possible now to imagine her as she might have appeared before the drug had ravaged her body.

The door creaked open, and Glustred spun, knife in hand.

A long, thin face framed by unwashed lank black hair poked through the opening, and frightened eyes took in the scene.

"Oh, bloody fang! Is she dead?"

"Yes." Whitsun got to his feet.

"Bloody fang! Was it that man?"

"What man?"

"The man." The speaker came far enough into the room for Whitsun and Glustred to determine it was female.

"The man with the white hair."

"Was he in this room?"

"Dunno." She shook her head. "I seen him runnin' for the stairs." She pointed.

"Was he carrying anything?" Whitsun's voice was tense.

"Uh, yeah . . . bundle under one arm. Bloody fang! He killed her, din't he?"

Whitsun was halfway through the door, pushing past the woman. "Which way?" he shouted.

The girl stuck out an arm. Whitsun shoved her and crashed through the small crowd that had been gathering behind her. Some, having heard what happened, were already dispersing. Death was too common an occurrence in Tumbledown to attract attention for long.

A few cries followed Whitsun as he raced along the alley and turned onto the main street. He grabbed a man lounging against a lintel.

"A man with white hair came out of here. Which way did he go?"

The man blinked stupidly, and Whitsun shook him. "Which *way?*"

"There!"

Whitsun dodged down the street. Though stocky, he moved with surprising ease through and around small knots of people that dotted the way. He lunged up a wide flight of stairs and into a broad square lined with grubby market stalls.

"Dolurrh!"

He halted, chest heaving. His eyes surveyed the crowd. He started and craned his head. A white-haired man was pushing his way through the throng, which had been slowed by a large-wheeled garbage cart that was stuck in the mud. The driver lashed his whip at the horse, and the animal, neighing and rolling its eyes in pain, struggled to pull the vehicle free while the onlookers offered helpful advice interspersed with curses.

Whitsun slipped easily through the crowd. Now he was within five feet of the white-haired man.

His quarry turned. Their eyes closed with one another.

Recognition flared in the man's face, a mixture of alarm and anger.

Whitsun bent. His hand went to his ankle. When he came up, there was a knife in it. He flicked his wrist, and the knife flew in a flash of silver. It struck the white-haired stranger's left wrist, pinning it to a wooden pole beside him. The man howled as the crowd parted, each looking for the source of the skillfully thrown knife.

Whitsun lunged toward the man. The white-haired man gritted his teeth and pulled the knife. The blade came free as the man gave a grunt of triumph. With his right hand, he snatched a sword from his side. It snaked from the scabbard with a hiss. The crowd about him scattered, pressing back against each other as the blade darted for Whitsun's chest.

CHAPTER 5

Whitsun's sword was out, and his blade met his opponent's with a clash and ring that sounded above the babble of the marketplace. A quick glance showed him he had room to maneuver. Of Glustred, there was no sign.

The white-haired man was nimble, darting in and out, thrusting and cutting. He held his left hand to his chest to stanch the flow of blood from the knife wound, but it never seemed to affect his balance or his swordsmanship. Whitsun's sword work was more solid but had a mechanical skill that matched his opponent's erratic brilliance.

The white-haired man clutched his bundle to his side beneath his left elbow. Whitsun's strokes, more often than not, were aimed at that side, and he edged toward it at every opportunity.

Hardly unaware of his tactics, the white-haired man made a thrust at Whitsun's thigh, which Whitsun barely avoided. The movement brought him to one knee, and his foe rained a series of blows on him from above. His aim was evidently to achieve by sheer force what he could not gain by skill.

Whitsun fought his way out of danger, though by the time he regained his feet he was bleeding from cuts on the right cheek and arm. He resumed menacing his enemy's burdened side, and the fighters circled again and again.

The crowd shouted admiration at noteworthy displays of sword play and roundly booed those they considered not up to standard. None interfered with the match.

Gradually, as Whitsun struck at the bundle and the injured left limb again and again, he forced his opponent against the line of stalls behind him. Each blow now was carefully calculated in its effect. The white-haired man's strokes were still vigorous, but his breath was coming heavier, and scarlet tinged his cheeks.

The man's thighs pressed against a wooden stall, and his motions were constricted by the other stalls next to him. His teeth were bared in a grimace. Whitsun's blows increased in strength and speed as howls from the audience predicted his victory.

The white-haired man's glance skewed sideways. His blade flashed out, slashing a rope. A stall wavered and collapsed, and a pile of melons larger than either man's head rolled forward. Whitsun leaped back and fell as the melons rolled along the pavement to the agonized screams of the stall's owner.

The white-haired man lunged to his right, and the crowd parted to let him through. Whitsun, recovering his feet, ran after him, kicking melons out of his path. He saw his quarry slip through a narrow opening between two buildings and followed him.

The alleyway twisted, curled around itself, and opened into a semicircular space ringed by a slender, wrought-iron balcony. The white-haired man stood, his back to his pursuer, staring out, looking for somewhere to jump. At Whitsun's footsteps, he spun.

"You don't have anywhere to go," said Whitsun. "Just give me what you've got there."

The man's sword point described small circles in the air between them.

"I don't give a toss about you or the girl back there. All I'm after is what you've got under your arm."

Steel flashed as the man lunged and thrust. Whitsun parried and replied, keeping himself between the man and the alley entrance. They exchanged a dozen blows and broke apart. The man stepped back a pace against the railing and looked over it. Whitsun stared.

"Dolurrh!"

The man leaped over the rail, hurling his blade at Whitsun as he did so. Whitsun struck the blade aside and jumped after him, one hand snapping around the rail while the other grappled his foe's collar. The white-haired man wriggled to break free. He struck at his captor with a fist then brought up the bundle in a stroke aimed at Whitsun's face.

Whitsun released the collar and snatched the bundle as the man's fingers slipped from it. The man fell, and Whitsun could see his lips moving in a spell.

His lips stopped moving.

A spike of iron, the top of a narrow steeple twenty feet below the balcony, protruded from the man's chest. He writhed for an agonizing moment, shrieking a wordless cry, then was still and silent.

Whitsun stared down. Hands from above pulled him back off the railing, and he smelled a familiar scent of sour wine and onions.

"About bloody time," he remarked to Glustred. "I was wondering—"

He stopped.

Behind them, members of the Watch filed onto the balcony, swords drawn, blades pointing toward the two men.

➤

"What was he after?" The Watch captain—a dwarf named Belar, whose belly hung low over his leather belt—glared at Whitsun. His beard was unkempt and his uniform was stained. His breath smelled of tobacco and bad wine. He leaned back in his chair.

"I've no idea." Whitsun stretched. The Watchhouse in Tumbledown was undistinguishable from its fellow in Boldrei's Hearth. The same battered tables and chairs. The same badly whitewashed walls. The same questions in the same disbelieving tone. The Watchmen who had escorted Whitsun there had been polite but firm. Leaving Glustred to kick his heels outside, they'd brought Whitsun before the captain, who showed no inclination whatever toward politeness.

"Bloody fang, Whitsun! If you don't know anything about the man, why were you chasing him?"

"He stole something. I was trying to recover it."

"Something of yours?"

"No. It belongs to a friend."

"This friend have a name?"

"Not right now."

"We know all about you, Whitsun."

"Really?"

"You were clean-up man for House Medani last year after the blackmail scandal."

"The—? Oh, yes, I heard something about that."

"Four members of the baron's personal guard found with their throats cut. Yes, I think you did hear something about it. More than heard something. We *know* what happened, Whitsun, even if you managed to get away with it. But now you're playing in my patch, and I don't like that."

Belar thrust his face to within an inch of Whitsun's. "Who's your client?"

Whitsun shook his head. "I have no client. Just a friend. His name is my business."

"His?" Belar pounced.

"Very good. Of course, I might be lying. I wouldn't put it past me."

The dwarf glared at him for a moment then went to the door and banged on it. Two men entered—one another guard, the other . . .

Whitsun came out of his seat, but the guard stepped forward and with an easy motion pushed him back.

"What's a wizard doing here?"

"What do you think?" Belar retorted. "I don't care for wizards much myself, but they're useful if you want to get the truth out of a suspect."

"You can't use a truth spell on me! Not without orders from the head of the Sharn Watch!"

"Yes, well, here in Tumbledown," the dwarf observed, "we aren't so particular about rules when we're questioning a suspect. You're stone lucky it's a truth spell and not some other kinds of things I can think of. Now, you want to tell me on your own, or do I have Saleh here go in an' rip up bits of your mind into tiny pieces?"

Whitsun said nothing but set his jaw. On either side of him, guards clamped hands around his arms, holding him in place. The dwarf looked at him a moment, then nodded to the wizard.

Whitsun groaned. Sweat poured down his forehead, and his body writhed. He shuddered, a movement that ran from the top of his body right down through his feet. Saleh, with one hand resting on Whitsun's forehead, the other inscribing semicircles in the air, twisted his mouth in mirthless amusement. The wizard was tall and thin with lank black hair plastered down the sides of his head ending in two waxed curls on either side of his face. His face was pale, and his nose was hooked. With his clawlike fingers, he looked like a vulture hovering above the body before him.

"Who is your client?"

"A . . . a . . . human."

"Good. Name?"

"Del . . . Dral . . . Desh . . ."

Drool oozed from the corner of Whitsun's mouth. Captain Belar, watching from a corner, growled. "Come on, Saleh. Curse you, you've been at it for half an hour. Let's get some answers."

The mage ignored him. A long furrow appeared in the center of his forehead, and he bent toward Whitsun.

"What . . . is . . . the . . . name . . . of . . . your . . . client?"

Whitsun shook his head. Blood ran from his ears. The mage turned to the dwarf.

"How far do you want this to go?"

"Don't kill him. Disposing of bodies is inconvenient."

The guards had been dispensed with as unnecessary once the process of truth-spelling Whitsun got underway. Whitsun lolled in the chair, arms dangling at his sides, while the wizard loomed over him.

Belar got up and paced. "Let's try something easier. What's this thing he's looking for?"

The mage turned back to Whitsun and put the question. Whitsun's eyes rolled back into his skull, but he answered. "A valuable."

"What sort of valuable?"

"Don't know. It's got gold and jewels on it."

The dwarf snorted. "Hah!" He walked to the cell door, opened it, and called, "Bring me that!"

A large guard appeared with the bundle over which Whitsun had fought the white-haired man. The dwarf unwrapped it and showed the contents to Whitsun.

Two copper disks fell out. One was punched through the middle, while the other was corroded and practically falling apart. Both were battered and rough looking.

"That's what you were chasing."

Whitsun, eyes half closed in pain, reached out a hand and touched the disks. He was open mouthed. Belar chuckled nastily.

"So that's the kind of thing you go after," he remarked. "Can't say as I'd risk my life over it, but I guess you know your own business. What's next? Picking up a bundle of laundry for someone?"

There was a flash and a scream. The wizard shot backward through the door of the cell and crashed into the corridor wall. A large, charred hole smoked on the front of his robes, and he clawed at the flesh underneath. His mouth worked in a spell. The burned flesh knit, though it left a scar with red and raw edges. The dwarf stared.

"What in Dolurrh . . . ?"

Saleh came to his feet, eyes staring at Whitsun. Carefully he backed away down the corridor.

"Come back here, curse you!" roared his master.

The wizard was gone. Belar stared at Whitsun, with something very much like fear in his gaze.

"What did you do to him?"

Whitsun straightened up painfully and groaned. The dwarf

jerked his head at the other guard, who left the room only to come back in a minute with a bucket of dirty water. He splashed some of it in Whitsun's face, wiping away the trickle of blood from his ears. Whitsun bent over, retching, This was followed by a fit of coughing. He spat a gob of phlegm onto the floorboards. At last he straightened up and looked at the dwarf with bloodshot eyes. "What?"

The dwarf repeated his question.

"Nothing much." Whitsun stretched and did his best to assume a light, carefree air. "I take it that since you can't find anything I'm free to go?" He turned abruptly on Captain Belar, who flinched and nodded.

"Get out of here!"

Whitsun picked up the bundle containing the copper disks and started to leave. He looked back at the dwarf.

"When you touched these . . ."

"What?"

"Did anything happen?"

The dwarf looked at him curiously.

"Yes, now that you mention it."

"What?"

"I got grease on my fingers and had to wipe 'em clean. Enough of this!" Belar opened the door. "Get out!"

Whitsun picked up the bundle, being careful to avoid touching either of the copper disks, and left. Outside in the street he found Glustred. The big man was lounging by a lantern post, munching a meat pie.

"So they let you go," was his only comment.

Whitsun ignored him. He stalked down the street, brows drawn down in an angry bar. Passersby scuttled out of his way.

Glustred strode in his wake, wiping away juices from his mouth. "You look like a cat chewed you up and spat you out." This got no response either. "Where are we going now?"

Whitsun ignored him. Glustred struggled to keep up for a moment then halted. "I'm going home," he said.

"No, you're not." The words were spat out between clenched teeth.

"What's to stop me?"

Whitsun spun on his heel. His face was within an inch of his companion's as he spoke.

"You're going with me. You're going until I say you're not. You're doing what I say to do, and if I say to shut up, your mouth is staying shut."

"And why am I doing that?"

"Because if you don't, you'll come home to a smoking hole in the ground where the Bone and Bristle used to be. Because I can make life so bad for you you'll wish you'd never heard of me. *That*'s why." He turned again and continued walking.

"I already wish that," the big man muttered.

➥

Back inside Paaltova's shop, Whitsun locked and barred the door behind them and shuttered the windows. Outside a thin rain was falling, spattering on the cobbles in a vain attempt to wash them clean. This deep within the city moisture drained constantly from the higher levels and poured relentlessly downward until it found its way at last to Dagger River.

Whitsun lit several lamps. He turned Paaltova's corpse faceup and methodically went through the dead man's pockets and anywhere the shopkeeper might have secreted something. At last he sat down on a three-legged stool. His anger seemed to have passed, and he looked about him at the chaos of the ransacked shop.

"Let's think about this," he said.

Glustred grunted and righted another stool, lowering his massive bottom onto it. He kept his back to the body of the shopkeeper, whose sightless eyes stared at the low ceiling. Whitsun continued.

"Sharessa, needing money for lilyweed, looks around for something to take to Paaltova. Would she try to fool him with a couple of copper disks? No. First, because Paaltova, presumably, isn't an idiot and is going to examine anything he's given to check for value. Second, because he *did* pay her, which was why she was off on weed when we found her.

"So. Paaltova's sitting in his shop, and our white-haired friend comes in. He's been tracking Sharessa. Why he hasn't just killed her and taken the object, we don't know, but we'll leave that for a moment. Instead he marks Paaltova as easier. He asks for what Sharessa left.

"Paaltova's bright enough to realize there's profit to be made here, though not smart enough, I think, to understand that White-Hair is willing to do anything to get his hands on the bundle. So he tries to put White-Hair off. Our friend engages in a little aggressive questioning. Paaltova realizes it's not worth hanging onto the object—at least not apparently. He agrees to give it up. White-Hair looses him, and he goes to get the bundle and has time to pull a substitution. What he doesn't think of is that in giving up the bundle—even if he really hasn't given it up—he's made himself expendable to White-Hair.

"The question is, why didn't White-Hair examine the bundle? He was in a hurry. Probably. But that much of a hurry? Or was he interrupted? Ah! Of course!"

Whitsun smiled.

"He hears or sees two intrepid investigators on their way. Realizing he's got to get out of here, he leaves without looking closely at what he came for."

Glustred stretched and groaned as his shoulders creaked. "Very well. Where does this get us?"

Whitsun ignored him. "If he didn't examine it closely, it must have been about the size, shape, and weight of what he wanted. So we know approximately what we're looking for, even if we don't know exactly."

"So?"

"Let's start from Paaltova." Whitsun stood by the corpse. "He's struck down here, and he was facing away from his killer."

"How do you know?"

Whitsun gave the big man a look.

"Because his wound is on the back of his head. His killer, White-Hair, is standing *here* and bashes his head in with something. Whitsun picked up a poker and examined its end. "This, in fact. There's blood and hair all over it. Stand here, Glustred."

The big man obeyed with every sign of reluctance. Whitsun shook his head. "You're too tall. Crouch a bit."

Glustred bent at the knees.

"Good. Hold that."

Whitsun swung the poker and stopped just a fraction of an inch away from Glustred's head. The big man seemed frozen in place.

"Yes. That's the way it happened. Our friend walked up behind Paaltova when he was standing where you're standing now and struck. Now, where did he walk *from?*"

Whitsun tossed the poker away—to Glustred's relief—and backed off behind the shop's wooden counter toward the back. He bent, examining the floor. "Yes," he called. "I can see traces of shoes here. Not mine. Not Paaltova's. And too small to be your boots. And if any further proof were wanting, here's the rack where the poker stood. He used the first thing that came to hand." He nodded, satisfied with himself. "All right. Come over here."

Glustred approached, and Whitsun maneuvered him into position. "Stay there," he told the innkeeper. "Watch me." He walked toward Paaltova's corpse. "Can you still see my hands?"

"Yes."

"What am I doing?"

"Flapping them about."

"What about now?"

"Can't see."

"Move around some."

Glustred started to go to one side.

"Crouch again. The killer was shorter than you. Otherwise he'd have hit the top of Paaltova's head, not the back. A bit taller than you were before but not as tall as you are."

Glustred lurched from side to side, maintaining his crouch with difficulty.

"No good," he said. "If I stand here, your back's to me, and if I move over there, the pillar blocks you."

"Excellent." Whitsun looked around him. "So this is one place Paaltova could have carried out the substitution."

Glustred joined him. "Would he have kept more of those disks in this part of the shop?"

Whitsun stared at him. "You know, Glustred, there are times—not many—when your intelligence is almost human. Let's see if there are any more of these things around."

A search yielded a small heap of the copper disks piled untidily next to an assortment of boxes and flasks, most of the latter cracked or broken. In the same area were two or three old books, their pages crumbling with age. Whitsun lifted them and thumbed through each one before tossing it aside.

The two men cast their search a bit wider but without results. All the objects in the shop were well covered with dust, and examining them stirred it into clouds that lingered in the lights that illuminated the interior. Over everything the dead man kept a ghastly watch.

Whitsun moved slowly, his hands making arcane gestures. Every now and again he muttered words in another language. Once or twice he stopped and examined an object more closely, and once he set a vase on a bare counter space and stood in front of it for several minutes, lips moving with spells. Nothing happened to the vase, and he abandoned it.

There was a flash and a burst of light. The vase exploded, driving shards of glass across the shop. Glustred howled and clutched at his ear. Whitsun, who had been bending over at the time, escaped the effects of the blast. He came up, knife in hand, eyes twitching from side to side.

"What the . . . ?"

Glustred snatched up a scrap of cloth, trying to stanch the flow of blood from his injured ear. "What did you do?" he demanded.

"Nothing. I . . ." Whitsun's voice faded as he stared at the spot where the vase had been. He walked over and examined it carefully and shook his head.

"Is *that* what we're looking for?"

"No. Certainly not. We haven't yet found it. It *must* be here."

"Maybe Paaltova disguised it," Glustred observed.

"The thought *had* occurred to me." Whitsun was obviously irritated at being outsmarted by Paaltova as well as still startled by the explosion of the vase. "I've been spell checking every object in this part of the shop. Nothing." He stopped again. "Spell checking . . . I wonder . . ." He shook his head.

Glustred looked about. "Including that?" he asked, pointing to the pile of copper disks.

"Including that." Whitsun stretched, beginning at one end and letting the movement ripple slowly through his body. He rubbed his ear fretfully.

"What's wrong with you?"

"That damned truth spell gave me a splitting headache."

Glustred snorted. "At least your ear's still in one piece." He tied the cloth around his head in a clumsy bandage.

Whitsun's eyes moved about the shop. "Surely I can't be wrong," he muttered, picking up two of the disks and tapping them against one another.

"Hah!"

He strode over the dead shopkeeper, snatched up the two copper disks taken from the white-haired man, and returned to the corner. He slipped them into the heap of disks and shuffled the pile, then turned to Glustred.

"Pick out the two we started with."

The big innkeeper turned the disks over in a half-hearted way and shook his head.

"No idea."

"Watch! But stand back."

Glustred needed no second invitation to move into the farthest corner of the shop, well out of reach of another explosion. Whitsun too positioned himself as far from the pile of disks as possible as he murmured unheard words. Two of the disks glowed poisonous green for a moment. The color faded, leaving a silver ring enclosing a gold sphere in their place. Jewels glinted here and there on the artifact. Whitsun let out his breath.

Glustred whistled. "How'd that work?"

"If someone spell checked the disks by themselves, they resisted the magic and looked just like two ordinary objects. But if they were next to or touching the objects they were with when they were bespelled, they responded." Whitsun smiled. "Very clever, our Paaltova, to come up with that on the spur of the moment. I hope someone gives him a good funeral."

"What now?"

Whitsun looked at the object but did not pick it up. He found a clean cloth—as clean as anything was likely to be in Paaltova's shop—and wrapped it, being careful to keep it away from himself. This done, he looked at Glustred.

"Ready to go?"

CHAPTER 6

lustred insisted on returning to the Bone and Bristle. The innkeeper had grown increasingly nervous after they left Paaltova's establishment, and he showed his disinclination to stay with Whitsun while the latter contacted Freylaut and Delru. Whitsun equally displayed no great desire for the big man's company.

They parted accordingly, and Whitsun made his way up several long flights of broad stairs to a higher level of the city. The lanterns were burning brighter now, signaling the approach of dusk—though this far down in the City of Towers, sunlight never penetrated, and a perpetual gloom reigned. As Whitsun ascended, the streets grew wider, and in some windows a few flower pots were displayed. After the blackness and death of Tumbledown, even a few levels higher meant a welcome change.

Whitsun found a message station with little trouble and, rousing the sleepy clerk, who was just ending his shift, sent a brief message to Delru. He waited patiently in the station as the old clerk was replaced by the night worker. At last, a reply came through.

> Meet at the Bone and Bristle in two hours.
> Freylaut

No mention of the woman. Whitsun read the message over several times, tapping his fingers together. At last, he rose, tossed a coin to the clerk behind the counter, and set out for home.

The inn was filled as usual when he arrived. Glustred, busy behind the bar, ignored him. Whitsun mounted the stairs to his room.

He sat for a while, had a small drink, then unwound the wrappings around the orerry and examined it all over. He tried several spells on it without getting any results. His forehead creased. At last he brought one hand cautiously down to within an inch of the golden sphere that sat within the ring.

Nothing happened.

He moved it closer. Still nothing. At last, with a slight grimace, he touched the sphere. Then he picked up the orerry. He performed the same operation with the silver ring, moving with exactly the same degree of methodical caution. Again, no spark, no rush of magical energy.

The gold sphere was about six inches across. Around its equator were etched tiny symbols of the same type as Whitsun had seen on Norn Maresun's ring. The silver ring that encircled the sphere was twelve or thirteen inches in diameter and was also covered with symbols. The sphere floated in its center with no visible means of support. Whitsun pressed them and twisted them in various ways, but he could not get them to touch one another. The sphere also resisted all efforts to detach it from the silver ring.

Whitsun's face retained an expression of scholarly detachment. He went to the chimney and retrieved Norn Maresun's ring from its hiding place. He examined it closely, but it was unchanged from the time he had last examined it. Next he brought it close to the jeweled pieces of the orrery, but again nothing happened. No magical spark, no flash or—to his relief—no cataclysmic event. Whitsun touched the two objects together, first Maresun's ring to the sphere, then to the silver ring, then to both at once, without results.

He shook his head, laid them on the table in front of him, and sat looking at them for a time. At last he rose, found a piece of parchment and a quill, and made a tracing of the symbols—with some difficulty, since the symbols on the golden sphere were so small. Finally, Whitsun fetched from his chest the tracing he'd made from his earlier discovery and compared the two drawings. His lips moved slightly as he looked at them side by side. He spread out his hands and placed them over the two pieces of parchment, closing his eyes. His brow wrinkled in concentration. A faint glow emanated from his fingertips. Carefully he brought his hands down until his fingers touched the parchments.

The glow flared brightly, and Whitsun snatched his hands back with a curse. The glow disappeared. Whitsun wrung his hands then wiped them with a cloth rag. His face was puzzled. He examined the parchments and was satisfied with the results.

Whitsun sighed, rewrapping Maresun's ring and placing it once more in the chimney flue. The parchments he folded and put in his pocket, and he covered the orrery with cloth, putting it in the remains of one of his chests. He poured another drink.

"Shifter's coming," announced Glustred's voice through the speaking tube.

There was a knock on the door, followed a moment later by Freylaut.

"Have you got it?" were the first words out of his mouth.

Whitsun raised an eyebrow. "Nice to see you too. Where's your . . . partner?"

The shifter's sharp teeth champed together. "Never mind her. Have you got it?"

"Have you got my fee?"

Freylaut pulled out a bag and tossed it on the table. Whitsun counted the gold inside, taking his time.

"That makes it a nice evening so far."

The shifter said nothing. Whitsun rose and bent over the chest in which he'd placed the recovered object.

He dodged just as Freylaut's knife cut through the air, stabbing where his neck would have been. The shifter, overbalanced by the momentum of his blow, staggered forward, giving Whitsun time to twist and roll out of the way. He came to his feet facing Freylaut, holding the bundle that concealed the orerry in front of him like a shield. The two cautiously circled the room, keeping the table and chairs between them.

"Cutting down expenses?" Whitsun asked.

Freylaut made no answer save a lunge, shifting the knife from right to left hand as he did so. His eyes glowed yellow, and fangs grew over his lower lip.

Whitsun snorted. "Is that supposed to impress me?"

Freylaut leaped over the table, knife forward to slash, fangs gleaming.

Whitsun, twisting aside a chair, dived under the table. As he came up his hand went to his boot and drew a knife, not as long and deadly looking as that carried by the shifter but serviceable for a fight. He now clutched the bundle in his left hand, keeping the knife in his right.

Freylaut was beside the window but began to sidle again. Whitsun moved with him until he felt the door against his back.

He opened it and was through just as Freylaut made another high leap and cleared the table.

Whitsun plunged down the stairs and into the crowded common room. Glustred, from the far end of the bar, looked up just in time to see the shifter come flying down the stairs, long hair drifting behind him in a cloud, fangs gleaming against his red lips.

"Balls!"

The innkeeper's exclamation cut through the excited babble of the customers as they scattered out of the way of the combatants. The shifter, seeking to gain an advantage of height, jumped on the bar. Mugs and earthenware pitchers and plates went crashing to the accompaniment of agonized yells from Glustred.

"Outside! Outside, blast you!"

The combatants ignored him. Freylaut launched himself from the counter, blade flashing. He made a daring feint, and Whitsun, caught off guard, thrust out the bundle to parry it.

Swift as thought, the shifter snatched the bundle from him and sprinted for the door. Whitsun dodged and kicked a bench between the shifter and the exit. Freylaut, having seized his prize, was careless and went head over heels across the obstacle. Whitsun, with his free hand, grabbed a bottle and shattered its lower half, leaving him with a jagged-edged piece of glass in his left hand and his knife in his right. As Freylaut disentangled himself from the bench, Whitsun placed his body between the shifter and the door. He waved the bottle menacingly.

Freylaut grinned. "I'd expect that kind of beer-brawl fighting from you. Did you learn it in the brothel where your mother worked?"

Whitsun ignored the gibe. Freylaut's fangs were now fully extended, his hair bristling. He moved left while Whitsun matched him.

The shifter darted forward. Whitsun backed as much as he was able. The solid wood of the door was behind him. Eager shouts from the crowd filled his ears.

"Six crowns on the shifter!"

"Twelve on Fangs!"

"Watch your right, human!"

Taking his opponent off guard, Whitsun dived forward, tucking his body in a compact ball, surprising for one of his bulk. He slid under Freylaut's knife and slashed the shifter's leg with the broken bottle. Freylaut howled in pain and bent toward his injured leg. Whitsun came up again and spun just to see the shifter, blood pouring from his leg wound, wrench open the door and stagger through it. Eager faces stared through the opening into the inn, seeking the cause of the ruckus.

"Out, please!"

Knife in front of him, Whitsun threw himself forward. Spectators sprang back to give him passage to the cobbles. He rolled again and came up facing away from the inn's entrance. He glared about, seeking the course of the shifter's flight.

Freylaut burst at him from one side. Rather than running, the shifter clearly intended to finish the assassination he had begun upstairs. A good portion of the crowd from inside the inn, anxious to see the outcome and collect on their wagers, spilled through the doorway into the street.

The shifter's ragged trouser leg was soaked in blood, but his strength and energy appeared undiminished. He held the bundle containing the orerry tucked beneath one long arm, while the other hand described slow circles with his knife. Whitsun backed away, creating room between himself and his foe. His heels slipped on the cobblestones, and he fell backward.

The shifter was on him, long teeth bared in a snarl of triumph. He lifted the knife to strike . . . and stopped.

The blade fell from his hand and clattered on the stones. He plucked at a slender shaft that sprouted from the base of his neck. His dark eyes took on a puzzled expression as he fell forward.

Whitsun rolled on one side and got to his feet. The crowd had gone suddenly silent. The victor looked about for the archer.

There was a whirr and a thump. A second arrow struck the doorway of the Bone and Bristle, scoring Whitsun's shoulder. Without so much as a murmur, the gathering of onlookers dissolved, some slipping back into the inn while others melted away into nearby streets and passageways. Whitsun snatched the bundle from the shifter's lifeless hand and, ignoring the blood trickling down his back, dived back through the inn's door only to be brought up by solid wood as Glustred slammed it in his face.

Another arrow struck the door, penetrating it a full inch. Whitsun cursed and ran down a narrow passageway to one side of the inn's entrance. The two buildings that bordered it leaned toward each other as if whispering secrets. He heard the thump of one more arrow behind him, then silence save for his feet on the pavement.

A quarter hour later Whitsun was standing at the edge of a small plaza. On three sides, towers rose, while on the fourth a graceful staircase with an intricately carven balustrade rose in broad steps to another street level above. A steady traffic of well-clad folk moved up and down the stairs, and Whitsun immersed himself in the crowd. His breathing slowed, and the color returned to his face. Slipping into a niche where he would be unseen, he tore a piece of cloth from his shirt and, bending awkwardly, bound it around his shoulder where the arrow had struck. He covered the makeshift bandage with his cloak then tried out the arm once or twice, swinging it back and forth, wincing slightly. He looked around as if considering.

A few members of the Watch passed down the stairs, and Whitsun bent as if tying his boot, keeping his face averted. The Watch passed in a burst of laughter and stale beer.

Whitsun glanced back down the way he'd come and hesitated. A slight smile curved his lips. Turning, he climbed the stairs. At the top he surveyed the street, more out of caution than need, and set off down one of the side avenues that opened from the main way.

A short burst of walking and climbing brought him into a maze of streets in which a happy throng surged and roared as it entered and exited buildings adorned with flaring torches and flanked by muscular men and slender, half-clad women. Gaudy signs advertised entertainment, while from doorways females of every race and species beckoned to passersby. A tall woman with pointed ears and the build of a half-elf sidled up to Whitsun.

"Looking for a party?"

Whitsun shook his head and strode on, ignoring the catcalls behind him that impugned his virtue and his manhood.

Another few twisting streets that seemed to meander aimlessly, and he found himself in an alley whose sign grandly proclaimed it Kingsway. Halfway down the street, two balls knocked together as a street sign creaked in the breeze. Whitsun knuckled the door and waited patiently.

A slit in the heavy oak door flew open at his waist level, and a pair of black eyes stared out.

"Yeah?"

"Merimma."

"Never heard of her."

"You should get out more then."

A pause while the eyes considered.

"What's the word?"

Whitsun leaned against the oak. "How about if I kick down this door and walk over your ugly face?"

Another pause then a click of a latch, and the door opened.

The halfling—for so he was—on the other side considered Whitsun with the gloomy air of one who foresees trouble.

"Whatchu want wit' her?"

"Just tell her Taliman is here to collect his debt."

The halfling disappeared, shaking his head. Whitsun looked around. The room was lavishly furnished in contrast to the homely aspect of the entrance. Furniture of dark, rich wood lined the walls, and everbright lanterns shed a golden glow over all. Paintings and engravings on the walls showed couples engaged in a variety of interesting acts. Whitsun had just moved closer to examine one of these when a voice, soft as rabbit's fur but tinged with something stronger and sharper than a scalpel, spoke from behind him.

"Taliman?"

Whitsun's mouth curved upward at the sound. "Merimma."

He turned and paused to admire the view.

The woman who stood in the doorway was almost six feet tall with auburn hair that swept nearly to her feet. Tiny threads of silver among the red glistened in the lantern light. Her eyes were a startling blue, the blue of sapphires on a moonlit night, with long lashes that made them seem even longer. She stood in the doorway with a studied motionlessness and waited for him.

"Merimma," he repeated.

She smiled. "My Taliman. Welcome."

He moved toward her. She suffered him to come within six inches then struck him full in the face with her open palm. His ears rang with the blow. He rubbed his jaw.

"Been a while."

"Yes." She turned. "Come in."

They passed down a corridor and through several rooms equally lavish in furnishing. They arrived in a small room dominated by a massive desk. Merimma gestured to a large leather armchair, and Whitsun sank into it gratefully. She seated herself and looked at him.

"What do you want, Taliman?"

"To stay."

"How long?"

"A few days. No more."

She smiled. "Who is after you?"

"Don't know." He frowned. "Someone with arrows."

She rested her chin on her folded hands. "I do not like having you here, Taliman. You attract the attention of the Watch."

"What d'you care about the Watch? I'm sure you pay them enough."

"For this business—" she spread her hands to take in the room and its surroundings—"yes. For my other business . . ." She shook her head. "They always want more. My affairs are in a delicate state at the moment. I prefer to remain obscure."

It was Whitsun's turn to smile. "You can be many things, Merimma, but obscure isn't one of them."

She acknowledged the compliment, bowing her head gracefully. "Nonetheless, I prefer that the Watch not come to my door just now. Besides, they are crude . . . pigs. They smell. And they insult the girls."

"The girls aren't part of the bribe, then?"

She snorted. "Never! I love my girls as if they were my own daughters. Never would I force one of them to go with one of those—" She spat an elven word that referred to a body part. "So, Taliman, if I do as you ask, I must be sure it is not the Watch that is after you."

He shook his head. "Not the Watch, no. I told you, I don't know who it is. All I need is a place to lie quiet for a few days."

She considered and nodded. "Very well. Fifty galifars."

"Twenty."

"Forty."

"Thirty."

"Done."

From an inner pocket, Whitsun produced the bag Freylaut had given him and counted out the money. Merimma placed it in a drawer, rose, and led him to a bedroom. Its windows were tightly shuttered.

Merimma paused at the doorway. "The room does not come with company. That would be extra."

Whitsun grinned. "Don't worry. I want to be alone."

When the door closed, he took several turns around the room, his face a mask of concentration. He took out the package he had snatched from Freylaut's body, unwrapped it, and examined the orrery again. He shook his head. Then, without removing his clothes, he put the orrery beneath his pillow so that anyone putting a hand on it would wake him. He lay down on the bed and closed his eyes. From time to time he stirred and opened an eye, but at last the sound of his regular breathing filled the chamber.

He awoke with a start and glanced about the room as if reassuring himself where he was. Everything was as he had left it. The orrery was still beneath the pillow. He checked the door to make sure it was still fastened.

He undid the shutters and opened the window, avoiding as much as possible showing himself. He looked out on a typical Sharn cityscape. Below him was a precipitous drop of several hundred feet. Opposite a tower rose into blackness, its few lighted windows glowing like a cat's eyes. Most were curtained, but a few showed interiors. Whitsun examined these closely, his gaze moving methodically from one to the other while he kept his own body, as much as he could, behind the window frame. At last, satisfied, he closed the window and shutters.

He sat for a time drumming his fingers, thinking. As if from far off, there came a scream and then another. A few minutes later, he heard distantly the sound of sobbing, quickly hushed.

There was a tap on his door, and Merimma entered. His quick ears had not heard the tumblers of the lock move. The woman had changed her clothes to a skintight dress of bright green, cut low in front and back. Whitsun smiled as he looked at her.

"Full house tonight?"

She inclined her head in a graceful gesture. "A party of orcs. Some girls do not like to have orcs as customers. They say they are too rough and smell."

"But you persuade them otherwise? Even though you love them as your own daughters?"

She shrugged. "Sometimes even one's daughters require correction. I show them where their best interests lie." Her nose wrinkled. "It is true, I suppose, that orcs are an acquired taste."

Whitsun leaned forward. "Have you heard anything about me?"

"You have many names, Taliman." She sighed. "Under which might I have heard something?"

"The old one."

"Ah."

She sat, parting her dress in front to reveal shapely legs. "Yes, I have heard a few things."

"Such as?"

"You found an object of great value, but you failed to return it to its proper owner. In so doing you angered important figures." She looked appraisingly at his face. "It would be wise, I think, Taliman, to divest yourself of this object as soon as possible."

Whitsun gave a short, harsh bark of laughter. "I don't even know what it is I've got. I can't tell what the best way to dispose of it is or how it might profit me to do that."

Her delicate brows drew together. "I do not understand."

Whitsun hitched his chair closer to hers. Keeping his voice low and an eye on the door, he gave a compressed account of the events that had transpired since Norn Maresun first staggered into his room. Merimma listened without comment. When he had finished, she sat in silence for a time. A clock ticked loudly and chimed the quarter hour.

"What is the connection," she asked at last, "between what Maresun brought you and the object for which the shifter tried to kill you? You speak as if they are part of a whole, but I do not yet perceive that."

Whitsun shook his head. "They *must* have something to do with one another. Look."

From his inner pocket he drew the two parchments on which he had traced the hieroglyphics from each object. He laid them side by side.

Merimma bent forward to examine them and nodded. "Yes. You are right. Though this—" she tapped the first parchment, the one containing the symbols from Maresun's ring—"seems different from the other. Older, somehow."

"Yes. I need someone to look at this text and tell me what it means." Whitsun's voice changed a bit. "I tried to read it myself with a spell but something . . . went wrong."

Merimma raised a delicately drawn eyebrow. "From what you say, something has been going wrong with magic around you since you acquired these objects. Still . . ." She considered, tapping a finger against her lips. "There is one who might help you read it."

Whitsun grunted. "I thought of him. How much of his mind is left?"

"Some. He fades fast. But enough for this, perhaps." She rose. "Where is the ring Maresun gave you?"

"In my room at the Bone and Bristle." He nodded. "I know what you're thinking. But it doesn't seem to like being found. Except by me."

"Nonetheless, I think you are mistaken in leaving it there. From what you have told me, far too many people are interested in it. You should retrieve it. You may keep it here. I have many ways of keeping objects secret within this house."

Whitsun thought for a bit then nodded. "Very well. Maybe you have a point." He stood and walked over to the bed. Lifting the pillow he retrieved the bundle he and Freylaut had struggled over. "I want you to guard this."

Merimma took it without opening it. "Very well. I will take both. But not for too long. I have my own safety to consider, Taliman." She walked to the door. Whitsun watched her, mouth twisted in a cynical smile. "Tell me something, Merimma," he said.

She turned.

"What price would you accept to betray me?"

She considered for a moment. "Two thousand galifars," she said. "But there is some room to negotiate."

He sighed and shook his head in mock chagrin. "Underestimating the market, love."

She went out, locking the door behind her.

➽

Ringing the bell produced the halfling who, after some chat, supplied Whitsun with a coil of rope. He left, and Whitsun, opening the window, dangled the rope from it. After securing it to a ring driven into the brickwork around the fireplace, he slid down and dropped into the courtyard at the bottom of the shaft. He tied off the rope behind a few pipes where it was largely out of sight and slipped down a long, dank passage, smelling of human waste and rotting food. He emerged into a narrow street that was, for once, deserted. He stopped and listened but heard nothing but the soft dripping of moisture from above and the occasional clatter of some pedestrian's footsteps above or below his vantage point. After listening and watching for a short while, Whitsun slipped like a shadow onto the side of the street and passed rapidly down it.

Noise and a glow from ahead made him slow his steps. In the middle of the lane, a bonfire was burning, its light illuminating a ragged group of figures around it. Two were women, their dank, unwashed hair draped over their dirty faces and ragged clothes. The other three were male. One, taller than the others, was better dressed and had an air of command. He stood, and the others ranged in front of him. He walked before them, inspecting them, touching their hands, shoulders, faces, hair, as if looking at a row of cattle for purchase at market. Finally he stopped in front of one of the women. He pushed her hair aside, baring her neck. His long, gleaming teeth flashed in the firelight as he bent and bit. The woman gave a low groan—whether of pain or of ecstasy Whitsun could not be sure. The others stood passively, watching as the vampire fed. He drank his fill then pushed the woman back, half fainting, into the arms of her companions.

"Tomorrow night then," he growled through bloodstained lips.

One of the men said something. The vampire laughed and

turned his back. The man sprang forward, wooden stake upraised in one hand. The vampire turned and chopped the stake from his attacker's grip in an easy, unhurried motion. He grasped the man's hair and lifted him off his feet. The man squealed with pain. His companions looked on, frozen. The vampire carried the man back to the fire without apparent effort. He thrust the man's face into the flames and down into the fire so the victim's head blazed.

An animal howl of pain came from the dying man. The others scattered like shadows into the darkness. The vampire tossed the dead man aside. His red eyes stared balefully into the dark where Whitsun stood motionless. The vampire bared his teeth in a mirthless grin and vanished.

Whitsun continued, stepping around the dead man, holding his nose against the continued stench that came from the burned, disfigured corpse. At the next passageway opening to his right, he turned down it and, after some twists and turns, came to a long, narrow flight of stairs leading down. He made his way along them, careful not to slip on their slime-covered surface. The steps broadened and emerged from a doorway onto a street where a few people, faces wrapped in cloaks, rushed to and fro, doing their best to ignore one another.

Whitsun breathed an unconscious sigh of relief and turned along the populated street. Whatever the dangers of traveling Sharn by night, the perils were less in places where there were witnesses.

He made his way without hesitation along streets, down lanes, and across bridges. At last he began to climb a shallow hill lined with shops and inns. From the other side, hidden from his sight, was the Bone and Bristle. Ahead he could see an ominous glow. A wisp of smoke drifted by him.

He surmounted the hill and looked. Flames, yellow, purple, and green, blazed from the building that had formerly housed the

Bone and Bristle, as well as Whitsun's living quarters and office. A crowd had gathered to watch the fire, a fine one even by the exacting standards of the middle levels of Sharn.

Whitsun surveyed the crowd, looking for some sign of Glustred. The innkeeper's big frame should make it easy to spot him, even among so many. Suddenly Whitsun stiffened. Amid the crowd, he caught a glimpse of a wave of dark red hair. He plunged down the street, pushing bystanders out of his way.

"Delru!" he shouted. "Delru!"

A wave of bodies surged toward him as people pushed and shoved against one another. Some struck out against their neighbors. A fist took Whitsun in the ear, but he seemed unaware of the blow.

"Delru!"

Unreasoning panic seemed to have seized him, and he struggled frantically against the human tide, shouting. People parted before him, but he found no sign of the mysterious elf woman.

A crash and roar turned his attention back to the fire. The lower roof of the tower fell in, smashing dozens of bottles of liquor, which fed the fire. The crowd ran shrieking from the inferno. Whitsun stared at it, his face a picture of gloom.

A hiss came from the flames as a steady rain began to fall, stifling the fire and sending a thick, black smoke up to coil around the towers of Sharn before escaping into the distant sky.

CHAPTER 7

Much of the night had already gone by. Whitsun consulted a clock. While smoke rose from the remains of the Bone and Bristle, he found a narrow doorway from which he could watch the site and settled down to wait out the rest of the dark hours. Despite the ashes from the wreck that still smoldered, the night turned cold, and he wrapped his cloak about him to ward off the chill.

The crowd remained, trying as best they might to pick through the rubble and find unexploded bottles of liquor, scraps of food, or odds and ends they could carry off. As dawn broke, a company of the Watch appeared and chased them away—reserving for themselves the right to loot the smoldering ruins. Whitsun watched from his doorway, keeping himself concealed. The Watch tramped over the smoking rubble and, after an hour or so, departed, doubtless to find a tavern that had not been destroyed so they could take their breakfasts.

Whitsun emerged from his hiding place. A few narrow

shafts of pale sunlight managed to make their way down from above, lightening the street, filled with coiling smoke and drifting ashes. He approached the ruin and kicked over the remains of a charred bar stool. Glass crunched underfoot as he made his way through the scattered bricks and ash-covered timbers.

"Hey!"

A growling voice hailed him from behind. Whitsun turned and found Glustred, his face begrimed with smoke, his clothes sodden with rain, glaring at him.

"What're *you* doing here? Last I saw, you were about to become a pincushion."

"No thanks to you I wasn't." Whitsun's demeanor was equally hostile. "Good to know I can count on my *true* friends when I'm in danger."

Glustred made no reply but looked about. He bent, picked up a bottle of amber-colored liquid that miraculously had survived, knocked it open, and took a long swig. He glared at Whitsun again.

"Did you have anything to do with this?"

"How? As you said—I was too busy being chased by some-body. Still—" Whitsun broke off, staring upward. Glustred followed his gaze.

The fire had gouged an enormous bite out of the square tower in which the Bone and Bristle had been located. Three sides had fallen in, while the fourth stood, perilously wavering with barely any support, its stones blackened and charred. Against it . . .

"Isn't that my chimney?" Whitsun asked.

"What if it is?"

Without replying, Whitsun scrambled toward the wall. The innkeeper followed, hanging back to make clear he had only a tepid interest in his fellow's activities. Whitsun reached the wall, tested it, and began to climb, looking for bits and pieces of rock sticking out to provide handholds. Glustred watched from below.

"That'll come down on you, you know," he called up.

Whitsun made no answer. He was now some twenty or twenty-five feet off the ground and needed all his concentration to make his way upward. He scrambled up ten more feet then climbed sideways a bit, looking like some large, ungainly spider as he clung to the brickwork. A few pieces of stone came spinning down from above.

"Steady there!" snarled Glustred. He began to back away so as not to be under the wall when it fell.

Whitsun clung to a projecting piece of stone with one hand. His other groped up into the darkness of the chimney that at one time had been in his room.

"Hah!"

He pulled out the bundle containing Maresun's ring. Clutching it between clenched teeth to free his hands, he began to descend. This was harder than going up, but he managed it until he was fifteen feet above the ground, at which point he lost his grip and fell.

His body flipped back into the air, and his shout of dismay was cut off as he floated gently down, coming to rest on the ground with no more disturbance than if he'd been a feather.

Glustred joined him. "Lucky you still had a spell," he observed.

"I didn't, you idiot!" Whitsun pulled himself to his feet. "This is getting very interesting. Magic around me doesn't seem to work the way it's supposed to, and when it's not even supposed to be there, it turns up in spite of itself." He looked at the bundle containing the ring. "And it's started happening since Maresun gave me this."

Glustred grunted. "It doesn't seem to want you to get hurt, whatever it is."

Whitsun considered. "It's a bit unreliable about that," he said at last. "The last time I used a falling spell, it stopped working. I used a spell to detect magical disguise and the vase blew up— though only you got hurt, so maybe something does care about me. Still, I don't think I'd care to trust my life to this."

Glustred looked at the ruins of his tavern and sighed. "Well, I suppose I better start clearing this lot away."

"What then?"

The innkeeper shook his head and seemed at a loss. "Don't know. Everything I bloody owned was in the bloody inn. Balls!" He kicked a bit of wood savagely, slamming it against a pile of stones from one of the collapsed walls. "I could go to Zefinn for money to start again, but—"

"But he'd want most of your takings," Whitsun finished for him. "In fact that'll be true of anyone you go to—even a bank, though they're at least legitimate. Well, I suppose you could come with me."

Glustred stared at him. "What?"

"I find myself in need of a bodyguard again, preferably one who looks intimidating as well as being able to hold off attackers. You fit the bill on both accounts."

The innkeeper was shaking his head. "I know the sort of business you're mixed up in, Whitsun. Don't think I don't. I don't want any part of that. I'm an honest businessman."

"Who rented his upstairs room to me." Whitsun's voice was dreamy. "And who served as an early warning system—at least some of the time. I wonder, Glustred, how that would look to people who are trying to kill me. Don't you think they might come to the conclusion it was safer and simpler to wipe you out as well? Or burn you out, as the case might be."

"Balls!" the innkeeper roared, his face red. "Are you telling me that this fire *was* your fault?"

"Hardly my fault, Glustred. But it wouldn't surprise me to find that the people who are after this—" touching Maresun's ring—"didn't care very much about burning down a sleazy, fourth-rate pothouse to get it."

Glustred struggled for utterance. "The Bristle's not fourth-rate," was the best he could come up with.

"Fine. Third-rate. Come along." Whitsun turned and walked off.

Glustred stared after him, eyes blazing with anger, then followed.

❦

As they made their way to the Firelight District, Glustred's temper improved. He stared at the women who swaggered by them on the street, hips swaying, suggestive smiles playing about their lips. Several called out to the innkeeper, making tempting offers. On one occasion Glustred turned to follow a woman only to have Whitsun's hand grapple his collar and pull him back on the path.

"You don't have the money," he informed the innkeeper, "and I don't have the time."

Whitsun's step was firm, despite not having slept during the night, save for his brief nap at Merimma's establishment. He seemed to have an excess of energy and whistled softly between clenched teeth. As they walked, his eyes flicked from side to side, examining windows, alleyways, anywhere someone might be posted to make an attempt on him.

"If you could," he remarked to Glustred, "keep your eyes off the merchandise wandering around and get your mind—what passes for it, anyway—focused on what you're supposed to be doing, which is guarding me."

The big man shrugged. "I wouldn't mind being attacked by some of the women walking around here. Dolurrh!" He stopped to goggle at a scantily dressed specimen lying seductively along the sill of a low window. Whitsun shook his head and frowned at the woman, who pursed her lips and blew him a kiss.

"Next time, Ulther!" she called in a pretty accent.

"You *know* her?" Glustred asked as they walked on.

"Professionally. Not *that* kind of professionally, though." Whitsun's mind was running in other channels. "We need to get the symbols translated. They're clearly the key to whatever these things are. Once we do that, we'll have a better notion of what to do with them."

"Mph! Yes. Who's going to translate them, though?" Glustred asked.

"I know someone. He might take a bit of persuading though."

"You expect me to . . . persuade him?"

"No. Not that kind of persuasion." Whitsun refused to answer any more of Glustred's questions until they reached the door leading to Merimma's house.

The halfling let them in without hesitation, especially upon seeing Whitsun's large companion. The front hall contained several women in various states of undress lying on couches or sitting demurely on chairs. They stared curiously at Glustred as he accompanied Whitsun down a long hallway, led by the halfling.

"Jesseq!" one of the women called after the halfling. "Is that your little brother?" There was an explosion of giggles that followed them down the hall.

Jesseq stopped outside a door. "She's in," he said, jerking a thumb. "But she doesn't like to be disturbed. If she gets angry, it'll be on your heads!" He chuckled, his voice breaking oddly midlaugh, and disappeared.

Whitsun tapped on the door. There was no answer. After a few moments, he knocked again and, receiving no response, tried the handle. The door swung open silently, and the two men entered.

The room was fitted in silks and satin pillows, in gaudy but good taste. Draperies hung about, creating small chambers in which pillows were piled to form divans. A large hookah sat on a low table in the middle of the room, the fluid in it gently bubbling.

Merimma sat at a dressing table, her back to them. Her hands rested on the table next to an elaborate collection of brushes, pots, and jars. She did not turn as they came in.

"Merimma," Whitsun said. "You were right. It was a very unsafe place to leave it. But I had some luck, and now I've got it."

The woman still said nothing. Whitsun approached her, stared down at her, and moved back.

"What's the matter?" Glustred muttered. "Doesn't she understand you?"

Whitsun said nothing, and the big man looked more closely at the still figure of the woman. In the mirror before her he could see her face reflected clearly, her beautiful sapphire eyes staring at him.

Around her neck was a string of pearls. Something seemed wrong with them. Glustred started to say something and stopped.

The pearls had been twisted and pulled so they sank deep into the flesh. The string that held them must have been strong, and the killer had struck suddenly. There were no signs of struggle. Merimma sat, frozen, before her dressing mirror, looking out into eternity.

Whitsun walked over and stood beside her. He put one hand over her small, white still one and closed his eyes. His face looked old, and deep lines appeared about his brow. His lips moved silently.

He looked at Glustred. "Ring the bell."

"But—"

"Ring the blasted bell!"

Glusted pulled the bell. Jesseq responded in a few moments. "Well?"

Whitsun stepped back. Jesseq advanced, stopped, and exclaimed something in his own language. He leaped back, drawing two knives in the same motion.

"Lathon! Halfor!"

Two other halflings appeared. Both were bigger and stronger than any Glustred had seen before, and both were armed. Short swords leaped into their hands as they saw the body of their mistress.

Whitsun held up a hand, palm out. "Calm down."

"She's dead! She's bloody dead!" Jesseq groaned.

"No getting anything past you, is there?" Whitsun's voice was a mixture of sarcasm and conciliation. "Now let's figure out who did it."

"Seems to me we don't have to look very far for that," growled one of the halflings. He moved to put himself on Glustred's flank, while the other positioned himself within striking distance of Whitsun.

Whitsun smiled. "Do you think if we'd killed Merimma we'd ring for you?"

The halfling thought. It was an effort. "Might," he said sullenly. "Might be part of the plan."

"What plan?"

"How should I know what plan? It ain't my plan."

Whitsun sighed. "Let's leave it that there wasn't any plan. Someone came in here, murdered your mistress, and stole something."

"How'd you know that?" Jesseq asked. "How d'you know they stole somethin'?"

"Because I asked Merimma to guard something very valuable. And I'll wager it's missing now."

"What was it?"

"An artifact. Magic." Whitsun gave up the words with an appearance of reluctance.

"It missing?"

"I don't know. Probably. Where would Merimma keep something valuable?" Whitsun's tone was patient, but Glustred could see his fingers working back and forth against each other.

Jesseq looked at his companions for help and, finding none, shrugged. "C'mon."

He led the way along the corridor, down a flight of stairs, through a narrow passage, and to a small door. This Jesseq unlocked with a key from a large bunch he carried on a ring at his waist. The other two halflings followed the humans, swords still out.

In the center of the room a large crystal block rested atop a stone pillar. The block seemed to glow from within, as if a fire were burning but glimpsed from very far away through a thick fog. Jesseq placed a hand on the side of it, the other in his left pocket. He rested his forehead against the pillar and muttered something. The block wavered and vanished, not suddenly but as if a breeze had blown away a mist. On top of the pillar was the bundle Whitsun had left with Merimma. Several other small bags and bundles rested there as well.

Whitsun breathed a sigh of relief and reached for it but was brought up short by Jesseq's hand.

"Just a minute," said the halfling. "How do I know this here thing is yours?"

Whitsun said nothing but stared at the halfling's hand gripping his own. After a few seconds Jesseq nodded and released his wrist, stepping back. Whitsun picked up the bundle.

It fell apart, showing nothing but rags and some scraps of silk. Whitsun uttered a curse.

"Gone!"

Glustred shook his head. "So now you've got the thing Mare-sun gave you and you're missing the thing the shifter wanted."

"So it would seem." Whitsun stood motionless in thought. The others waited.

"What—?" began the halfling.

"Shut it!" Whitsun thought some more. "All right," he said finally. "Who would have known about this hiding place, Jesseq?"

The halfling shrugged. "Nobody. I don't know. Mebbe one of th' girls."

Whitsun shook his head. "Unlikely, I think. Merimma wasn't inclined to take her girls into her confidence about anything. And this place is connected to her other operation."

"What're you talking about?" Glustred asked. "What other operation?"

Whitsun spoke, keeping his eyes on Jesseq. "Merimma ran the brothel as a cover. In fact, this is the headquarters of the Copperheads."

"Copperheads!" Glustred's eyes swiveled around him. "Damned burglars! Bloody thieves!"

"Exactly. Merimma found her other business a useful source of information about wealth in the city. Her clientele were inclined to give up secrets to the girls, who passed them along to Merimma. She assigned tasks to her gang members, who carried out the burglaries." Whitsun smiled. "She was a remarkable organizer." He looked at Jesseq. "She wasn't a fool. She wouldn't have been caught sitting at her table by just anyone. It would have been someone she trusted. Someone who knew about her hiding place."

Jesseq made a dart for the door, only to be brought up short by one of his fellows, who held a sword against his throat. Jesseq was sweating, rivulets of perspiration running down and staining his collar.

Glustred walked over to him and lifted him up, pinning him against one of the chamber's stone walls with a single hamlike hand. The halfling's toes dangled three feet from the ground.

"Who?" the big man asked.

"I . . . I . . ."

Glustred slapped him with his free hand. Jesseq's face jerked, and he began to cry.

"Who?"

"I . . . don't know."

"Not good enough." Whitsun walked over to stand next to Glustred. "How did you get your orders?"

"It was a man. I met him in an inn."

"Which inn?"

"Bone and Bristle. In Boldrei's Landing."

Glustred and Whitsun exchanged glances.

"What did he look like?" Whitsun asked.

"Tall. Thin."

"Human?"

"Er . . ."

Whitsun took it as an affirmative. "Distinguishing marks?"

The halfling appeared to be thinking as much as anyone in his position could.

"Scar on 'is forehead and cheek. Long and white."

"Name?"

"No."

Whitsun nodded to Glustred, who let the halfling slide slowly down the wall while keeping a hand on his throat. The other two halflings sheathed their swords and moved to either side of Jesseq, hands resting on his shoulders, guarding him in case he made any attempt to escape.

"What did he tell you?"

"I met wit' 'im last night. He wanted the t'ing you gave Merimma. He said to get it and bring it to 'im."

"And you did?"

"No. He was at the corner of Kingsway and Battle Lane. I tol' 'im I couldn't get it. Then he give me money to go back." Jesseq fumbled in his pocket and pulled out a handful of galifars. Whitsun glanced at them.

"Why'd you kill Merimma?" he asked.

"I din't. I din't kill her."

One of the other halflings twisted Jesseq's shoulder. Jesseq screamed and staggered.

"I *din't!* The man did. He came back with me."

"Very good." Whitsun considered. "Evidently he thought he'd have better luck than you at getting into this place. So you led him to Merimma. She would have been relaxed with you present. Maybe you were talking to her, telling her something important. He got behind her as she was putting on her pearls. And . . . is that what happened?"

The halfling guard twisted Jesseq's shoulder again and was rewarded with another shriek of pain.

"Yes! Yes! Leave me 'lone!"

Whitsun nodded. His voice was almost gentle. "Why, Jesseq?" he asked. "Even if you didn't strangle her yourself, you led her killer to her and stood by while he did the deed. Why? What did he promise you? Was it just for the gold? Or was there something more?"

Jesseq began to cry. Snot and drool rolled down his face. "Somethin' of mine she had. She had no *right* to it. It were mine. I needed it. I *needed* it."

"What was it?"

Jesseq's reply was inaudible. Glustred's hand went back for a slap.

"A book," the halfling yelped. "My secret book."

Whitsun put out a hand. Jesseq hesitated then looked at Glustred again. He dug beneath his clothes and produced a small book bound in leather. Whitsun took it, opened it, and glanced swiftly through the pages. He held it out.

Glustred released his grip on the halfling and stepped back, wiping his hands on his shirt. He took the book and opened it. He looked at the halfling in disgust.

"You . . ."

"Yes." Whitsun's voice was mild but his expression echoed something of his companion's emotion. "Our little friend here likes to watch the girls at work, it would seem. How do you do it, Jesseq? Create magical images of what you see through peepholes? Then blackmail the girls? Is that the idea?"

Jesseq was sullenly silent.

"Merimma found out, didn't she? She didn't want to lose whatever talents you have as a thief, but she put a stop to this." Whitsun gestured to the book. "But she made the mistake of retaining you in her service."

"It were *my* book!" the halfling snarled.

Whitsun looked at the taller of the two halflings who had stood watching the interrogation. Both released Jesseq and drew their swords, holding them steady.

"Come see me when you've finished," he said. He and Glustred left the chamber.

They heard Jesseq shriek, cut off as the door closed behind them.

➽

Lathon and Halfor rejoined them in Merimma's chambers, accompanied by another of their race. Whitsun had summoned several of the girls and ordered them to clear away the body and wrap it in sheets so it could be safely disposed of with a minimum of fuss. The girls did not seem overly upset at the death of their mistress and readily carried out Whitsun's orders. Glustred sat and watched Whitsun pace back and forth, unceasing, between the door and the window. Once or twice he started to ask something only to be cut off by Whitsun's snarl.

Glustred stared at the halflings. On the front of the jackets worn by Lathon and Halfor were splashes of blood, and the shorter one was dabbing at his face with a rag as they came in, wiping away traces of red that had sprayed him. Whitsun raised an eyebrow, and the new halfling—he whom they hadn't met before—nodded.

"There are some shafts in the cellars," he said. "They go all the way down to the harbor. These two weighted him down with some rocks. Nobody'll find him for a couple of weeks at least."

Whitsun nodded and apparently put the matter from his mind. "What's your name?"

"Thavash."

"Very well, Thavash. We have a convergence of interests here. You want to find the man who was behind the murder of your mistress, and I want to find the man who stole the thing she was keeping for me. So what I suggest—"

"Just a moment."

The halfling's voice had a tone of authority. Whitsun stopped. The halfling cleared his throat. "Fact is," he said, "I don't give a dire rat's ass who Jesseq did his dirty business for. We took care of the traitor, and now that's done we just need to go on. Nothing changes, 'cept now Thavash is running the Copperheads instead of Merimma."

Whitsun considered and inclined his head. "Very well. But I still want to find this man. What do you suggest?"

Thavash pushed past them and sat down. He looked incongruous in Merimma's chair, dangling his feet amid silks and perfumes.

"Merimma told me a little about you," he said. "I hear more from others, Taliman. What I can tell is that you don't want to be seen on the streets just now. But you've got to find the man who took your bag. We'll supply your eyes and ears—for a price."

"How?" Glustred asked.

Thavash looked at him scornfully. "We know every dip, newpthumper, and slash artist in this part of Sharn. If you want to find this man, we'll find him."

Whitsun pondered for a few moments then nodded. "Very well. How much?"

"Five hundred galifars."

"Two hundred."

"Three."

"Two fifty."

"Done."

Thavash and Whitsun shook hands, and the halfling and his deputy disappeared. Whitsun and Glustred returned to the room in which Whitsun had originally been deposited upon his arrival the previous day. Whitsun stretched out on the bed.

"What are you doing?" Glustred asked.

"We won't hear anything for some time. I didn't sleep last night. So now I am."

"Why do you get the bed?"

"Because." Whitsun closed his eyes.

The first reports did not arrive until the next day. After a long sleep, Whitsun roused himself long enough to eat a meal brought by one of the girls. Glustred attempted to make small talk with her, but she ignored him and vanished after delivering the food on a tray. Whitsun, having finished eating, slept again for a time then awoke and whiled away the time with some dice he brought out of an inner pocket. Glustred also slept—on the floor—ate, and tried to devise schemes for getting some of the girls to pay him a visit. Whitsun listened to his companion's plans without comment but always with a faint derisive expression on his face.

Thavash came in from time to time to check on them. Reports from his spies trickled in, none of them encouraging. The thin man with the scarred face had apparently vanished.

"D'you think he's gone for good?" Glustred asked.

Whitsun shook his head. "We still have the ring. Without it, the orerry is useless. Or, at any rate, without its full potential."

"How do you know?"

"Intelligent guess. The markings show they are connected. It stands to reason their magical powers are linked somehow. He knows we have the ring. He'll show up sooner or later."

Glustred shook his head. "You told me you had them both together and nothing happened."

"I know." A faintly worried look showed on Whitsun's face. "I'm missing something." He stretched. "I think it's time for us to make a foray out of here. We're not accomplishing anything by staying, and at this point some of the interest in us may have died down. In any case, I need to find out more about these things. We'll take a trip."

Glustred got up. "Where to?"

"Morgrave University."

Glustred had never ventured as far up in the city as the Upper Menthis District, home to Morgrave University. He looked around with interest as he and Whitsun made their way up narrow flights of stairs and along spidery bridges overlooking vast urban chasms. Here the air was clearer and brighter, though towers still stretched far above them into the morning sky. The streets were cleaner than below, and young men and women in the robes of students hurried along the streets, arms filled with books, quills, parchments, and magical devices. They stopped at an outdoor eatery to snatch a quick bite to eat in the fresh air. The innkeeper brought seed-covered rolls, sausage, and beer as good as anything Glustred could imagine, and they sat and munched and sipped, breathing deeply as the sun slowly rose overhead.

Whitsun appeared to know his way around this part of the city, and he led them across several courtyards filled with pleasant, well tended lawns covered with trees, fountains, and benches. These were fascinating to Glustred, who, having lived his entire life in the lower city, had never seen trees, though he'd heard of them. Before them loomed a large building whose impressive portico was flanked with pillars and enormous statuary that frowned down on the stream of people entering and leaving. It was surmounted by a dome that dominated the surrounding buildings.

Glustred stopped to look up, shading his eyes. "What's this?"

"Dalannan Tower. Most of the administrators of the university have their offices below us. The library is located here. The university archives are here as well."

"Oh."

Whitsun looked at his companion and sighed. "I know, Glustred. I know. Bringing you here is like taking a mermaid to a desert. Some things just don't belong together."

They entered and made their way across an impressive entrance hall of great marble pillars and spanned by enormous arches whose pillars framed statues and paintings of the great events of Khorvaire's past. A great stone staircase before them swept up to the over levels. They mounted it, following streams of robed students and masters whose footsteps over the centuries had worn the steps lower. At the top of the staircase, they passed through several halls, climbed two other stairways, though not as broad or impressive as the first. At last they emerged onto a railed landing, on one side of which were great wooden doors carven in a complicated pattern of flowers, leaves, animals, and people. The door frame was painted in gold leaf, and the fittings were of polished bronze. Whitsun said something to an ancient attendant in dark purple robes who stood to one side, examining the credentials of all who passed beyond the doors. The attendant listened, nodded, and waved them through.

They pushed back the doors, entered the hall, and Glustred, looking up, gasped.

The room was round and ten stories in height. Far above them the ceiling was decorated in ivory and marble tracery that framed a vast painting in which clouds raced across a blue sky. Lines of carven leaves and flowers made their way up the wall, twisting and tangling one another until they spread across the roof. Set into the walls between these were row upon row of shelves built of dark wood and crammed with books. The volumes were of every shape, size, and color—some vast folios bound in leather or less identifiable substances, while others were tiny, no more than a hand span in width. They filled the air with a scent that combined dust, vellum, and rotting leather. Here and there, set in alcoves within the shelves, marble busts gazed solemnly down upon the tomes and their readers.

Balconies encircled the room with stairs leading from one level to another. The books mounted to the very top of the room. In the middle of the room, a large wooden cage sat with small windows. At each window, a gnome librarian took requests from the library's users for books. Other gnomes flitted up and down the staircases, plucking from the shelves those volumes the readers requested and returning to the collection those that had been used. The gnomes scurried hither and yon, arms full of books, pushing impatiently past the visitors, bent on their errands.

"Impressive, isn't it?"

Whitsun's voice startled Glustred, who'd been staring at the sight with rapt attention.

"Of course," Whitsun continued as his eyes ranged thoughtfully over the scene, "this isn't nearly as large as the Korranberg Library. That's said to be the biggest one in all Khorvaire. But this is adequate for the needs of the university's students. I suspect that a student who can't find the answer to a question in this library is told he's asking an inconvenient question and gently guided to some more . . . productive . . . line of research."

Glustred shrugged. "It's a sight more books than I've ever seen."

"Yes," Whitsun retorted. "I rather thought it might be." He strode forward and accosted one of the gnomes.

"Where's Lamonn Scorpeth's chamber?"

The gnome gave him an odd look and pointed upward. "Fifth level. Door six. Room fourteen. But you'll need a pass." He waved them to the wooden cage in the room's center.

Whitsun approached the gnome sitting at the window. "Good afternoon, friend. I want to see Lamonn Scorpeth."

"Business?" The gnome's voice sounded like crushed walnuts rattling against broken glass.

"Private consultation."

"Denied. Next."

Whitsun did not move. "It's quite important that I see him," he said. His voice was still friendly.

The gnome looked up in surprise. "Denied," he repeated. "Next."

"I don't think so."

The gnome, whose experience evidently did not encompass this sort of confrontation, looked around in confusion. "Request denied," he said to Whitsun, evidently hoping that altering the order of the words would produce the required result. "Denied. Your request. Your request is denied." A slight note of panic entered his voice.

Whitsun reached into a pocket and brought out a small piece of parchment. He unfolded it and pushed it across to the gnome.

"I *really* need to see him."

The gnome held the parchment so close to his nose he appeared to be sniffing it. He read its message, reread it, tapped it against his chin, read it for a third time, and sighed. "Approved." He scribbled a note and handed it to Whitsun along with the parchment. "Next!"

Whitsun and Glustred approached one of the staircases leading to the next level.

"What did you show him?" Glustred asked.

"Nothing you need know about." Whitsun showed the note to the gnome guarding the bottom stair. The gnome officiously examined the note, nodded, and waved them upward.

Along the balconies, framed by the cases of books, were wooden doors. Whitsun and Glustred, having made their way to the fifth level, opened the door that had a "6" painted on it in white. This entered onto a narrow passageway with doors on either side. Whitsun led the way to room fourteen and knocked.

There was a rustling noise from within but nothing else. Whitsun knocked again.

"Lamonn! Open up! It's Dasquith."

Glustred glanced at him. "Dasquith?"

"Shut up. Lamonn!"

There was more rustling. At last a feeble voice said, "Dasquith? Come in."

Whitsun and Glustred entered. The room was small and filled from top to bottom with an array of parchments, manuscripts, and books. Some of the latter were jammed into bookcases while others lay on the floor in piles or were stacked nearly to the ceiling. A wooden table in the middle of the room was covered with papers heaped untidily about. Next to the table was an old leather chair, its cushions burst and straw stuffing sticking out. The room smelled unpleasantly of mold and neglect.

Its inhabitant was slumped in the chair. He had cleared a small area on the table in front of him, but he seemed so buried in the detritus of scholarship that it was difficult to make out his form.

He stood slowly, revealing himself to be a human of about fifty, balding, with black and silver thinning hair, a short, straggly beard, and moustache. He had once been thin but now bore a mild paunch that comes suddenly with middle age. He stooped, as one accustomed to long study. His eyes were red-rimmed, and his hands shook with palsy.

"Dasquith. Good to see you, old fellow. Long time."

His voice was a mumble, the edge of which grated and set Glustred's nerves quivering.

Whitsun seemed unaffected. "Lamonn," he said. "I need your assistance."

"Glad to oblige. Only too glad." The man sank back into his

chair, lips working in and out. "Push those out of the way," he said to Glustred, gesturing to a heap of books balanced precariously on top of a wooden chair. The innkeeper removed them to the floor and sat down, eyeing the chair a bit nervously, unsure if it would support his weight.

Whitsun perched his bulk on a pile of moldering manuscripts.

Lamonn lifted a large leather-bound book and began to turn the crumbling pages. "Interesting work, this," he observed, pulling it around so Glustred could see the pages, covered in fine, spidery handwriting. "Study of early giantish ruins in Xen'drik by a member of the Heleffinn Expedition. Prewar, actually, so less influenced than one might think by vulgar political considerations."

Whitsun cleared his throat. "Lamonn—"

"Now here's something interesting." The scholar dived into a pile of loose manuscript pages that adorned one of the tables and pulled out a dirty parchment covered with writing and arcane symbols. "I *think*, but I'm not quite sure, that this is a spell for summoning a creature of the outer planes, one that can appear simultaneously in several—"

Whitsun harrumphed loudly, and Lamonn reluctantly stuck the parchment back into the pile. "Yes. Sorry. I do tend to ramble sometimes. But you've no idea how fascinating some of this is. I think with a bit more effort and a few more resources from the university, I might just be on the track of some variant forms of early Giant, without the southern influences one finds in the later dialects. Fascinating stuff. Still. What was it you wanted?"

Whitsun pulled out the parchments of the tracings from the ring and the orerry. "What do you make of that?"

Lamonn glanced at them carelessly at first, then with

greater attention. With more concentration than he'd shown so far, he pushed a pile of papers off the table and spread the parchments side by side. He studied them for a time in silence, then turned and grabbed several books from a shelf, seemingly at random, and consulted them. He scribbled a note on a piece of paper and resumed his study. He took another book, flipped expertly through its pages, made another note, pursed his lips, and continued reading.

Whitsun watched in silence. Glustred allowed his attention to wander about the room. There were no windows, and the only light came from two everbright lanterns set into the wall. The remainder of the walls were covered with shelves housing an impressive collection of leather-bound books. The volumes were stacked in piles on the floor as well, some leaning drunkenly against others, in imminent danger of collapse. A piece of slate was propped against one wall, covered with chalk rock scribblings, most of them in other languages.

Lamonn ignored both of them as he continued his study. Finally he looked up. "Interesting."

Whitsun nodded. "Yes. I thought so too. What is it?"

Lamonn examined his notes. "Do you have the object this came from?"

"I have one of them."

"One?"

Whitsun pulled out the ring and handed it to the scholar. Lamonn examined it carefully, running his hands over it, tapping it against the spine of a book, holding it up to the light. He pulled out a large glass mounted on a leather band, put it around his head, and looked closely through the glass first at the symbols incised into the ring and then at the gem at its center. He consulted a few more books, then looked at Whitsun. "From Xen'drik. Definitely Giant in origin. There are a lot of top administrators in this place who'd give their left hands for a chance to hold this. But this is only half of it."

"How do you know?"

"There are some indications here." Lamonn touched the writing.

"You can read it then?"

"Not well. I can make out a little of what it says, but the dialect is very old, and many of the words aren't familiar. But there's a description that clearly implies there is more to this than what you have here."

"Yes, I know. The other half is . . . elsewhere." Whitsun held out his hand, and Lamonn, with every appearance of reluctance, returned the ring to him. "What is it?"

The scholar considered for a time. "I don't want to say just now. I could be wrong. Can you leave these with me?" He tapped the parchments.

"How long?"

"A few days."

Whitsun hesitated then nodded.

"And that?" He gestured at the ring.

Whitsun shook his head. "I don't like that. The last time I left part of this with someone she ended up dead."

Lamonn's face paled, but he said, "Morgrave is safe. Safe as anywhere in Sharn." His former manner of fussy scholarship seemed to be returning, but now it was mixed with something else. He sat down, and one hand began to pick unconsciously at his robe. Glustred watched, eyes narrowing.

Whitsun thought some more. "Very well. But you need to make me a promise."

"What?"

"Stay off the weed."

"Oh, for the sake of the Host!" Glustred exploded. "He's

another bloody weedhead. Haven't we learned our lesson about that?"

Whitsun glared at him and didn't answer. Lamonn looked up at the innkeeper and smiled. "Harder to give it up when you've used it for twenty years." He pulled up his sleeve to show his right arm, mottled with tiny red dots. He turned to Whitsun. "For two days. I promise. After that . . ."

Whitsun handed him the ring. Lamonn opened a drawer concealed beneath a pile of manuscript, and shoved it in.

"Now, go. I need some sleep. And to think."

Whitsun turned to leave then looked back. "Lamonn."

"What?"

"Take care."

The scholar raised a hand in farewell.

Outside the room, Glustred looked at his companion with a mixture of incredulity and rebuke.

"You really, *really* want to do that? Leave that thing with a weedhead? And he told you it's from Xen'drik. I don't know a lot about Morgrave, but I know half the people here are buying and selling things from Xen'drik. Talk about a dangerous place to leave it."

"Exactly."

"What?"

"It's called hiding in plain sight. Put something where your enemies don't expect to find it, and they won't search for it there."

Glustred shook his head. "*I* call it being too clever by half."

As they entered the brothel they'd unconsciously come to think of as home over the past few days, Thavash came up to them.

"Good news."

"You've spotted him?"

"Aye." The halfling was smiling. "Hope's Peak in Dura."

Whitsun tapped his chin. "Interesting. Good. Have an address?"

Thavash handed him a piece of parchment with a rough quill scrawl. Whitsun glanced at it and crumpled it into his pocket. "Glustred, let's go."

"Just a moment." Thavash stepped in front of him, between him and the door.

"What's the matter?" Whitsun's face betrayed his impatience.

"Soorlah and Chemsh are going with you."

Two halflings stepped forward. One, at four and a half feet, was almost big enough to be mistaken for a short human. Both had tough expressions and wore swords.

"Why? Too many of us are going to put the wind up him?"

"Think of it as protecting my investment." Thavash's mouth curved in a sneer. "You still owe me half the money. What's to stop you walking off without paying?"

"You have a suspicious nature, Thavash," Whitsun sighed. "You should fight against it. You really should." He looked around at the two halflings. "Try to be subtle. I know it's hard, but try."

CHAPTER 8

ope's Peak was in the Upper Wards of the city, a climb too long for any of them to contemplate with equanimity.

"We'll pick up a skycoach," Whitsun said in answer to a question from Glustred.

The halflings were evidently pleased by this decision. Soorlah had his hand half raised to hail a coach from the busy line of traffic running along the way, but Whitsun, whose eyes had been wandering over the crowd that filled the street in front of them, pushed his arm down.

"Not here."

"Where then?"

"Follow me."

Falling in line behind him, they followed Whitsun as he plunged into a maze of alleys and passages that led down rather than up. Even Glustred, who had a good head for such things, was quickly disoriented by the many twists and turnings they took, seemingly at random. Whitsun never hesitated, and at last they emerged from the darkness into another street, just as crowded as the first.

"Where are we?" Glustred asked.

"Cogsgate. Near the station." Whitsun made the reply absently as he carefully watched the folk hurrying by them. After a few moments he appeared to relax. Glustred had been watching him closely.

"We were being followed?" It was more a statement than a question.

"Possibly. I don't know. It was a feeling. But I don't like taking chances." Whitsun looked about. "We'll take a coach from here."

They made their way to the lightning rail station. This was a tall, imposing building, entered through a great archway. Within was a wide space covered by a marble floor inlaid with brilliant stones. The usual crowds of travelers rushed to and fro, frantically pushing against one another in an effort to secure tickets and seats on the line. Through one large opening, a stready stream of bales and crates poured under the watchful eyes of customs inspectors. Other arches led to the station itself where several lightning rail coaches were taking on passengers. The crackling of magical energies from the conductor stones that kept the rail running filled the air. Porters raced through the station, piles of trunks balanced perilously on floater carts. Handlers shrieked the names of coaches departing, while under Whitsun and Glustred's eyes, dippers worked the crowds and plungers and nobblers created distractions to allow them to ply their trade.

Amid this frantic chaos, Whitsun hailed a skycoach and told the driver to take them to Hope's Peak. They rose and scuttered above the thronging hundreds, rising gently up a shaft and scooting around and between towers and bridges, moving higher and higher through the slowly clearing air. Sunlight filled the coach as they rose, and the two halflings, who had evidently never been much higher in Sharn than the middle levels, rushed from side to side of the coach, staring out the windows, commenting.

"Lookitthat!"

"I never seen nothin' like it!"

"Who's that then?"

"Who?"

"The fellow in the yellow skycoach. There! By the double tower!"

"I dunno!"

"It's Lord Klaventine, an't it?"

"Ur!"

Glustred did his best to look casual, though he too couldn't resist glancing about. "What's this Hope's Peak region we're going to?" he asked Whitsun.

His companion had lit a long, thin, twist of weed and inhaled the smoke easily as the skycoach flew between the towers. His eyes were half closed as if he were memorizing their route.

"What?"

Glustred repeated the question.

"Hope's Peak is a temple district. Full of them." Whitsun blew out a cloud of smoke that was whisked away in an instant by the momentum of their journey. "Every god that exists in the pantheon has its share of worshipers who send up sacrifices to it. And they all require temples. Mark my words, Glustred, religion is an industry that will never lack for demand."

"You make it sound like a business," Glustred observed.

"So it is, for the most part. I dare say there are some priests who really believe in the gods, but most of them are in it for money and benefits."

"That's pretty cynical, even for you."

"Just realistic." Whitsun leaned over the side of the coach to gaze about. "Look at that building coming up on this side."

"The big one?"

"Yes. That's a temple dedicated to Dol Arrah, sovereign of sun and sacrifice. Impressive, isn't it?"

Glustred's eyes took in the soaring towers, the massive dome, and acres of delicately wrought window glass that filled the interior of the temple with light. The building shone as if it were made of gold. Its tower rose above any others nearby, and atop the highest pinnacle, there were flashes of greenery as if the temple's top were adorned with a garden. "Aye," he admitted. "That it is."

"Probably took ten years to build. Thousands of craftsmen working day and night to put that up. Someone has to pay all of those folk."

"Of course. The church."

"And how does the church get the money to do that?"

Glustred stroked his chin. "Contributions?"

"Ah, yes." Whitsun's mouth curved in a mirthless smile. " 'Come, good sir. Make a contribution to the temple of Dol Arrah. If you do, the goddess will smile on you. If not, your life won't be worth living.' That temple, Glustred, is built on the fears and terrors of Dol Arrah's worshipers. Most people are afraid of hunger or poverty. The church has found something that scares them even more—a goddess."

Glustred ruminated on his companion's words for a few minutes. "What about you?"

"What about me?" Whitsun leaned back against the pillows that lined the seats of the coach.

"Which god do you worship?"

"None."

"None?"

"None." Whitsun flicked his weed over the side to fall into

121

the void. "Religion's a dangerous thing, Glustred. It's a force that can move men to kill or be killed. Let it into your life and it takes over. I prefer to stay in control of what I do, thanks very much."

"But suppose . . ." Glustred moved a little closer to his companion. "Suppose you're wrong. Suppose there really are gods. And someday you're called before them to answer for your deeds? What then?"

Whitsun stared at him. "You're awfully contemplative all of a sudden, Glustred. Is this a side of you I haven't seen before?"

"I'm just wondering. That's all."

"Well . . ." Whitsun looked thoughtfully at the towers that rose around them. "I suppose if it came to that . . . I'd just have to have a quick answer."

Glustred snorted. "Trust you. What's that dome on the left?"

"Church of the Silver Flame. The one beyond it to the right is the Sovereign Host."

Both buildings were smaller than the temple dedicated to Dol Arrah, but they were still striking. The Church of the Sovereign Host was a mass of towers, some broad, others slender, like fingers groping toward the sky. All were ringed with marble shot through with gold and silver that reflected the sun's rays this high in the city.

As they passed the Church of the Sovereign Host, Glustred's hands moved in a quick gesture. Whitsun stared at him and smiled cynically. "Really. I didn't know you adhered to that particular faith. We can stop by the church and you can give some blood or pour water over the altar or whatever it is you people do."

Glustred's voice was low. "You shouldn't mock things you don't understand, Whitsun."

"I don't." His companion sat calmly, watching the city around them. "But I don't overestimate its power. Religion is a tool, Glustred, like anything else. If you know what to do with it, it will serve you well. In the wrong hands, it's dangerous, just like a sword. The sword doesn't have any inherent capacity for good or evil. That's what's brought to it by its owner. The same's true of religion."

They passed several more temples, some smaller and dingier than the ones they'd seen previously. Whitsun watched them float past.

"The temple down there—that's the church of Olladra. God of good fortune. He hasn't been doing awfully well of late. Look. There are warforged around it."

Sure enough, several of the large, slightly ungainly figures of warforged constructs gathered around the entrance to the temple. They looked like oversized ants. Around them people scurried in and out of the temple entrance, though Glustred could see there were fewer of them than at the temples to other gods.

"And those—over there! Unless I miss my guess, those are adherents of the Dark Six."

A line of black-clad figures wove along a narrow balcony and passed over a bridge to disappear into a small opening in one of the smaller establishments. Glustred spat in their general direction.

"Glustred! Really! Religious bigotry. I'd never have expected it from you!" Whitsun, having exhausted the subject, brought his gaze inside the skycoach and stared at nothing. The two halflings, who had been listening to the conversation, also drew inside.

"You'd better watch it," the taller one remarked.

"Why's that, Soorlah?"

"The Host'll strike you." He said this with an air of great contentment, as one happy to pass along an unpleasant task.

"Ah. Well, until he does, I'll wait." Whitsun settled back and closed his eyes.

❦

The skycoach deposited them in front of a large inn, whose signpost, in startlingly large letters, proclaimed it to be the Royal Octogram. Whitsun sent the two halflings inside to inquire about rooms while he and Glustred remained in the street and surveyed the prospect.

As in all of Sharn, the streets were crowded with a variety of races. Here they were somewhat better dressed and had a swinging, careless demeanor about them that was at odds with the furtive movement of their counterparts lower down in the city. Numbers of them were dressed in robes marking them as acolytes of one or another of the faiths. These moved in groups, hands clasped before them, eyes devoutly downturned. Whitsun watched them, mouth quirked upward. At last he stepped forward and tapped one on the shoulder.

"Excuse me, brother."

The man turned. He was clad in a white robe, his hair shorn, and his face thin, wearing a benevolent expression.

"Yes, my brother in the Host?"

"I'm looking for someone."

"We are all looking for him, brother. But when we find him, we find the most extreme ecstasy we can know."

"Yes. But this is someone a little closer. A thin man with a scar on his forehead."

The man shook his head. "I've seen no one fitting that description. My apologies, brother."

"No matter."

The man moved on. Whitsun looked at Glustred. "This is apt to prove a bit tedious."

Glustred nodded. "Let's try in here." He gestured to the common room of the inn. "People here see a bit more and tell a bit more. If you give them the right incentive."

Whitsun followed his companion. They passed into the interior of the Royal Octogram. It resembled the common room of the Bone and Bristle inasmuch as both served drinks, but there the resemblance ended. The Octogram was large and airy, with benches set around tables kept clean by an attentive staff of waiters who moved swiftly and silently around the room, clearing empty mugs and carrying ones full to the brim of foaming liquid.

Glustred sauntered over to the bar and hailed the master of the house, a slender man with a tankard in either hand. He was wearing a clean white apron, and his cheeks were shaven. His blond hair was pulled back in a long ponytail to keep it from his eyes—or his customers' drinks.

"Hey, friend. A couple of ales here."

"Aye."

The innkeeper of the Octogram drew two ales and placed them in front of the pair. Glustred sipped his and nodded appreciatively.

"Ah! Nice!"

"Last year's crop of hops." The master settled against the bar, prepared to talk shop. "Michelar Sprat's my name. You've a liking for good beer then?"

"Urmas Glustred. Had. Until my inn burned down."

"Rough luck. Still . . ."

Whitsun allowed his attention to wander. A pair of elves were chatting, leaning against the wall, ostentatiously ignoring the rest of the crowd, though Whitsun could see that under cover of their talk they were carefully watching it. Ten feet away, a small group was gathered around a drunken dwarf who evidently gave good entertainment. His voice rose and fell over the crowd's noise.

"I . . . there, I tell you . . . left hand of death . . . dragon's breath."

Whitsun allowed his attention to slacken. His eyes passed over the patrons.

Glustred's voice drew him back to their quest.

"So who's been around lately, Sprat? You got dips and other magsmen up here, same as elsewhere, I reckon. See 'em round in here?"

Sprat, the bartender, stepped back a pace. "Here! You inquisitives?"

"No, no. Just interested customers. That's all." Glustred pulled out a sovereign and began to bounce it on the bar, letting the lamplight catch its gleam, playing it against the wall. "So?"

Sprat ran a hand over his ponytail while he thought. "Usual crowd, really. Left Hand Roff. Slippery Joch. Usual."

"What about a new one? Tall. Thin. Scar on his forehead and face."

"Oh, that one." Sprat looked disgusted. "He's new, all right. But he's not a dipper. Slash artist. He's been around for a few weeks or so."

"Name?"

"None. No one talks much to him. And he don't talk to no one. Lets his razor do the talking."

"Killed anyone?"

Sprat spat. "Well, no one we seen. But some people gone missing since he showed up, if you know what I mean. People who was asking questions or talking about him too much. Long-fingered Stalch was one. They found him in an alley with his fingers cut off and his throat slit."

Glustred nodded. "Interesting. Sounds a good man to stay

away from." He tossed back his drink. "Do you know where he lodges?"

The innkeeper looked around to make sure no one was listening and leaned forward. "I might. If there was something in it for me."

Glustred took out another coin and began to spin it on the counter. The innkeeper's eyes followed it.

"I don't know for absolute certain," he said, "but some around here have seen him in and out of the Church of the Silver Flame."

"Where's that?"

"Entrance is across the square. But be careful. One man who talked to him in the common room here was found next day with both eyes gouged out and his throat cut."

"I'll keep that in mind." Glustred tossed the coins on the counter. "Thanks, friend." He turned to Whitsun. "Come."

They made their way to a bench and sat down, sipping their ales. Glustred leaned forward so he could speak in Whitsun's ear.

"Well?"

Whitsun shook his head. "I don't know. Why's he waiting around here? What is there in this district that attracts him? Or is this home?" He took a draught of ale. "And what is he doing in the Church of the Silver Flame? One would think that's the last place a slash artist would hang about. Unless, like you, Glustred, he's especially devout. Well, we'll wait a bit and see if he shows up."

Soorlah and Chemsh approached. "Two rooms," grunted the shorter one. "You owe us two galifars."

Whitsun stared at Chemsh. "Really?"

"Uh huh."

"Because the last time I was here, a room only cost four silver sovereigns."

"Finder's fee." Chemsh was not in the least embarrassed. "We done the work, so we gets paid for it."

Whitsun slipped some coins out of his pocket. "Consider that I've deducted taxes from your fee and call it even. Where are they?"

"One front, one back. Second floor."

"Does the front room overlook the street?"

"Aye."

Whitsun nodded in satisfaction "You two take first watch from it," he told them. "Keep your eyes on the Church of the Silver Flame across the way. If you see him come in or out, one of you come up and get us from the other room. The other of you stick close to him. Don't approach him, and don't speak to him. Let's play this out nice and easy."

He drained his mug, and he and Glustred mounted the stairs.

The next day passed slowly. They changed watches every three hours. Glustred's head began to ache from cups of ale. Whitsun disposed of his drinks in some way that did not appear to affect him. When not watching, he sat and stared out at the wall that was three feet from the window of the back room or lay on the narrow bed, eyes open, gazing at the ceiling. Glustred slept or smoked a noxious pipe, for the smell of which Whitsun ordered him outdoors. After that he found a comfortable corner of the common room and sat watching the patrons of the inn pass in and out.

On the morning of the second day, Whitsun came into the common room to find Soorlah, the taller of the two halflings, sitting by himself at a table.

"Who's watching? Where's Chemsh?"

Soorlah jerked his head. Whitsun turned and froze.

Chemsh was wandering around the fringes of a crowd of dwarves who were drinking heavily and shouting at one another in thick accents. The halfling's hands dangled by his side and, as Whitsun watched, one darted into the pocket of one of the dwarves and came out with a purse, which instantly vanished into the halfling's jacket.

Soorlah shrugged. "Chemsh used to be a dipper before Merimma found him. Reckon he wanted to see if he still had it."

Whitsun shook his head. "He doesn't. He'll be caught."

"Nah. Not him. He's too fast. Them's dwarves. Slower'n pigs in a mud storm when they're drinkin'." Soorlah chuckled and turned back to his drink.

"Not as slow as you think. For one thing, I don't think they're very drunk."

"Huh! What makes you say that?"

Whitsun jerked his head slightly. "The one on the end there. He's been watching our little friend. He's just waiting for . . . ah!"

The dwarf's hand shot out and grasped Chemsh's wrist, twisting it and pulling the halfling next to him. Chemsh gave a loud squeal and struggled. Soorlah started to rise but was jerked back by Whitsun's hand on his shoulder.

"Sit still!"

The dwarf's left hand was on Chemsh's collar while his right hand held a knife to the halfling's throat. The bar had suddenly become very quiet.

"A dipper!" The dwarf twisted Chemsh's collar, and the halfling's face began to turn red. "A dipper right here in the Octogram! Hey, Sprat! What d'ye think o' that?"

The barman stared hard at Chemsh then transferred his gaze to Glustred. "I think dippers should keep out of my house if they know what's good for them."

The dwarf looked about. "Well, I don't know about the rest of you, but I've had all I care to of dippers. A halfling, too. Nasty little buggers. Like rats. And we all know what to do wi' rats, don't we?"

There was a half-hearted cheer from the other patrons. The dwarf jerked his head at one of his companions. "Hey, Tosh. Run and get the Watch."

Tosh disappeared, and the other inhabitants of the room returned to their conversations, all the while keeping a watchful eye on the dwarf and his captive. Chemsh twisted helplessly in the dwarf's grip, but each attempt he made at conversation was met with a buffet in the mouth. After the third time, he gave up and let the blood trickle down his chin. Another of the dwarves, meanwhile, went through his pockets, relieving Chemsh of the money he'd stolen.

Tosh returned, accompanied by two large men wearing the red and gold uniform of the Watch. Their swords were drawn, and both had grim expressions. Whitsun and Glustred turned their faces to their ales. Soorlah continued to stare balefully at the dwarf until Whitsun jogged his arm.

"Careful, fool! D'you want to get us arrested?"

There was a muttered colloquy between the dwarf and the Watch, and Chemsh changed captors. His hands were secured behind his back with a bit of rope and he was led off. The dwarves sat down again and loudly called for more ale while Soorlah turned a wrathful face to Whitsun and Glustred.

"Why din't you let me get him? We coulda done it, no problem."

"This isn't a concern of mine." Whitsun's voice was smooth. "I'm paying you people to track a man. If one of your gang gets into trouble, that's his lookout." He took a sip of his ale and made a wry face. "Besides, if he's going to try dipping, he might at least be good at it. I'm no expert, but I could have spotted him from half a street away."

Soorlah looked for support from Glustred, who buried his face in his mug.

"Well," Soorlah observed, "I'll tell you one thing."

"What's that?"

"Thavash won't like this."

Whitsun lifted an eyebrow. "I could learn to live with that."

"Won't like it a bit. And that could make things a bit uneasy for the pair of you in Firelight and surrounding districts."

"Oh, come." Whitsun's tone was filled with scorn and ale. "Are you really telling me that Thavash gives a Host's damn about the fate of one of his gang? A failed dipper at that? And he's aspiring to be chief?"

"Aye." Soorlah seemed slightly embarrassed. "He's funny that way. 'Sides, it's good for business."

"How?"

"Lets us know he cares, y'know? That 'e'll protect us'n all."

Whitsun shrugged. "I suppose there's some sort of warped logic there." He looked at the door out of which Chemsh and his captors had vanished. "Are you saying you want to get him back?"

"Aye."

"Very well. Come along."

The Watch house in the temple district was not dissimilar from its counterparts farther down in the city, though it was somewhat better kept up. The captain's desk had fewer obvious scars, and the room looked as if it had been swept at least twice in the past year.

Soorlah did the talking, and Whitsun and Glustred were glad to let him.

"So y'see, Cap'n, it were a misunderstandin' is all. Me friend's mind were just a wanderin' type on account of an old war injury. I wonder, were you in the War at all, Cap'n? Aye? Well, then, you'll understand me friend 'avin' this problem, y'know."

Soorlah's accent seemed to have gotten heavier. The Watch captain, a surly man with a low brow surmounted by an oily fringe of dark hair, was unimpressed.

"That's going to do no good for him. They're stretching him in the morning."

"What?" Soorlah's outrage was genuine. "Not wit'out a trial they ain't!"

"There's already been a trial."

"When?"

"When he was brought in here. All we require here is a hearing before a priest or a magistrate. We've had one, he was found guilty, and now he's going to die tomorrow morning."

Whitsun intervened. "Bit of a drastic penalty for dipping, surely?"

The captain turned his attention to him. "Perhaps. But we've had a problem lately with dippers from other wards coming here for new business." He glared at them. "That brings me to the question of what you three are doing here in my ward."

Whitsun spoke easily. "My employee here—" he waved at Glustred—"is considering becoming a monk of the Church of the Silver Flame. He'd never been to this part of Sharn, so I decided to show him about a bit. Show him where the temple is and so forth."

The captain grunted. "No need to come all the way up here for that."

"Perhaps, but this ward has the greatest Silver Flame church in the entire city."

The captain digested this then asked, "What about the two halflings?"

"Servants we hired at the lightning rail station in Cogsgate. I'm afraid I can't vouch for them. They seemed honest enough." Whitsun shrugged. "Still, you know how it is these days. After the War, all sorts of unsavory characters are looking for work. I had no idea one of them was a dipper."

The captain's fingers, with their dirty nails, drummed on the table. "Name?" he asked Whitsun.

"Buresh."

"Occupation?"

"Innkeeper." Whitsun jerked his head at Glustred. "This is Wordd, My potboy. A bit slow but an honest chap. Still, not the sort of person to be left on his own to wander around the city, if you know what I mean."

Glustred's face turned red, but he was silent.

The captain thought then said, "My advice to you three, since you're friends or employers or whatever of a convicted criminal, is to get out of my ward before I take it into my head to make life very difficult for you. I'll give you until after the execution tomorrow. Then I want to see your backsides heading back down where you belong."

Whitsun nodded. "Thanks for the advice, captain. But I've some further business, so we'll be sticking around."

The yellow eyes glared at him. "What business?"

"Traders," Whitsun said. "I'm from Firelight, and I'm looking to arrange a shipment of girls up here for work at my inn—"

With a roar, the captain came half out of his chair. Whitsun backed away hastily. "Just a joke. We'll be going now."

The three hurried through the station and converged in the street outside. Whitsun drew them into a corner away from the passersby.

"That's it, then." He seemed unmoved.

Soorlah shook his head. "No. Ain't it. We gotta rescue him."

Whitsun frowned. "We're here to find the man who was behind Jesseq, the murderer of Merimma and the man who stole something belonging to me. If your friend was stupid and careless and it costs him his life, that's no concern of mine."

Soorlah looked at him with narrowed eyes. "Is if you wanna come back to Firelight," he retorted. "We don' like leavin' companions inna lurch. You help me get Chemsh out before t'morrow, or else don' come back to Firelight."

Whitsun stood irresolute. Glustred shrugged. "Doesn't seem as if it could be that difficult to stop the Watch from hanging a halfling."

Whitsun shook his head. "It's not that it's difficult. It's that it calls attention to us when we should be quiet." He sighed. "All right, all right. Here's what we'll do." He glared at the halfling. "You're confounded lucky I know how to throw knives."

❧

Several shafts of rosy light penetrated the clouds far above their heads, signaling dawn's advent. The light made its way down into the City of Towers to shine on the square. A scaffold on one side of the square had been cleaned and readied for service overnight, and Whitsun and his companions had watched the activity from the shelter of their front room in the Octogram.

A small crowd gathered in the square. Evidently, hangings were common enough in the area that they had ceased to excite public interest. Most of the onlookers were poorer, clad in ragged clothes, their thin, starved faces watching eagerly as members of the Watch marched in unison into the square.

"Come." Whitsun stood and went downstairs and out into the street. His companions followed him, then left him and circled around the fringes of the crowd. Glustred stood out by reason of his height and bulk. Soorlah vanished completely.

Chemsh appeared, hands tied behind him. His eyes flickered wildly about the square. A cloth was bound about his mouth. He stumbled several times and was jerked to his feet by members of the Watch, who too clearly wanted to get the business over with as quickly as possible so as to get back to their breakfasts.

Whitsun continued to circle, keeping his pace casual, his eyes fixed on the scaffold and the drama unfolding there. He stopped at one side of it, seeing Glustred on the other side. Their eyes met briefly. Glustred looked down, then up at Whitsun and nodded slightly.

Chemsh was on the platform by this time. The hangman, a stout, jolly-looking man, placed a noose around his neck. He reached down and plucked off the gag.

"Any last words, thief?"

Chemsh's voice burst in a stream of obscenities, pleas, promises, and requests for another trial, a lawyer, a pardon, a stay, anything.

The hangman stepped back, and the crowd grew silent, waiting.

A movement at the edge of the square caught Whitsun's attention. The door of the Church of the Silver Flame opened. Out of it strode a tall, thin man. He was just close enough for Whitsun to make out the long, narrow scar that split his countenance. The man looked, with interest, at the scaffold and the crowd. Whitsun's fingers twitched. The man turned to go.

The hangman threw the lever that opened the trap.

CHAPTER 9

olurrh!

Whitsun's lips formed the word but did not speak it aloud. Already, his hand had found the knife in his boot and held it balanced in readiness on his palm. Glustred, as they'd arranged, lunged forward, scattering people this way and that, shouting something incoherent. The Watch, both those standing on the platform to help with the execution and those stationed in the crowd, were gazing at the big man, and some were converging on him as he flailed about.

Whitsun threw the knife. A shaft of sunlight caught it as it flew, bright as a swallow skimming a pond. It flashed past the nose of the executioner and sliced the rope as Chemsh shot downward. Though it did not sever the rope completely, it was enough. The rope quivered and snapped, and the executioner gave an angry shout. A moment later, Whitsun saw Soorlah, hand on Chemsh's shoulder, scurrying through the crowd. The condemned halfling's hands were still tied behind his back. He was coughing from the impact of the noose on his neck, but his legs moved quickly.

Whitsun looked back at the cathedral. The door was shut and there was no sign of his quarry. The crowd was shouting, pleased at the entertainment it was getting. Glustred managed to evade the Watch who were closing on him. The big man climbed up on the scaffold, heaving the startled executioner off into the crowd. A Watch member sprang up on the platform, and Glustred kicked him in the stomach. So far, all the attention of the Watch was on the drama unfolding on the scaffold.

Not quite all. A sword swished through the air just where Whitsun's neck would have been had he not ducked. The angry purple face of the Watch captain stared at him.

"Bloody dip!"

The sword slashed again, and Whitsun leaped backward, barely evading its path. He looked about for weapons and saw none.

The Watch captain leaped forward, raised his sword for another blow, and stumbled. Soorlah stood behind him, a heavy stick in his hand half raised for another blow. The halfling gave a prolonged yodel celebrating his victory. Members of the crowd spun around to find the source of the unearthly noise.

Whitsun reached forward and grabbed the captain's sword as the man's eyes closed peacefully on the cobbles. "Shut up, idiot!" he snarled to Soorlah. "Shut it! Don't draw attention to us!" It was too late. The rest of the Watch were looking at the source of the shout, waving their weapons, calling to one another. A second later, Glustred landed on the street beside Whitsun, clutching another purloined sword.

"Which way?" he shouted.

Whitsun took off running. His companions pounded behind him. They dodged into an opening, across a short bridge, and down a narrow street.

Glustred looked behind. "I think we're—"

Members of the Watch poured across the bridge, yelling. Whitsun fumbled in a pocket, pulled something out, and tossed it into the air with a word of command. Four bright bolts of energy formed and streaked toward the Watch, the front rank of whom tumbled to the ground, trying to avoid them.

The maneuver was meaningless. The bolts, suddenly arrested in their flight, turned and headed for Whitsun. At the last instant they split apart and smashed into the buildings on either side. Shards of brick and glass from shattered windows up and down the street flew, and angry shouts resounded.

Whitsun wasted no more time. He ducked into a series of narrow openings between buildings. Glustred, Soorlah, and Chemsh struggled to keep up, the latter still coughing and swearing. With his hands bound behind him, he was awkward and bumped into the walls on either side of them with dismaying frequency.

Panting, they staggered into a small courtyard and threw themselves against a wall. Chemsh turned slightly to let his fellow thief cut his bonds. He massaged his wrists and neck as his chest rose and fell. Glustred's eyes were closed. Whitsun sat, breathing hard, brow drawn.

At last Glustred looked up. "All right," he announced. "No more bleeding magic until you figure out what's going wrong. Agreed?"

Whitsun ignored him. He took some items from his coat pocket and examined them, turning them over with a finger, counting them, and finally replacing them. He shook his head and muttered something to himself.

Glustred looked around. "Any idea where we are?"

Whitsun nodded. "Yes. We're far enough from the Watch right now not to worry for the moment, but not far enough to feel complacent."

"Thanks. That makes me feel better." Glustred closed his eyes again.

Whitsun glared at Soorlah. "We might be farther away from danger if it hadn't been for your yowling. It's hard to see how more could have gone wrong with this escapade. For a burglar, you've no idea when to keep quiet."

Soorlah ignored him. Chemsh was chattering away with his companion. Finally Soorlah looked at Whitsun with something like respect. "So the plan worked. I din't think it would. Where'd you learn to throw a knife like that?"

Whitsun ignored the question and got to his feet with a grunt. "Come. We can't wait here all day."

They got to their feet and, led by Whitsun, made their way down a passageway that led out of the courtyard. Narrow iron grates hung over their heads. Whitsun looked up at them and grabbed Chemsh around the waist.

"Here! What d'y think you're doin'?"

"Shut up and grab on!"

Whitsun held the struggling halfling up to the grate. Chemsh grasped the iron and pulled himself up. Glustred, meanwhile, performed the same office for Soorlah. Following the halflings, the humans pulled themselves up and mounted a twisting iron staircase that led steeply upward. It wound around a tower then darted across an abyss to land them on a stone walkway.

"Tha's better!" Soorlah bent to massage his calves. "We're half a bleedin' level above the Watch."

"You know something of this area?" Whitsun demanded.

"A bit. Come on."

The halfling strode forward. He disappeared between two walls that seemed to enclose him. The others followed without hesitation. Their way led through a long, dank tunnel that smelled of garbage, urine, and rainwater. It snaked upward then turned abruptly to the left and spat them out onto another street.

Chemsh looked about. "This better. Where's—?"

A company of Watch rounded the corner. Soorlah, kneeling to catch his breath, almost tripped one of them.

"Balls!"

Glustred's choice exclamation was lost as they took to their heels. Shouts followed them. An arrow, loosed at venture, pinged against the stone near Glustred's shoulder. The big man tried to make himself smaller as he ran.

"Do something!" he snarled at Whitsun.

The two halflings ducked into a doorway, and Glustred and Whitsun followed. The oak door slammed shut, a bar fell, and the four companions groped in the dark.

"Light!" came a plaintive voice belonging to Chemsh.

A pale light sprang up as Whitsun lit a tindertwig. It glowed enough to illuminate their surroundings. They'd stumbled into a warehouse of some sort. Piles and bales of cloth surrounded them, stacked in ghostly shapes against the walls.

A body crashed against the door. It was joined, a moment later, by another. Whitsun wiped a hand across his brow, dripping with sweat, and glowered at the halflings.

"They'll have it down in a moment."

Chemsh vanished behind one of the bundles of cloth. Soorlah followed him. Glustred ran down a narrow way and vanished around a pile of rags. Whitsun, with one backward glance at the door, which was bending to repeated blows, followed him. He found the former innkeeper huddled against a large stack of silk.

The door crashed into the ground, and there was a tramp of feet.

"Scatter, men, and find 'em!" shouted a voice. "They're in here somewhere."

Watchmen raced through the warehouse, overturning goods and smashing what furniture they could find. Glustred and Whitsun stood very still and listened.

A shout came from a far corner of the building, followed by a scramble of feet.

"Do 'em!" shrieked the captain's voice.

There was the clack and rustle of a crossbow missile, followed by the unmistakable thud of a bolt entering flesh. There was a horrid groan and then silence.

Whitsun took advantage of the commotion to slide along the wall. His groping hands touched a ladder. With Glustred behind him, he began to climb, keeping as silent as possible. Fifteen feet off the ground, he could see the dim glow of a torch below and to the right. The Watch seemed huddled around some shape that lay on the floor of the warehouse.

"What about the other ones?" demanded the captain.

On the ground, dim forms moved about, passing through the passageways created by the crates. One approached the bottom of the ladder and stopped. Glustred held his breath. There was silence for a few minutes, then the form moved away. The big man quietly sucked air into his lungs.

"No use, captain. They got away." The voice was flat, holding neither disappointment nor satisfaction.

"Well, one's better'n nothin'. Come on, let's go."

"What about 'im?"

"Vellig an' Wreck, you stay wit' 'im. We'll be back in a while wit' a sack for 'im."

There was a shuffle of feet and a door closed. After a time, Whitsun and Glustred descended the ladder. They peered around a bale of clothing.

A small bundle lay sprawled on the floor, a shaft sprouting from its neck. Glustred could see the crimson shoes that identified it as Chemsh. On either side of it, tall figures of the Watch stood, staring off into the dark recesses of the warehouse.

Whitsun gestured with his head to Glustred, who nodded and moved stealthily to the right. Whitsun, at the same time, breathing heavily, paced to the left. They approached their prey from the back. The two Watchmen looked intently into the darkness in front of them.

Glustred picked up a bit of wood. Without a sound, he leaned back and smashed the stick into the head of the Watchman. The man crumpled without a sound. Satisfied, Glustred looked to his right.

The other Watchman was lying at a slight angle, his head staring off into the distance. Whitsun was stepping back from him, wiping his hands on his tunic.

"Hey!" Glustred stepped over and examined the fallen man. He straightened and glared at his companion. "No need for that!"

Whitsun turned to the man fallen by Glustred's blow. "Well, there's no point in taking chances." He pulled out his knife and bent over the man. He made a quick movement then turned. "Now, let's get out of here."

Glustred examined him as if he'd never seen him before then nodded slowly.

They sidled along a street that led away from the warehouse, ears and eyes alert for any further sign of the Watch. Whitsun seemed unconcerned, but his companion stayed well behind him. After they'd gone a few blocks, Whitsun turned.

"Well?"

"Well?"

"You know damn well there's something bothering you."

Glustred nodded and swallowed. "I didn't know you . . ." He had trouble finishing the sentence.

". . . were that sort of man?" Whitsun's voice held only scorn. "For the sake of the gods, Glustred, what did you think? You've watched me work for two years. How d'you think I earn my living?" He ran fingers through his thinning hair. "It's curious, though . . ."

"What?"

"Why they didn't find us. Anyone would think they didn't want to." Whitsun shook his head. "Too many curious things happening lately. I don't like that."

He turned and passed down the street. Glustred followed him.

They arrived at the entrance to a broad plaza, seemingly deserted. Whitsun scanned it carefully. He seemed to find what he was looking for and turned to his partner.

"Just be careful. We're going for that alley over there." He gestured.

There was a commotion to the north of the square and a small figure shot into it as if pushed.

"Soorlah!" Glustred called in a deafening stage whisper.

The halfling looked in every direction but the right one and finally located the source of the voice.

"Oooer!" he gasped, running up to them. "Where's Chemsh?"

Whitsun shook his head and pointed behind them. Soorlah made a noise in the back of his throat and stamped hard on the pavement. "Thavash ain't gonna like this," he warned.

"I'll see if I can sleep nights." Whitsun's eyes, large in his pale face, were examining the plaza. "Where did you come from?"

"Stairs. Down there. There's Watch at the bottom of 'em."

"Down the alley then."

"Which one?"

"Right there. By the portico."

They scurried across the plaza and arrived at the entrance to the alley. Whitsun held up a hand.

"Wait!"

A tramp of boots on stone echoed off the walls. Whitsun spun to head back the way they came just as a shout resounded from the far side of the square.

"Make ready weapons!"

Glustred looked about with the air of a trapped animal. "Which way?" he snarled.

Whitsun stepped back into the portico. Tall pillars rose on either side, surmounted by a graceful pediment. Two tall doors of carven bronze panels extended upward. The party shrank against them as the Watch hove into view.

Whitsun pressed against the door with his shoulder. It gave silently inward, moving on oiled hinges. Making his bulk as thin as possible, he slipped inside, followed a moment later by Glustred. Soorlah scurried through just as the door shut with a soft click.

They looked around. A long hallway stretched in front of them. Its pillars reached high above their heads. Glustred looked up, eyes widening. "That's not right," he muttered. "The roof outside wasn't that high."

Before them, the hallway extended so far that its end could only dimly be glimpsed, ending in a high marble wall, adorned with a mural, executed in inlaid stone. To either side, the hall extended to an unknown length, and at the far walls, strong brass doors gave promise of hidden chambers. The floor on which they stood was a mosaic composed of thousands of tiny stones, cunningly laid so that they formed a picture of a long, silver flame extending down the length of the hallway. So realistic was it that Soorlah moved to one side to avoid scorching his feet in its heat. The same motif was etched in the pillars that supported the roof and along the walls, dimly glimpsed in the shadows.

The ceiling far, far above them soared majestically, seeming to fly free of gravity's constraints, reaching beyond anything that could be grasped by mortal minds. A few birds soared across it, and their cries came down faintly to the watchers below. The three observers stood as if transfixed by the vastness of the room.

"Err," whispered Soorlah. "The church. The Church of the Silver Flame."

Glustred kept his voice low, either out of reverence or fear of being heard. "I never knew the cathedrals of the Church were this big."

Whitsun, who seemed the least affected of the three, looked about him. "Yes. The church is immensely wealthy—enough to afford the sort of spells that would conceal its true size from prying eyes." He took a few steps forward and swayed. "I don't imagine they have to worry over much about running out of room to expand."

Glustred pointed overhead, where great windows, filled with colored glass, let in the afternoon sunlight and spread it in jeweled patterns on the polished floor. "Those must be visible from outside. Why didn't we see them?"

"Because they're enspelled to be hidden." Whitsun was likewise impressed, though he showed it less. "I don't even know if what we're seeing is the real size of the cathedral. It might be. It might be smaller—or bigger. The point of illusion spells is to create an effect. In any case, the Watch don't seem to want to come in." He looked back at the solid bronze door that led back to the plaza then turned to his companions. "Let's look around."

They followed the hall, moving gradually to one side of it as its size and silence proved oppressive. Rows of stone benches lined it, all facing toward an altar at the eastern end. Glustred moved along the benches, knife drawn but concealed in his hand, doing his best to appear nonchalant. Soorlah made no such effort, and his mouth hung down to his breast.

Below the cathedral's dome, they hesitated. There seemed something almost blasphemous about crossing such a vast empty space. The floor was fashioned here of chalcedony and red marble in interlocking patterns that formed a swirl, ending in the exact center beneath the dome's apex. They sped across it as if the Watch were still on their heels. Three quarters of the way through the enormous space, Whitsun spun on his heel.

"Soorlah!"

The halfling was wandering blindly around the center of the circle, his feet guiding him without heed. He staggered as if drunk.

"Glustred!"

The big man sprang forward and gripped the halfling by the scruff of his neck. He dragged him across the floor, the halfling's shoes scuffing the stone.

"What's wrong with him?" Glustred demanded.

Soorlah wailed a low soulless sound. Drool poured from the corner of his mouth.

"I've seen it before," Whitsun grunted. "Get into a space that's larger than you're used to and you get disoriented. Even sick. His brain, what there is of it, can't comprehend the size of this space. It's completely outside his experience. It's harder when you're small. There's a different perspective on largeness. Not to mention coming from the lower city, where everything's crammed together." He rubbed his face, which had turned pale. "It seems to be catching. I don't feel well."

Glustred shook his head. "I feel fine."

After a few steps, Soorlah seemed to recover, though he

resolutely refused to look up at the distant ceiling. Making their way cautiously, the trio reached the far side of the opening and hesitated. From ahead of them, there opened the sound of male voices lifted in a chant. A few moments later, the chorus hove into view.

There were about twenty of them, men clad in white robes bordered with green and silver. Their hoods were thrown over their heads to conceal their faces as they marched down the long center aisle of the church. The monk leading them waved a censer that spread its perfumes through the still air of the room.

Whitsun and his companions watched them from behind a pillar. Soorlah sat up and started to cough, but Glustred clapped a large hand over his mouth, stifling the sound. As the last of the monks passed, the acolyte sniffed the air and turned, as if in answer to an unheard signal or sound called something in a language that the party did not recognize, and the monks swept backward in a unified movement, seeming not to hesitate or question their leader's command. They surrounded the pillar behind which the companions had sheltered, their hands raised in attitudes of self defense.

A tall monk stepped forward and tipped his hood backward to reveal a pair of dark eyes.

"Hail, friends! What seek you?"

Whitsun, as the spokesman, stepped forward.

"Hail! We're looking for sanctuary. We are much sought after by one who wishes us harm."

The acolyte listened hard as if his ears heard sounds beyond the range of mortals. "Who would that be?"

"A man named . . ." He hesitated.

"Fear not, my son." The acolyte's tone was patronizing. "You will come to no harm here."

"Lassar Redhand."

"The acolyte's smile wavered, and his hand made a small, involuntary gesture. "Gods! The Redhand himself?"

"Aye. We met him on the street, face to face, and I recognized him. We tried to go about our business, but he saw something in my face." Whitsun coughed, his whole body shaking, and wiped his forehead.

"We must notify the Watch at once." The acolyte started toward a doorway.

"No! Wait!" Whitsun coughed again and recovered. "I thought to tell them as well, but . . ." Again, he hesitated.

"Well?"

"The Redhand, when we met him, was already in the company of the Watch—or rather, one of its commanders."

The acolyte was puzzled. "I don't understand."

"May I sit?" Without waiting for permission, Whitsun sank to the floor, his back against a marbled pillar. The acolyte crouched by his side while his companions waited, faces alert, for instructions.

"When I first saw the Redhand, I knew him for who he was. He was a frequent guest at an inn in which I used to lodge. Many times I saw him in the common room, watching the guests with those eyes of his. Those eyes . . ." He shuddered.

"Yes, yes!" the acolyte said impatiently. "Come to the point, my son."

"As I gazed at him, I saw he was accompanied by two other men. One I don't know. The other . . . the other is Captain Belar of the Watch in Tumbledown." Whitsun sighed. "I confess freely to you, brother, that I've had a few differences with the Watch in my time. Belar knows me. When he saw I recognized Lassar, he shouted. Lassar tried to hide his face, but both of them knew it was too late."

"Are you saying," gasped the acolyte, "that this Captain Belar actually is in league with a killer like the Redhand?"

"It looks that way, doesn't it?" Whitsun closed his eyes. "They gave chase to us. Somewhere along the way, Belar must have put out the word to other members of the Watch because when we arrived in the temple district, they were ready and waiting for us." He reached up with an effort that made his face glow and touched the acolyte's sleeve. "Brother, I know the monks of the Silver Flame cooperate with the authorities under ordinary circumstances. But my life, and those of my comrades here, is in danger. If we fall into the hands of the Watch, we'll be dead. Belar has certainly given orders that we be slain on sight. Surely we can claim sanctuary here for a time. Just long enough to recover and decide what to do."

The monk thought. "What you say has force," he conceded. "We will take you to the High Priest Hallah. He'll know what to do with you."

Whitsun nodded. His head sagged.

"You're ill!" The acolyte gripped his arms and set him on his feet. Whitsun's bulk did not seem to bother the monk at all, and he lifted Whitsun as if he were a kitten.

Glustred looked hard at his companion. Whitsun's face was ash white. Sweat poured off his brow and dripped onto his jerkin. His knees trembled.

"What's wrong with you?" Glustred whispered.

Whitsun shook his head. "Don't know." He put his hands out in front of him. Around the left one, a very faint glow could be seen in the cool darkness of the church's interior. Whitsun lifted the hand, examining it as if it belonged to someone else. The acolyte appraised him through narrowed eyes.

Whitsun's legs bent. He collapsed in a heap. Glustred sprang forward, at the same time as the adherent of the Order of the Silver Flame moved from the other side.

"Do not touch his hand!" the priest warned.

Glustred needed no warning. Avoiding the hand, which was glowing brighter now, they lifted the unconscious form and, under the acolyte's directions, carried him down a long corridor lined with doors. Soorlah followed, looking about him nervously. At length they passed through one of the doors into a small chamber with narrow walls. Even here the richness of the temple was on display. The walls were of chalcedony inlaid with an intricate mosaic of abstract designs. The floor was marble, covered in a thick rug of Talentan craft. A single high window in the far wall was blocked by two iron bars set in the masonry.

The priest and Glustred placed Whitsun on the narrow bed that filled half the room. They placed pillows behind his head and covered him with a blanket. The glow around his hand had faded somewhat, but his breath was still stentorian and his eyes were closed.

"Has he been ill before this?" the priest asked.

Glustred shook his head. "I thought he was looking a bit pale, but he seemed well enough. Do you know what's wrong with him?"

"No." The acolyte went to the door. "I will take word to the high priest. He will know the proper thing to do. Meanwhile, watch over him and do not touch his hand." He smiled. "You need not fear. Strong spells bind every part of these walls. Those who pursue you cannot enter without our leave."

"Yeah," Glustred muttered as the door closed. "Without your leave. That's what's worrying me."

Time passed slowly. Whitsun slept fitfully, tossing and turning. The light from the single window faded to the gold of afternoon sun then sank into the velvety dark of evening.

Whether because of the spells surrounding the cathedral or for some other cause, no sounds from the street came up through the window, and the room was bathed in a silence that might have been restful had it not been for the sick man's labored breath. The glow around Whitsun's left hand waxed and waned. As the night passed, it grew fainter until by the time the first rays of dawn peeped into the cell it had faded altogether. Whitsun's breathing slowed and grew normal, and some of the color returned to his face.

Glustred and Soorlah had long since fallen asleep, Glustred sprawled on the rug and the halfling curled up in a corner like a cat, when their companion sat up and looked about. He kicked off the blanket and rose, prowling around the cell like a cat examining its new surroundings. He tried the door, which was locked, looked out the window, and glanced through his own pockets as well as those of his companions. He flexed the fingers of his left hand a number of times, touching it with his right, pushing it against the walls as if to test its strength. Finally he returned to the bed and sat down.

Glustred was the first to stir. He rolled over on the floor, groaned, and pushed himself up on one elbow, glowering at the light streaming in through the bars. He looked over at Whitsun.

"So. You're up."

"Yes," agreed Whitsun. "As are you. He rose and kicked Soorlah none too gently in the ribs. The halfling squealed and came to his feet in a fighting attitude. "Well," Whitsun observed, "now that we're all up, suppose you tell me what happened."

"Starting when?"

"The last thing I remember is getting into the cathedral and having Soorlah here collapse on us."

Glustred looked at him in surprise. "You don't remember meeting the monks? And the story you told them?"

"Story? What story?"

Quickly and without elaboration Glustred related the events of the past ten or twelve hours, including the tale Whitsun had devised to explain their presence in the cathedral. Whitsun listened without comment until the end, stroking his left hand with his right.

"Ingenious of me," he observed at the end of Glustred's narrative. A bit of truth but not too much in it. That's the art of lying effectively, Glustred. Don't falsify more than you have to. He examined his left hand closely, flexing the fingers and moving it about. "It doesn't *look* any different," he said thoughtfully. "But it feels . . . it feels . . ." He broke off, frowning. Glustred and the halfling waited.

Whitsun rose and went to the door. He beat on it with his left hand and, when that produced no apparent result, kicked it vigorously.

"Hello! Anyone! How about some breakfast?"

Footsteps approached the door, and there was a rattle of keys. The same acolyte who had locked them in the night before entered, smiling. He addressed himself to Whitsun.

"Good. You are recovered. The high priest thought you might be."

"Nice of him to be concerned. Who's the high priest?" With Whitsun's health, his old manner had returned.

"Hallah. The high priest here. We are of the Order of the Silver Flame," the priest explained slowly and carefully, as if talking to people suffering from feeblemindedness. "Hallah is our high priest. He has been much interested in you and your story."

Whitsun's eyes flickered toward Glustred. "Ah. And is he willing to grant us the sanctuary we requested?"

"I believe he will look upon all of you with favor." The acolyte smiled. "Such a story is of great interest, even to we who have largely withdrawn from the affairs of the city. The name of the infamous Lassar Redhand is not unknown within these walls, as you observed yesterday. High Priest Hallah is much interested in your experience."

Whitsun shook his head without comment. "I'd like to meet this high priest of yours," he said.

"Certainly. Come with me."

They left the cell and traveled down a series of corridors and up several narrow staircases. Everywhere they went, they saw evidence of the great wealth of the Church. Floors were paved in marble and chalcedony; pillars were of jasper shot through with gold and silver filigree. Furniture was of dark polished wood, and here and there jewels gleamed from settings above doorways and windows. They passed other priests, and to each their guide bowed, hands clasped in front of him, while the others returned the salute. Several looked at Whitsun and his companions, but no one asked anything or spoke to them. Curiosity was evidently not a virtue encouraged by the Order.

At last they passed through a large hall where the arches of the roof met far above their heads. Glustred again marveled at the fact that such an enormous structure could exist within the cramped confines of middle Sharn. He wondered aloud, softly, if some sort of magical spell was at work, making the rooms seem larger than they were.

Whitsun nodded. "It's entirely possible. In this sort of outfit, appearance is everything. They want to intimidate their followers, and nothing intimidates like large open spaces."

"What do you mean?"

Whitsun gestured at the area through which they were passing, keeping his voice low. "In a place like this—or that hall we were in yesterday—the individual feels as if he's nothing. He can be intimidated, manipulated, ordered, betrayed, and he'll accept all of it because he feels insignificant. I've got a theory that one of the reasons thieves flourish in the lower parts of Sharn is because something like thievery, which requires individualism and a focus on your own needs and desires, works best in small, narrow spaces."

Glustred laughed. "That's ridiculous."

"Maybe. It's just a theory, anyway."

Whitsun looked around as if making a survey of the cathedral. The hall's floor was a complex pattern of inlaid stones, each joined so carefully to the next that no space could be detected between them, and the pattern they formed seemed to flow into a seamless whole. Everbright lanterns shed a golden light that preserved mysterious shadows where the marching pillars formed arches. High above them, something swirled and dipped in the air.

"Bat," Soorlah observed. Glustred flinched. Whitsun looked at him curiously.

"Really, Glustred! First rats, now bats. How do you possibly live in the Bone and Bristle?"

"I don't anymore. Remember?" snarled the innkeeper.

They had fallen a bit behind their guide, who waited patiently for them to catch up. Along one of the hallways formed by the arches, a group of hooded figures was moving, chanting softly. Their leader swung a silver censer, filling the air with sweet perfume.

Soorlah sneezed loudly.

Their guide led them around an altar and into a curving passageway running behind it, framed with pillars. In the space between the pillars were stone circles, each holding a glass portrait of a figure. The guide pointed to them and said in a half whisper, "Founders and great figures of our Order."

He stopped before a wooden door, intricately carved with

designs and symbols. "High Priest Hallah will receive you in here."

The door swung open without visible command, and the three visitors stepped inside. They found themselves in a smallish room, cozy in comparison to the vast space through which they had just passed. Its walls were paneled in wood, and a comforting fire burned in the grate of an enormous fireplace. The floor was paved in rough stone tiles that glowed in the ruddy firelight and seemed to embrace the visitors. Against either side of the hearth were two tall wooden settles that beckoned invitingly to them. Other walls were filled with bookshelves housing a large collection of volumes, the spines of which gleamed in the light cast by several everbright lanterns scattered about the room. Several birdcages hung from hooks in the ceiling, and their inhabitants stared at the intruders, clucking busily to themselves.

"Welcome! Welcome, friends!"

From behind a stout desk came an equally stout figure clad in a white tunic edged with silver. Around his thick neck was a heavy chain bearing the symbol of the Order. He extended a fat, ring-crusted hand and gripped each of their hands in turn. His other hand hung stiffly by his side, and as he emerged into the light of the fire, Glustred could see that the first and last two fingers of the hand had fused into one another, making it look for all the world like a misshapen lobster claw.

The high priest, as he came closer, revealed himself as not merely stout but fat. Flesh dripped from his chin and ran in ripples over his neck and shoulders. His cheeks were bunched up, almost hiding his eyes, which remained tiny pinpricks of dark light that glittered in his face. His hair had thinned over his high forehead, and what there was of it was white, though a few threads of black still showed themselves among the silver.

Whitsun showed no signs of being taken aback by the effusive greeting. "The name is Samoval," he said calmly. "Artrus Samoval. This is Magraford, proprietor of the Dragon's Keep Inn in lower Sharn, and our associate Shaalha, formerly of the Talenta Plains and now a resident and trader of this city."

"Pleased, ever so pleased to meet each and every one of you! An especial pleasure, I assure you!" The words were jerked out of Hallah's mouth in long strings of sound. His entire body jiggled and bounced with each statement, and his cheeks quivered. "I only wish it was under more fortuitous circumstances. We'll have something to drink! Absolutely! I insist upon it."

He ushered them over to the settles, drawing out a short stool for Soorlah. He occupied most of one seat, putting his feet up on a small embroidered footstool and ringing a convenient bell pull while reaching with the other for a long white pipe.

"We'll have some of the new ale. Just brewed in our cellars. As an innkeeper—" he leaned forward toward Glustred—"I would value your opinion on it. As a special favor to myself, goodman. I insist!" He turned to Soorlah. "And for you, we have a cordial just sent to me from your cousins in the Talenta Plains. Something very special indeed. I know you'll enjoy it! I don't know what you trade in, Master . . . Shallha, was that it? But if you import wines and spirits, you might consider adding this to your inventory. So you are from the Plains originally? No doubt this will remind you of your home."

Soorlah wriggled on his seat, almost doubling over with anticipation.

"And for you," the high priest continued, turning to Whitsun, "I have something very special indeed. A wine imported from far south in Xen'drik. It's just beginning to make an appearance here in Khorvaire, but as a judge of the finer things, as I can see you are, you will appreciate it, I know."

Whitsun spoke for the first time, breaking into the high

priest's flow of speech. "That's a great deal of information to put into a bell pull."

The high priest thought for a moment then burst into laughter. "Ah, very good, very good indeed! Yes, you're perfectly right. I knew you were coming, of course, and my servants told me who and what you are so I could order these drinks prepared in advance. Very clever, indeed, for you to guess that! My small subterfuge is exposed! I apologize! I really do!"

Nothing could have been more charming and disarming than his confession. Soorlah nodded, beamed, and bobbed. Glustred, hands crossed across his ample belly, feet stretched out to the fire, appeared comfortable and content. Only Whitsun sat at attention, back rigid, eyes never leaving Hallah's face.

"But we didn't give our names or origins to your servants," Whitsun said.

"Well, my dear Samoval," the high priest replied, winking as if sharing a private and very amusing joke between two old friends, "there are more ways than one of discovering such things. Samoval. What an interesting name. Not Brelish in origin, surely. I should think your people must be from Darguun originally."

Whitsun ignored this speculation. "If you know that," he observed, "perhaps you know who is chasing us."

"The Redhand, eh! Of course. You told my priest yesterday. We've heard of him here, don't doubt it! And possibly allied with the Watch now. A serious matter, no question. But you're safe! The Watch has no power here." Hallah puffed on his long clay pipe, which he had lit with a glowing coal from the fire. "No real power. It contents them to think they do, but I am the absolute power within these walls. They enjoy entering from time to time and wandering about looking for malefactors, but we determine what and whom they see. So they are content, and we are content.

And all is right with the world!" As he said these words, his eyes glowed—but perhaps it was merely a trick of the firelight. "Now this fellow Lassar Redhand—did you really see him? You're sure? My goodness! A frightful man! They say he slaughtered an entire family because he thought the wife might have recognized him from ten years' previous. Dear, dear me! Well, we must certainly hope he's captured soon."

"So you are willing to grant our request for sanctuary?"

A cloud of smoke wreathed Hallah's face as he answered. "I will grant you sanctuary here, until I have decided what disposition to make of you and your companions."

Glustred stirred and looked somewhat more uncomfortable. "What does that mean?"

Hallah burst into a high peal of laughter. "Nothing, my dear Magraford, that you need concern yourself with in the least. You may well be correct in your assumption that this fellow Captain Belar is in league with the Redhand. It's not for me to say until I've made some inquiries. In the meantime, I hope you will look upon yourselves as honored guests of the church. I assure you, you are most welcome. You may look surprised, but you really are." The high priest puffed on his pipe. "I feel the church is sadly out of touch with everyday life in Sharn. We go about our business of worship, but we have no means of talking to ordinary folk of the city who come and go about their business."

Whitsun answered before Glustred had a chance to speak. "Are you really that interested in the ordinary people of the city?" he asked.

"Master Samoval, I assure you there is no one whose interests I have more constantly in mind." The high priest sat up a bit, and the smoke pouring from his pipe increased in volume. "In this great city of ours, while the houses such as Kundarak, Jorasco, Deneith, and so on thrash about, dealing out great questions of policy, who looks after the folk whose labors keep the city running? None but a few, who discount the maneuvers of the high and mighty and who stand with the people."

"The people!" Whitsun's voice was cynical. "Do you think the people know what's best for them?"

"If they don't, Master Samoval," Hallah returned calmly, "it's an excellent thing there are educated and wise men such as you and I to tell them." There was a knock at the door, and the high priest turned. "Ah, here are the drinks. Excellent! Come in!"

The door opened and a man clad in the outfit of a priest entered. Tall and thin. A scar divided his face, twisting his lip into a permanently sardonic smile.

Their quarry.

The murderer.

lustred rose slightly from his seat and, at a glare from Whitsun, sank back. Soorlah watched his companions closely, keeping one eye on the scarred man as the priest, with no sign he recognized the visitors, distributed drinks under the watchful eye of the high priest. The latter clucked and chuckled as the various potations were served.

"Now, my good masters," to Glustred, "I really must *insist* on an opinion on this ale. Excellent? Really? You think? I, myself, remain agnostic. It tastes a bit green to me, but perhaps in lower Sharn you prefer a rougher drink, no? And you, little master—" to Soorlah— "what of the cordial? Does it do justice to Talentan tradition? I have never been to that part of Khorvaire, though I long, positively *long*, for the opportunity. We must have a long talk, you and I, and you can describe it to me in detail. Very well. That will be all." This last was directed to the priest, who nodded and went out.

Whitsun sipped his drink with no appearance of hurry, a circumstance that clearly irritated his compatriots. Both were poised as arrows on the drawn bowstring, waiting for his signal for action of some kind, any kind, but it never came.

There was a short silence after which the high priest said, "I had almost forgotten to ask, Master Samoval, if you're quite recovered from your illness."

"Completely, thanks." Whitsun was the picture of courtesy. "I think I must have just been worn out with all the excitement. Some rest and relaxation was exactly what I needed."

"Ah, well," returned the priest, "if that's what you need, you'll find few places better. Our church here is known for the excellence of its table, if I may be forgiven for appearing boastful." He appeared to hesitate a moment and said, with some charm of manner, "It's an impudence, I know, but I can't help asking if I might examine your hand. I believe it was the left that appeared strangely affected during your illness."

Whitsun promptly held out his left hand. The high priest examined it closely, without, however, touching it. He looked up. "You permit?"

"Of course."

The priest waved a few fingers over Whitsun's hand and muttered a spell. His eyes appeared to grow brighter in his face, and he turned an intense gaze to the hand, which, however, seemed to yield him nothing. After a few minutes of study, he sighed.

"I can see nothing. Curious." He relit his pipe.

Whitsun took another sip of ale. "You mentioned the dragonmarked houses a few minutes ago. Do you have much news of them here?"

"Some. Little enough." Hallah chucked, and the billows of flesh on his cheeks wobbled. "One hears that House Cannith is making some experiments with magic that skirt the law."

Whitsun raised an eyebrow. "Really? What sort of experiments?"

"Oh, nothing *definite*, you understand. Merely some things that may have been frowned upon by the Treaty of Thronehold. But who knows the truth in such a matter. . . ."

Whitsun nodded, and the conversation turned to other matters. It seemed to Glustred that Whitsun was deliberately keeping the talk inconsequential. At the same time, he appeared to be enjoying himself. Soorlah, sipping on his cordial, which was refreshed several times at a signal from the high priest, had slipped into his own pleasant world and was quietly humming and singing to himself on his stool.

At long last the lazy interval drew to an end. Whitsun rose and bowed politely to his host, whose chins jiggled in merriment.

"You are welcome to enjoy the hospitality of the Order of the Silver Flame," he announced, "as long as you choose. Our reverend brother will conduct you back to your chambers. I regret that your first rooms were a bit spare. We have made . . . adjustments." He chuckled to himself.

Whitsun bowed again. "Too kind. I look forward to seeing you again, Reverend Hallah."

"As do I, Master Samoval. As do I."

The door opened, and the scarred-face man entered.

"Brother Stolach will conduct you to your rooms." The high priest bowed one last time, and the final glimpse they had was of his smiling face as the door closed.

The scarred man motioned for them to precede him. "If you would, masters."

Whitsun shook his head. "No, please, after you."

"But I insist."

"Very well."

They set out through the corridors and vaulted passages again, with the tramp of Merimma's killer echoing behind them. Several times Soorlah tried to stop and turn, but each time

Whitsun's firm hand on his shoulder prevented him. The man led them down a series of corridors that moved away from the cell in which they had first been housed. These areas were more sumptuous and more richly appointed than those they had first been in. The walls were hung with tapestries and paintings, and here and there a table held a vase or a silver candlestick.

Soorlah's hands twitched as he walked.

They stopped outside a heavy paneled door. The guide unlocked it and swung it open, motioning them inside. They entered. Whitsun brought up the rear and waved the guide through before him.

The room was as different from their previous lodgings as night is from day. Dark wood lined the walls, and silks were thrown carelessly here and there as decoration in the richly appointed chambers. The three beds looked soft and inviting, and by each was a robe made of thick wool and a pair of slippers. There were bowls of hot water, steam still rising from them, and a fire burned in the grate.

A window filled part of one wall, but it was made of stained glass in a complex pattern that blocked any view. It was impossible to tell if it opened to the outside or was merely another portal to part of the church, which seemed to them endless in its rambling corridors and vast, vaulting chambers.

The guide bowed and without saying a word disappeared, closing the door behind him. Whitsun at once moved to the portal and tried the door. It opened easily enough. He nodded as if satisfied and looked at the others. He held up a finger before his lips and began to search the room.

Glustred and Soorlah joined him. Between the three of them, they ransacked the chamber, pulled apart the bedding, drew furniture back from the walls, pulled aside the tapestries, and tapped the plaster. At length, satisfied, Whitsun nodded, though he still kept his voice low when he spoke so his companions were obliged to lean close to hear what was being said.

"It would seem they don't recognize us and don't associate us with anything that could be a threat. The question is why is the Order of the Silver Flame mixed up with a murderer and a thief?"

Glustred shrugged. "Could be what you said on the way up here. If they're in the business of power, maybe they want that magical whatever-it-is to increase power."

Whitsun shook his head. "The Order of the Silver Flame is among the most powerful religions in all the Five Nations. They're rigid in their morality. It makes no sense that they'd risk anything for this object—unless either it's far more powerful than we imagine or . . ."

"Or what?"

"Unless there's something else going on here." Whitsun shook his head. "I can't figure it out. It all seems very normal."

Glustred looked around. *"This* is normal?"

"To the Purified, probably. The Order is very rich. I don't know anything about this cathedral—they have them all over Sharn and beyond—but there's nothing here that seems out of place."

Glustred had been looking around, fingering the objects in the room as if assessing their exchange value. He looked around and spoke. "Just the high priest."

"What do you mean?" Whitsun sounded more interested than usual in the innkeeper's opinion.

"Well, it's odd, isn't it?" Glustred picked up a piece of silk, running it through his fingers. "I mean, he gets us up there, rescues us from the Watch, swallows your story about Lassar, and then spends all that time asking us about ale. He seemed barely interested in the stuff about Lassar. And that should be big news to him."

"Possibly he just wanted to feel out what kind of folk we are. Or the priest who brought us to him had given him the details of our story he wanted."

"That's another thing. That priest that brought us to the high priest. Whuff!"

"What are you talking about?"

"He's a dip."

Whitsun looked startled. "Really? You think so?"

Glustred's face showed scorn mixed with triumph at having scored over his companion. "How long have I been tending bar and watching common rooms? I tell you, he was a dipper. You could see it in the way his hands moved when he walked. He's not been long gone from it either."

Whitsun sat on a bed and stretched. "But there's nothing altogether unusual about a thief converting to religion. I'd imagine some dips pray a lot every time they go on the street." He smiled at Soorlah, who had the grace to blush. "What do you think, Soorlah?"

The halfling considered. "Right enough. 'E's right." He jerked a thumb at Glustred. "A dipper. 'Igh class, too."

"Right." Glustred paced. "What's a high-class dip doing becoming a priest of the Silver Flame?"

"Well, you do have a point. That is a bit odd." Whitsun stared into space. "In any case, it bears looking into. I don't trust the high priest, and that's a fact." He moved to the bed and swiftly, without wasted motion, pushed the pillows in a lump down the middle of the bed. He pulled the blankets over them, stepped back and examined his handiwork, and gave a poke or two to the resulting facsimile. Then he looked at Glustred and Soorlah.

"I'll be gone for a while. You two might want to get into bed as well, though I wouldn't recommend going to sleep. But be ready in case anything happens. If anyone comes through the door, don't forget your new names. There's no reason to take chances in case anyone here has heard of Ulther Whitsun."

"Or Glustred," observed the former innkeeper.

"Yes, that would be a big problem, you being so well known." Whitsun's voice held nothing but sarcasm. Glustred scowled at him and might have said something had not Soorlah intervened.

" 'Ow're you gonna get by all the magic they got 'round this place?"

Whitsun shrugged. "It won't be the first time I've made my way through a magically sensitive area, Soorlah. Trust me, I'll be careful. You two do the same. Don't leave this room."

Soorlah nodded and made a mound under the covers of his bed. Glustred kicked off his shoes and shook his head. "I hope you know what you're doing."

"Let's hope so." Whitsun opened the door a crack, peered through, and slipped out.

⬛

The layout of the cathedral proved even more confusing than Whitsun anticipated. He moved from corridor to corridor, from room to room, staying with his left hand against the wall as much as possible. In some rooms he found acolytes engaged in prayer or meditation. Sometimes he was able to slip through unnoticed. In others he had to pretend to be one of the crowd of worshipers until an opportunity presented itself for him to make his way into a less populated area.

Nowhere did he find magical traps and alarms, and though at first he proceeded cautiously, checking for them, at length he grew bolder. It seemed the Order was confident that anyone within the cathedral was under its control.

Everywhere Whitsun found activity, but nowhere did he see anything that might not have been seen in a half a hundred temples throughout the city. Priests conducted ceremonies, followers bent their heads and prayed to the Silver Flame. Smoke rose from altars, and incense burned in dozens of censers. In a few areas, monks sat together, silent in meditation, heads bowed, lips moving. Whitsun watched them all carefully before moving on to the next scene.

In several rooms, he found doors that were locked and sealed. Though he tried spells on them, he failed to gain entrance to the rooms or passages that lay beyond. In other places, he discovered windows that would not open to his touch, though others opened easily enough. There was no pattern to this; in one room, doors and windows sprang ajar at his command, while in an adjoining chamber, every window was shut fast. In several cases he tried to force the casemates and doors by brute force but was unsuccessful.

At last he came to a room with an altar toward the front, pillar lined, darkened. There were few lanterns burning here, and there were no windows to bring outside light—or the illusion of light—inside. Above the altar was the ubiquitous sign of the Silver Flame, this time painted in oils on a board and richly mounted with gold and jewels. Surmounting this was a portrait of a man dressed in monastic robes, looking in a dignified manner out of the canvas. A crowd of twenty or so acolytes knelt before the altar, their hands moving in prayer, their voices chanting a hymn of praise to Dol Arrah.

A movement at the other side of the room caught Whitsun's eye. The scar-faced man moved quietly among the rows of worshipers. His hands were in front of him, thrust into the sleeves of his robe, and his face was downcast, but Whitsun had caught enough of a glimpse of his countenance and its disfiguring scar to know this was his prey. The scar-faced man passed out of the chamber, leaving its devotees behind. Whitsun followed.

The two, the pursuer and the pursued, passed through many other passages and rooms. The assassin did not seem in any hurry as he moved along, and Whitsun followed at a leisurely pace, being careful to find cover to dodge behind if his quarry turned. But the scarred man never turned, never increased his pace.

They came at last to a large room with marble walls that was uninhabited. Here, for the first time, the scarred man exhibited signs of secrecy. He looked around and behind him. Whitsun watched him cautiously from behind a pillar.

The priest stepped up to a long panel recessed somewhat in the wall and placed his fingers on it in a delicate pattern. He pressed, and the wall melted away, revealing a blackness behind it. The priest melted into the darkness, and the wall closed silently behind him.

Whitsun waited for a hundred breaths then emerged from behind the pillar. He placed his hands over the panel as he had seen the priest do. Nothing happened. He closed his eyes, and his brow drew together. A faint glow enveloped his left hand, and the marble wavered and disappeared.

Before him appeared a long passageway stretching back an unknown length. Its walls were patterned in a complicated design of tiles whose swirls and interweaving lines seduced the mind as they beckoned him onward. Whitsun shook his head as if to clear it and walked forward.

The passage twisted and turned on itself, widening so that three or more men might walk side by side and not touch one another. Whitsun proceeded cautiously, keeping to one side and stretching his left hand in front of him as if feeling the way where unseen dangers lurked. The passage bent to the left, and he looked around the corner.

Another space opened up, not as large as some of those he and the others had traversed on the way to their room, but sufficiently great to lift the hair on the back of his neck. The pillars on either side of him bent inward and met above his head in a twisted rhythm of coils that seemed to draw the light of many cold fire torches upward into blackness. They bent and swayed in the thick air. Whitsun rubbed his eyes, staring at them. He reached out a tentative hand and touched the wall and seemed to find reassurance in its solidity.

The hall at whose entrance he was standing was taller than it was long. On either side, a line of statues sunk in alcoves, tall men, dressed in the robes of priests but with gold bands around their heads, marched, each one lifting a pallid hand as if in greeting to an intruder. The floor was cold marble; indeed the entire room felt chilly and clammy. The light came from torches that guttered and flickered in drafts.

Movement at the far end of the hall. Whitsun stole cautiously from statue to statue, concealing himself in the alcoves. The air still seemed absurdly thick and heavy, as if it were some sort of curtain that must be drawn aside to see clearly.

Twenty or so priests gathered at the end of the hall in a broad space somewhat better lit than the rest of the area. They wore dark robes edged in blood red silk, which rustled softly when they moved. Their backs were to Whitsun.

They moved in a kind of prearranged pattern, which to Whitsun seemed like the steps of some elaborate dance. Hands wove in front of each one in a tangle of thrusts and chops. Their bodies bent, leaned back, and moved forward. They generally remained in place, and each was separated from his neighbor to avoid striking each other. The man whom Whitsun had been following stood in the third rank, moving with the rest. He was somewhat taller than his fellows and easy to mark because of his scar.

One who seemed to act as the leader motioned the others to

halt. They stood easily in their spots while one selected by the leader came forward.

The leader priest—so he seemed to be, judging from the color and splendor of his robes—was a striking figure. Well over six feet, he had golden hair that flowed like water over his shoulders to hang halfway down his back. It was bound with a leather thong, and another thong encircled his left bicep. His eyes were of a brilliant blue and seemed abnormally large and all seeing.

The leader spread out his hand in a magical gesture. A knife rose from its place on the ground and shot across the space at one of the initiates. Just as swiftly, the initiate gestured, and the knife was parried in mid air by another. The leader moved his hand and another knife joined the others. It too was countered by his opponent. More and more blades whirled in the air, striking at one another in a resounding clash of steel that echoed and reechoed against the walls of the chamber. The pace of the exercise grew faster, and Whitsun's head whirled as his eyes followed the knives' movement.

All the other acolytes were still, watching the movement of the knives. Each combatant moved barely at all, fingers working in an intricate dance as their knives darted and struck at each other in the air between them. No one spoke. Indeed, no words could have been heard above the clash of metal.

Slowly the cloud of weapons controlled by the leader inched toward his opponent. The acolyte gave way reluctantly, his fingers fluttering more swiftly than before until they seemed to blur. But there was now an air of desperation in his motions. The leader pressed his advantage. One of the knives darted and struck, slashing at the young man's robe. He staggered as red trickled down his leg. Other blades swooped in, cutting and twisting. He howled as one struck at his hand, slicing off two of his fingers. A cloud of steel surrounded his body.

No one else spoke, and the cries and moans faded away to silence. At a gesture from the leader, the knives fell to the floor with a clatter. In their midst was a shapeless bundle surrounded by a red halo on the stone floor.

At a sign from the master, two of the acolytes produced a sack and encased the corpse in it while others picked up the knives and wiped them clean. The leader watched them all with an impassive eye. Whitsun could see the scar-faced man helping the rest with alacrity. When they had completed their tasks, they moved off down the corridors that exited from the chamber.

As one passed Whitsun, who stood in a niche concealed in the shadow, he stepped out and struck. The acolyte, warned by some movement in the air or light turned just in time to duck. His hand came up holding a blade. Whitsun, dodging it, reached with his left hand and pushed the man's head back.

The acolyte, without a word, crumpled to the ground.

Whitsun stared at him. Then he kicked away the blade, picked it up, and pointing it at the fallen man made his way cautiously over to him. He stirred the acolyte with his foot, then kicked him once or twice. When he got no response, he bent and put his right hand against the man's neck, feeling for a pulse.

At last he straightened, staring at the wall, his face a picture of confusion. He looked at his left hand, wiggling the fingers several times.

A spider scurried across the wall. Whitsun touched it, and it stopped. He poked it, and it fell to the ground.

He spent a little time seeking out another spider. He stood for a little time watching it move to and fro across its web, spinning its silken thread. Then he covered his fingers in a piece of cloth he tore from the dead man's robe and touched the spider.

Nothing happened. The spider moved as before. With some

arachnid sense of danger it scuttled sideways and disappeared into a niche between two of the stones.

Whitsun looked at his fingers again. Then, to himself, he said, "Well, who knows when that'll come in handy?" He looked at the body in front of him and added, "Now what to do about this?" He stripped the robe from the acolyte's body, girded on the man's knife, and dragged the corpse to one side, placing it behind a stone statue. He stood back, contemplating the hiding place then nodded as if satisfied.

He entered the room where the deadly contest had taken place. Three corridors led out of it besides the one through which he had entered. He examined the entrance to each, keeping away from the center of the room. Choosing the one on the left, he slipped along, one ear cocked for any noises.

Many doors lined the corridor, and Whitsun stopped to listen at several of them. He found nothing of interest and proceeded. His footsteps were noiseless against the polished marble floors. Once, from ahead, came the sound of voices, and he withdrew into the robe, hands clasped reverently in front of him. But no one appeared, and the voices faded to silence as the speakers moved up the corridor ahead of him.

The passage branched, and Whitsun chose which to follow with no sign of hesitation. He emerged into a broader passageway, the very one, in fact, leading to the high priest's chambers.

Here several acolytes and priests passed quietly along, and Whitsun moved among them. He found a position near a stained glass window from which he could see the High Priest's door. He waited.

An hour passed this way. Whitsun shifted from one foot to another and stretched. There was a pad of footsteps and he resumed his worshipful attitude, watching the door from out of the corner of his eye.

A tall figure with a scarred face moved along the corridor. The killer knocked quietly at Hallah's door, and even from where he stood, Whitsun could hear the cheerful voice of the patriarch bidding him enter. The door closed behind him, and Whitsun moved rapidly to stand by the door, one ear pressed against the wood. He stood for a few minutes, listening, then shook his head impatiently. From the High Priest's office, he had a good idea of the route back to his room, and he followed it with alacrity. He slid inside and threw back the hood of the robe as Glustred and Soorlah rose from their beds and stared at him in astonishment.

➤

"What are you talkin' 'bout?" Soorlah's voice was high with outrage. Whitsun gave him a look, and he lowered it. "Order of the Silver Flame monks would never cut someone, leastways one of their own. Musta been some kind o' mistake."

Whitsun's voice was even. "It was not a mistake, you moronic pile of rat droppings. I saw what I saw. I don't know who or what we've stumbled into, but I'll give my right arm that it isn't a church of the Silver Flame."

Glustred's slower mind was attempting to follow this. "It *looks* like a church," he observed.

"So it may very well be. Just not the kind of church we thought it was. The priests of the Silver Flame generally don't go about killing each other while practicing fighting techniques. It's possible, of course, that these men are Argent Fists."

Glustred looked puzzled. Whitsun explained.

"Argent Fists are members of the church devoted to battling enemies of the faith. They use spells, weapons, whatever's handy."

"I've heard of them," said Glustred. "Wasn't there some sort of scandal involving a couple of them a few months ago?"

"A bit of one. There was a brawl with worshipers of the Dark Six. It got out of hand, and two of the Dark Six followers were killed." Whitsun sniffed. "It probably wouldn't have made any difference except that the two were members of House Jorasco." The church had to do some quick explaining to make that case go away." He stretched. "In any case, we know Merimma's killer is here, he's part of the hierarchy, and he's got what we want." He looked meaningfully at Glustred. "The next step is to find out where his quarters are."

"Why?" asked Glustred.

"So we can search them. I don't think he's stupid enough to have hidden what we want there, but you never can tell. In any case, we may find something that'll tell us a bit more about what's going on here."

"Here!" Glustred said sharply. "Before we do anything, shouldn't we do something about that fellow you killed?"

Whitsun raised an eyebrow in query.

"Well, you said yourself he's bound to be found before long. There must be a way to hide him a bit more permanently. Isn't there someplace we can dump the body?"

"You know, Glustred," Whitsun said after a short pause, "I can see you have a natural turn for this kind of work. No, I don't think we need worry just now. I hid the body well—well enough to give us time to do what we need to do. By the time anyone finds it we'll be gone from this place." Whitsun looked at Soorlah. "I've been out and about this place. Now I think you're the lad to find out where our scar-faced friend resides."

"Me?" The halfling slapped a hand against the wall. "I ain't stirrin' from this room til you figure out 'ow to get around without bein' killed or stabbed or 'avin' a spell tossed at me."

Glustred put out a leisured hand and lifted the halfling by the scruff of his neck, leaving him to dangle two feet off the floor. Soorlah squealed and twisted about in a vain attempt to get down. Whitsun pulled his face toward him.

"Get this, rat brains. If I tell you to do something, you'll do it. Thavash told you to help me. Now I'm telling you what to do to help me. You'll do it without any backchat. Understand?"

Soorlah mumbled something. Whitsun slapped him, not hard but hard enough to leave a stinging red mark on his cheek.

"All right! All right! Put me down!"

Glustred lowered the halfling, who rubbed his cheek vigorously. Whitsun sat down on the bed.

"All you're looking for," he told Soorlah, "is where our friend with the scar sleeps. Stay out of sight. If anyone catches you, you were looking for a sanctuary to pray in and got lost. You know how to act pious, so that shouldn't be a problem." His voice held a world of contempt, but Soorlah didn't react to it.

"Questions?"

"No."

"All right, then. Don't mess it up." He opened the door. Soorlah, with a quick glance up and down the passage, scooted out, and Whitsun shut the door behind him. He looked at Glustred and yawned.

"I'm dead for a little sleep. Keep an eye on things." He lay down on the bed, put an arm behind his head, and closed his eyes.

❧

It seemed to be growing dark when he awoke several hours later. In the strange artificial light of the cathedral it was hard to know. Glustred was sitting in the same position in his chair, facing the door. His eyes were closed, and a little whiffling snore escaped from his lips. Whitsun sat up and looked at him with a sardonic smile. He stretched, rose, and slapped the back of the big man's head. The innkeeper came awake with a jerk.

"Huh? Wha?"

"If a job opens in the Guild of Night Watchmen, I'll be happy to nominate you for the position." Whitsun looked about. "How long was I asleep?"

"Two hours. Three. Not sure." Glustred rubbed his eyes. "I've heard nothing. Soorlah's not back yet."

"So I see." A frown creased Whitsun's brow. "I hope nothing's happened to him."

Glustred raised an eyebrow.

"I just don't want to have to go to the trouble of extracting him from any more trouble," Whitsun said. "We've enough to do without drawing more attention to ourselves. Speaking of which, I wonder why our friend Hallah hasn't asked to see us again. You'd think he'd show more interest."

Glustred considered. "Well," he said, "if you're right and there's something else going on here, he probably knows you've still got the ring. But he also knows if he sends you out in the street the Watch or someone else will pick you up and get it. If he's got the orerry, he just needs the ring."

Whitsun took him up. "Yes. He needs them both together for some reason. But he's only got the one. If he hasn't done anything to me yet, that means he knows I don't have the ring with me. But he can't just let me go and hope I'll lead him to it, because there's someone else out there looking for it as well, and he can't take the chance that person will get to me before he does." He rubbed his chin. "Interesting, if right."

"But why not just put you in a cell or something? Chain you up. That way he knows just where you are. If it comes to that, why not torture you to find out where you've hidden the ring?"

Whitsun lifted his left hand and turned it several times in the light, examining it. "Maybe," he said slowly, "maybe he wants to see what'll happen next."

"What do you mean?"

"That fellow I killed in the corridor. All I did was touch him with this—" he held up his left hand—"and he dropped dead. I seem to have picked up an interesting ability."

Glustred backed away from his companion. "Keep that hand away from me then."

Whitsun looked around the room. In one corner was a sumptuously appointed wardrobe. He opened it and looked through the cloaks and hats contained within. Seizing a pair of brown leather gloves, he put the left one on. It slid easily over his hand, almost like a second skin.

"There. That ought to be safe enough."

"You don't know that," grumbled Glustred. "Just keep away from me with that."

Whitsun sat down again. "So," he said, "if somehow I've got this power as a result of contact with the ring, why doesn't anything happen with the orerry? It doesn't seem to have any effect on me. Or I on it."

Glustred was silent.

Whitsun rose abruptly. "We've got to get back to Morgrave University," he said. "I've got to talk to Lamonn. Maybe he's been able to decipher those symbols or writing or whatever it was. In any case, I'm not easy in my mind about leaving the ring with him." He paced impatiently. "Damn him, where *is* Soorlah?"

"Why don't we just go without him?"

"Because I need to know what's going on at this end as well. And I can't just leave him here. For one thing, Thavash would probably have my throat cut if I lost him both his thieves. As it stands, he's going to be none too happy about losing Chemsh." Whitsun sighed. "I suppose there's no help for it. I'll have to go look for him."

The door opened, and Soorlah slipped inside. The halfling was breathing hard and had a streak of blood across his forehead.

"About time! What happened to you?" Whitsun stood over him.

Soorlah was sullen. "I got it?" he growled.

"What?"

"What you wanted. I got where the scarred man stays. In't that what you wanted?"

"Yes, but I wanted it before I died of old age. What happened?"

Soorlah sat down and caught his breath. He related his story clearly, interrupted now and again by questions from Whitsun. Glustred listened and kept an eye on the door to see they weren't disturbed.

The halfling had wandered through much of the cathedral. Everywhere he'd found nothing amiss. Priests and acolytes went about their business, and he found no shadowy monks in dark robes doing magical battle with one another. He was about to give up and return when he spied his quarry coming out of a chapel with a group of other worshipers.

Soorlah followed the scarred man down passageways and across courtyards. He was unobserved; at least he convinced himself of that. At last he saw the man enter a corridor with many doors opening off it. He watched as the man opened one of them and vanished inside.

"And no one saw you?"

"Nope."

"Umph!" Whitsun was plainly skeptical. "It sounds a bit too easy?"

"Easy!" The halfling was outraged. "Then next time you bloody well try doin' it!"

"You're *sure* no one saw you?"

"Not then."

Glustred intervened. "What do you mean, *Not then?*" he growled.

"Well . . ."

The halfling, having marked the door, was about to return when he thought he might as well peep into a few of the other rooms.

Whitsun groaned. "That's what I get for enlisting thieves as helpers. You just couldn't resist, could you? Wanted to see if there was gilt about you could lift."

Soorlah had found one of the monk's cells unlocked. Inside he'd discovered a chest containing several small but valuable articles. He took two of these and left the rest—"I ain't greedy!"—and was about to leave when the door opened. He had just presence of mind enough to conceal himself behind it. As the monk entered and looked astonished at his ransacked room, Soorlah slipped out the door and was away.

"And you were chased," Whitsun said resignedly.

"Well . . . yeah," the thief admitted. "But they din't catch me."

"Why do you think that matters, you imbecile? They saw you, didn't they? Enough to tell you were a halfling. How many halflings do you think are wandering about this place?" Whitsun stood. "We're leaving here."

"What about the Watch?" Glustred asked.

"We'll have to take our chances. As long as we stay away from public places and go by means of back ways, we should be all right. He turned toward the window.

"What 'bout that orrer . . . orar . . . sphere thing?" Soorlah asked. "You gonna just leave it here?"

Whitsun halted in thought then nodded. "No, you're right. We should get it back from our scar-faced friend. With luck he's out hunting for Soorlah here. I'm surprised no one's showed up at the door."

There was a sharp knock on the wood.

"Ah ha!" Whitsun spoke with the gloomy air of one who has successfully predicted disaster. He grasped a chair and hurled it through the stained glass window. Shards of colored glass flew, and the knocking on the door increased to a pounding. Whitsun picked up Soorlah and with no more thought than if he'd been a bundle of clothing, tossed him through the opening. He followed, and Glustred clambered out behind him, avoiding with difficulty the jagged shards of glass that littered the pavement.

They were in one of the corridors of the cathedral. Glustred looked about him.

"Dolurrh! How do you get out of this place?"

Whitsun paid him no attention. He set the halfling on his feet. "Do you know how to get to the man's cell from here?"

Soorlah hesitated a moment, then ran. Whitsun and Glustred pounded after him. From behind them they heard growing sounds of confusion and the faint shattering of wood that told them the door had been breached.

The halfling dodged down a series of passages, forking left and right, moving along with confidence. They slowed to a rapid walk to avoid drawing too much attention to themselves. Fortunately, they seemed to be in a part of the cathedral that for the moment was abandoned, and they met no one. At last they came to a hallway framed in dark paneling, its sides pierced by doorways. Soorlah led the way to one and pointed.

Whitsun pushed the door. It swung open and he stepped inside.

The scarred man sat facing the door, his face creased in a mirthless smile.

CHAPTER 11

Whitsun twisted backward, bumping into Glustred. The big man pushed him to one side and moved to get at the scarred man. Whitsun, with his right hand, reached for his left to pull off the glove.

A sound at his side drew his attention. Glustred was sprawled on the floor facedown. Soorlah stood behind him holding a long metal bar. Glustred stirred, and the thief struck him again on the head.

"What in the name of—" Whitsun's words were cut off as the scarred man surged out of his chair and motioned. A magic crackling filled the room. The air around Whitsun grew thick and cloudy for a moment then cleared, leaving Soorlah and the assassin coughing. The room seemed to be filled with smoke.

"I told you!" the halfling screamed. "No magic! Not around 'im!" He swung his bar at Whitsun, who dodged it and ripped the glove from his left hand. Soorlah backed away, and Whitsun, keeping an eye on him, turned toward the assassin.

"So you two have met already," he observed.

"Yes. Master Soorlah and I had a conversation earlier, and he told me of your plans." The assassin's voice was of a rich texture, like thick cream spread over polished silver.

Whitsun spoke to Soorlah without taking his eyes from the man in front of him. "Soorlah, you realize that if Thavash hears about this, you're dead?"

"Nope. Thavash'll be pleased. 'E likes money, and there's money to be paid out 'ere."

"You think he'll be happy you've joined forces with Merimma's murderer?"

The halfling shrugged. "What's done is done. Besides, Thavash don't like you much." He made another halfhearted swing with his iron bar. Whitsun caught it and jerked it. The halfling fell forward, close enough for Whitsun's left hand to grasp his throat. A tiny spark seemed to flow from Whitsun's fingers to the halfling's skin. Soorlah gurgled and went limp. His head sagged to one side, and his tongue lolled from his mouth.

"Well," Whitsun told him, "I don't think Thavash much liked you either."

He heard the whistle of air behind him and turned just as a wooden stick smashed into his head.

It might have been six minutes, six hours, or six days. Whitsun's head ached, and he could taste blood running down his forehead and trickling over his mouth. To one side, he could see Glustred, securely trussed like a turkey ready for slaughter. The body of Soorlah lay where Whitsun had let it fall. He himself was lying, bound, on the stone floor. He twisted his head and saw the assassin had replaced the glove on his left hand.

"Awake, are you?"

The question came from somewhere four feet or four miles above him. He looked up and saw the assassin's face staring at him. Behind it was a smoky cloud that resolved itself into the ceiling.

A pail of water was thrown over him, and he jerked to wakefulness. He tried to sit up and fell back against the bonds that held his hands and feet.

The assassin chuckled. "Relax," he said. "We have lots of time to talk."

Whitsun cleared his throat. "Who are you?"

The assassin ignored the question and pushed his chair a bit closer. "You're Ulther Whitsun."

It came as a statement, and Whitsun didn't deny it. "Well?"

"Where is the sacred ring?"

"I haven't the least idea what you're talking about."

The man kicked him in the ribs, without any particular feeling, as if it were part of a prearranged routine. "Answer the question."

Whitsun doubled up. "What ring?"

The assassin bent over him. "I don't like to take a long time with these things. But don't get any idea that anybody cares what happens to you. Now, either tell me where the ring is, or I'll find out on my own. But either way, I'll find it."

Whitsun spat at him. That is, he pursed his lips together and blew. They vibrated together, without producing any spittle. The hollow sound they made was a mockery of defiance. He kicked in defiance and only succeeded in shattering a glass vase that stood on a low table.

The killer shrugged and pulled out a large knife. "Very well. We'll do this the hard way. But you're making a mistake."

His voice was calm and cultured, coming from one of the upper reaches of the city. Again, he spoke with no emotion. He gave the impression of someone entirely uninterested in his job. He bent over Whitsun and plucked at his ear.

"This one first. Then the other. Then we start on the fingers."

"Gods curse you!" Whitsun's emotion was as close to being real as he could manage. "I don't know what you want!"

"I want the location of the ring."

"And after I give it to you, you'll kill me."

The assassin seemed to acknowledge the justice of this and stopped for a moment. "True. But it'll be quick. I can make it swift, so you won't even know you're dead. Wouldn't you rather have that than what I've got planned?"

Whitsun spat at him again. "Doesn't make a difference. I'm still dead."

"True." The assassin raised his knife again. A long ringing of silver bells interrupted him. The sweet notes blended with one another and melded to form a symphony. The killer's knife remained suspended in the air, and Whitsun's breathing slowed to normal.

The door to the chamber opened, and an acolyte entered. He paid no attention whatever to the scene before him—to Whitsun lying on the floor, Glustred trussed and gagged beside him, and the body of the dead halfling sprawled across the flagstones.

"The bells for evening service are calling, my lord."

"Very well." The killer rose in a smooth motion and handed the knife to the acolyte. "Keep them until I return. I shan't be long."

Whitsun twisted around and propped his back against the wall. "My lord? My *lord?*"

The acolyte made no motion. He stood, back to the wall, in

an easy stance, balanced on both feet, hands at his sides. His eyes never moved from Whitsun.

"Lord of what?"

"More than you can imagine, heathen." There was nothing hostile in the man's voice. He spoke the words without emphasis. Whitsun stretched and wriggled, as if scratching his back.

"All right, all right. If you won't tell me, you won't. But you might at least have the courtesy to scratch my nose."

The acolyte chuckled quietly to himself and didn't move.

"Oh, come! Do you really think I'm trying to trick you?"

Silence.

"If I were, do you think I'd—"

The tall figure of Glustred rose behind the acolyte. The man turned, as if sensing something, and collapsed without even a groan as the big man's fist descended on his neck. Glustred came forward, pushing the body to one side, and applied thick fingers to Whitsun's bonds.

"Next time you break glass, do you think you could do it a bit farther away? I've got cuts all over my hands."

"Next time, try not to get tied up and I won't have to provide you with something to cut the ropes." Whitsun's tone was irritated. "Is he—?" He motioned with his chin toward the acolyte.

"No. Don't think so. I didn't hit him that hard."

Whitsun rubbed his hands to restore circulation. "Well, at least our scarred friend seems to have guessed *this*." He gestured to his gloved hand.

"Careful with that thing." Glustred backed away, almost tripping over Soorlah's body. He looked down at the halfling. "What are you going to tell Thavash about him?"

"Thavash is a businessman. He'll understand completely— both Soorlah going over to the church and me having to dispose of him. The only question is how long ago Soorlah turned traitor and if Thavash is involved as well. If he is, the girls are going to be getting a new boss in short order."

Glustred nodded. "How did he know your name?" he asked. "The scarred fellow."

"He knows me by sight. That's clear. And with that knowledge, I'm sure it wasn't hard for him to figure out who you are. So there's no point in holding on to the Dragon's Keep." Whitsun stepped to the door. "Pity. It sounded like a place I'd like to visit sometime. Time to leave, I think."

The two men moved rapidly down the corridor. They had almost reached the end when there was a rustle of robes, and a group of priests rounded the corner in front of them, the scarred man in the lead. His eyes met Whitsun's.

He did not even bother to shout an alarm. His hand came up, and his lips moved in a spell. A net made of glowing energy flew from his fingers, shooting over Glustred and Whitsun. It enveloped them and faded into nothingness.

The scarred man cursed and hurled another spell. The bars of a cage appeared around Whitsun and Glustred, wavered in the air for a moment, and collapsed. The magical energies that formed it writhed on the floor for a moment like snakes then split apart with a deafening boom that knocked everyone to their knees.

Whitsun was the first up. He spun on his heel and raced down the corridor back the way they'd come. Glustred pounded after him. From behind them, they heard a cry from their former captor.

"Head them off!"

The two fugitives dodged down another passageway and turned at random at the next fork. The church was a twisted maze. Its walls fled by them as they ran.

At the next turning they met three acolytes, who flung up their arms in a vain attempt to stop them. Glustred swung a fist, and the worshipers went down in a pile of scrambling arms and legs. Whitsun leaped over them and raced on.

A small door loomed ahead. Without hesitation, Whitsun burst through it. A startled crowd of worshipers turned as the two men pushed their way through the throng gathered before a shrine. Several priests clad in the white and silver robes of the Order gaped at the intruders but made no move to stop them. Ahead of them, a large archway led down a broad stair to the street. They leaped down the steps, burst onto the street, scattering passersby, and, without hesitation, plunged into an alley and up another flight of stairs, this one darker and narrower. At the top the pair scurried across a bridge, down a slanting street, and in the front of a building and out the back. It left them in a narrow courtyard. Glustred sank to the ground, panting, while Whitsun leaned against the wall.

"What do you think?"

"I think . . . we lost . . ." Whitsun had no breath to complete the sentence.

The doorway of a tavern beckoned. The sign above proclaimed it to be the Dirty Duck. They entered and took a seat near the door. A large man in a filthy apron took their order for food and ale and slouched off to the kitchen.

The room was crowded, and Glustred had to lean close to Whitsun to be heard.

"What do you think?"

"It confirms, more or less, what we guessed." Whitsun's fingers of his gloved left hand drummed on the table. "Somehow touching that ring did something to me. It makes magic go awry near me. Sometimes it's harmful to me, sometimes not. It also gives me a deadly touch with this—" he lifted his hand. "But what we still don't know is who's after it, why, and what the orerry has to do with anything. We know scarface wants the ring. We know he's using the Order of the Silver Flame as a front. We know he knows who we are, and I have to presume he knows something about how I got the ring. We know all this has something to do with the shifter and the woman who asked me to find the orerry in the first place." He shook his head in frustration. "I can see the pieces but not how they fit together. It's a jumbled mess, like a broken window where all the shards of glass have been scattered about. We have them all, but we can't see the pattern to put them back together again. All I know is I'm an important piece, and I'm in the middle of it somehow."

"*We're* in the middle." Glustred grunted. The master of the house appeared with their food and drink and set it on the table with a crash.

They ate and drank in silence. Afterwards, Glustred pulled out a stubby pipe, lit it, and settled back in his seat. It looked somehow out of place in his big face. He blew out a ring of smoke and said, "What now?"

"Morgrave University. It's foolish to keep working in the dark like this. We have to find out something more about these things, the ring and the orerry. What do they do? Where did they come from? Why are they so important? Since no one looking for them will tell us, maybe the things themselves will have something to say on the matter."

"How far is the university from here?"

"We're in Dura, and the university is in Menthis Plateau."

Glustred looked blank, and Whitsun sighed. "A long way. Take my word for it. We'd best get started."

Glustred got to his feet. "Why don't we take a skycoach?"

"Because that's about the most obvious way I can think of to be spotted by the Watch or by our friends from the church."

Whitsun shook his head. "We need to stay out of sight and be careful."

They moved toward the exit. "Just try to be inconspicuous," Whitsun advised his companion as they ducked through the door. "Sorry," as he bumped into someone walking into the tavern.

The Watch commander stared at him.

"Hey!"

Whitsun twisted out of the man's grip and took off running down the street, Glustred pounding at his heels.

"Stop!"

The sound of running feet pursued them. Whitsun bent and rounded a corner, leaped over a low stone wall, and ducked into a doorway. He shoved open the door and raced through several richly appointed rooms, pushing aside startled servant girls. He dodged down a corridor and slammed open a door. From a broad bed, two startled faces looked up at him.

"Sorry for intruding. Won't be a minute." Whitsun, followed closely by the innkeeper, lunged out the window onto a narrow balcony.

"Dolurrh!"

He was looking out at a broad vista. To his left, stone towers rose into the air, framing a square of blue sky. To his right, a profusion of coaches and floating discs bumped and swayed against one another.

Glustred looked behind them, gripped his companion around the waist, and dived over the balcony.

"Hey!"

Whitsun wriggled to no avail as the wind rushed past them. Glustred mumbled something under his breath, and they slowed to a float. It lasted only a moment or two then they started dropping again. Glustred let out a squeal of fear. Whitsun, twisted left, kicked off a building while pulling Glustred's large frame with him, and alit on a passing skycoach.

"Dolurrh!" Glustred caught his breath. "Waste of a perfectly good spell." He looked over the side of the coach at the vast gulf of open air beneath them and shuddered. "Told you we should have taken one of these." He shook himself like a dog and settled into the plush cushions around them.

Whitsun looked above at the balcony from which they'd fallen, some hundred feet above. The small faces of the Watch could be seen peering from it as the skycoach sailed blithely around a corner. The driver acted as if it were the most natural thing in the world to have his passengers drop from the sky. He turned a toadish face toward them.

"Ur! Where to, gents?"

"Morgrave University. And be quick about it!" snarled Whitsun.

☞

The driver took him at his word, and the coach bent and soared around towers, making near misses and quick dodges around intruding towers and pinnacles. Whitsun seemed unperturbed by the ride, but Glustred kept his eyes firmly shut.

"Think we got away then?" Glustred asked. The coach dipped twenty feet and whizzed around an intruding tower in an almost vertical descent. The innkeeper's long hair streamed out behind his head.

"I think they'd have to be mad to follow us in this thing." Whitsun's face was pressed back due to the velocity of the coach, which now rose and hopped across a series of rooftops. A group of scantily clad women lounging on a balcony called insulting and delectable things to them. Whitsun ignored them. Before the vehicle, a wide space opened. Glustred, at last daring to open his eyes as the coach slowed a bit, peered over the side at a precipitous drop of at least five hundred feet. He clutched his companion's arm.

"They're mad!"

From far below, a coach rose after them. It was black, and in its passenger seats, the uniforms of the City Watch glistened in the sunlight.

Whitsun tapped the coach driver on the shoulder. "Holla, friend!"

"Ur?"

"Can you lose those people?"

The driver barely glanced at the pursuing coach. "Ur!"

"Good. There's some extra gilt in it for you."

Their coach hung in the air for a fraction of a second then began to really move. Walls, courts, and towers shot by at a dizzying velocity. The air rushed past them in a screaming wind. Glustred's eyes bulged as they rose, sank, and rose again, and he swallowed several times to clear his ears.

"H-how fast are we going?" He tried to make his voice casual.

"Fast enough." Whitsun was clinging to the seat as he half turned to look in their wake. They shot up a long shaft and burst into the midst of a complex of bridges that crisscrossed the upper city. Their coach looped one of the spans and streaked through a narrow arch. Behind them, the coach with the Watch skidded around a pillar and turned almost sideways negotiating the arch.

Glustred clutched Whitsun's arm. "They're gaining!"

His companion shook off his hand impatiently and shouted something to the driver that was lost in the wind whistling through their ears. The coach dived and climbed and hurtled straight for a wall, broken by a dark opening.

Glustred gave a squeal like an animal in pain. The coach shot through the opening, smashing the wrought-iron balustrade, and hurtled down a long hall. The passengers caught brief glimpses of startled faces in doorways and of a young man and woman hurling themselves out of harm's way as the coach thundered past. At the far end of the hallway, a bright spot of light grew larger. The coach burst through the opening.

Behind them, the Watch's vehicle fought its way free of the building. One of the Watchmen, standing in the prow of the coach, lifted his hand and gestured. Bolts of light shot from his fingers and streaked at Whitsun's coach.

"Dolurrh!" Whitsun sank back against the cushions.

"Aren't you going to do something?" Glustred roared in his ear.

Whitsun made no attempt to answer. The bright magical bolts came closer, following every move of the skycoach as the driver made desperate attempts at evasion. They neared—then burst, shattering into a cloud of spinning magical shards. One struck the driver on the cheek, and he howled in pain. Another cloud slammed into the side of the coach, scarring and burning the wood. Glustred and Whitsun ducked and covered their faces to avoid the pieces.

The blow seemed to affect the coachman like the touch of a whip against a horse's flank. The coach hung for a split second in the air and then leaped forward, breaking its previous speed record. Brick pillars, stone archways, soaring towers, and bottomless pits all seemed to blend into a blurred profusion of sight and sound. Glustred, clinging desperately to his seat, looked behind. The Watch coach was barely keeping up. Even as he looked, it swerved to avoid a bridge. The driver overbalanced just a hair, and the coach spun. A figure was hurled from it, and a dim shriek flew like a bird through the thin air of the city. Whitsun and Glustred could see him making frantic gestures as he cast a spell, but it failed. The falling body smashed against a slate roof a hundred feet below and rolled down to tumble another two hundred feet to the paved cobbles of a plaza.

The lightened load of the Watch's coach affected the driver badly. He swung too wide at the next turn, and his craft struck a wall, sending a shower of bricks and mortar into the air. Close as the two coaches were, the innkeeper could hear the Watch captain screaming at the driver, cursing him in the name of every deity in the pantheon.

Whitsun's coach dropped fifty feet, leaving its passengers' stomachs behind, and shot forward, turned left at a wall, and dived into a long circular tunnel lit with torches. The driver accelerated, and the walls of the tunnel flew by. The Watch commander, straining behind them to keep up, had evidently decided on one more magic spell. He lifted a hand. Whitsun turned to Glustred and mouthed, "Watch out!"

A spark started from the commander's hand, flew forward, and grew as it approached them. Drops of sweat from the driver's forehead flew back and struck Glustred's face.

"Fireball!" he moaned.

The massive fireball glowed, whitened, and turned to ice, filling the entire tunnel behind them.

There was a terrific crash. Dimly through the wall of ice, Glustred could see the shattered remains of the pursuing ship. Splashes of red told the fate of the Watch and the driver.

Their own vehicle slowed to a reasonable pace and emerged from the tunnel. The driver turned and moved back through the city at a sedate clip, finally circling a tall tower and coming to rest on a flat stone landing that on three sides dropped away into thin air.

"Ur!"

"Thanks!"

Whitsun pressed several galifars into the driver's hand and skittered out of the coach, followed closely by Glustred. Both men plunged across the coach landing to a narrow arch that connected it to the steps leading up to the Commons, a broad plaza atop one of the city's most impressive spires.

Glustred sank down on a stone bench and bent over, wretching. "Wait a moment!" he groaned. "I need to rest!"

Whitsun looked disapproving. "You haven't been doing anything," he reminded his companion. "Just sitting."

"No. I was reviewing my life since I expected it to end." Glustred wiped his forehead with a meaty hand. "Thank the Flame for whatever power you've got to disrupt magic. We'd have been dead otherwise."

"Yes. I don't understand it, but it seems to come in . . . handy." Whitsun lifted his gloved left hand and looked at it thoughtfully. "There doesn't seem to be much reason to it, though. I thought for a while it was protecting me, but it doesn't appear to have that effect—at least not all the time. It's almost . . ." He hesitated. "Almost as if it had a will of its own, some purpose we don't . . ." Again his voice trailed off. He stared at his hand as if it belonged to someone else then shrugged. "Well, after all, that's why we're here. To find out the point behind it all. Come."

Glustred rose to his feet wearily. "Do you think there's going to be trouble about that smash up back there?"

"My dear Glustred, an entire party of the Watch from Hope's Peak was just killed. You can't expect there *not* to be trouble about it." Whitsun considered. "On the other hand, the higher ups may want to hush up the whole thing. Especially if I'm right and there was someone behind the Watch's pursuit."

"What do you mean?"

"There wasn't any good reason for those men to chase us like that. They were out of their own district, and they could have turned around at any point and gone back. The fact that they didn't means they had very strict orders to capture or kill us—orders that must have had a lot of power behind them. The only reason I can think of for that is that there's someone or several someones involved with the Watch who want what we've got."

"The ring."

"Yes. And, for all we know, the orerry that our friends in the church have."

"Couldn't it be the church who set the Watch on us?"

"No. When we first got into the church, remember, our fat friend told us we were safe from the Watch in there. So we were, I suppose. Just not safe from him."

Glustred nodded. "So why didn't the church just kill us when they had the chance?"

"They don't know where the ring is. We do. And—" Whitsun again lifted his left hand—"for some reason they're frightened of this. Or intrigued by it. I don't know." He looked around them. "Let's go see if we can find some answers."

Students in their dark robes filled the plaza, strolling to and fro, many carrying books or tablets. Their heads were bent in converse, and they appeared studious and scholarly. Glustred looked at them with interest.

"What happens to people who study here?" he asked.

"Doubtless they go on to become teachers and teach others to become just as they were." Whitsun's tone more than his words betrayed his scorn.

"Were you one once, then?"

"Nonsense!"

Whitsun's response came a bit too quickly for his comrade, who grinned at him in unalloyed humor.

They headed toward one of the more impressive staircases in the university, a flight of at least 150 steps, thirty or forty feet broad, leading up to a pillared and domed hall. Students and masters passed along the steps, conversing of learned matters in quiet voices. One, clad in the dark red robe of a professional scholar, looked up as they passed and hailed Whitsun.

"Dasquith!"

"Sa'maat!" Whitsun returned the greeting with no great show of enthusiasm. "Still plodding among the dead and decaying thoughts of genius, I see."

Sa'maat showed no more enthusiasm than Whitsun. "I'm surprised seeing you here," he said. "We'd heard you left Morgrave. Happier in lower parts of the city. Of course, there are some who say it was a scandal. The death of the rector, was it?"

Whitsun shrugged. "People believe what nonsense they want to. I'm busy with other matters now. We're looking for Lamonn."

"Him!" The man's voice held contempt mixed with admiration. "Yes, you two were thick as thieves in the old days, were you not? Such a man for languages. They say he's one of the only living scholars to read Old Quori. Remarkable." He shook his head. "You'll find little good said of him today. He's been keeping to his rooms since sunup. The next stage in a long downward slope, I fear. A sad decline of a brilliant mind. I shouldn't think you'll get much out of him, in any case."

"What are you talking about?" Whitsun's manner was easy and conversational. "We spoke to him a few days ago and nothing seemed amiss."

"Has no one told you?" The scholar turned to go. "It's best you see for yourself, Dasquith. Perhaps he was better when last you saw him, but from what I hear, today is a bad day." He bowed and hurried away.

Glustred looked curiously at his companion. "You seem well known here."

"I used to work here." Whitsun's voice was slightly apologetic. "It was a long time ago, though." He looked about. "We turn left and go into that building there to find Lamonn's residence."

"What was that about his not going out of his rooms?"

"Ah. Well. You'll see."

Whitsun led the way with no more conversation.

The door yielded no response to their knockings. They entered, and Glustred surveyed the accumulated mess. As in Lamonn's office, books and papers covered most of the surfaces. A few battered chairs and a table occupied one room, along with a sagging bookcase. Several plates of half-eaten food filled the air with a sickly rotting smell, and flies buzzed thickly around them.

"Doesn't anyone around here know how to keep things clean?" Glustred inquired.

"It's a privilege of scholarship." Whitsun poked through some of the piles of parchment and moved half-open tomes. In one corner, a bale of manuscript tied with string showed signs of nibbling by mice. Quills were scattered freely over what could be seen of the table, and a half-empty inkwell stood open, the ink within it congealing. Everbright lanterns shed their glow across books and papers.

"If he never goes out of the room, where is he?" Glustred asked.

Whitsun made no reply but continued to poke through the contents of the room, looking at the manuscripts and books in boxes and baskets. The detritus of Lamonn's scholarly career—such as it had been—had been allowed to accumulate undisturbed in his sanctum.

The atmosphere was one of decay and age, but floating above it was another miasma. Glustred sniffed and wrinkled his nose. "Something else here," he grunted. "Smells like—"

A sound from the far wall made both of them turn. "What's that?"

The noise had come from behind a pile of books. Glustred shoved them aside, and they saw that a stone archway led to another room. It was blocked by a wooden door that yielded to Glustred's none-to-gentle shove.

They found themselves in a small sleeping chamber. A narrow bed was set into the wall on one side, while a noisome chamber pot protruded from beneath the filthy coverlet. An empty ewer and basin stood on a rickety table. Here too, books were scattered about and piled on the floor.

Lamonn was lying on the bed, propped up on one elbow. His eyes were closed in concentration. Glustred started to move toward him but stopped at Whitsun's hand on his sleeve.

The scholar's left arm was bare, and he held in his right hand a long, slender needle-like branch. One end was sharply pointed. He jabbed it into his arm a full inch, winced, and blew hard into the other end. There was a tiny *whoosh!* and the skin around the puncture darkened for a moment then faded. The branch itself dissolved into a thin cloud of brown dust, and Lamonn sank back on his bed, eyes rolled up beneath his eyelids. His chest rose and fell.

"Dolurrh!" Glustred wheeled on Whitsun. "And you told him to stay off the stuff! Why go to him if he's such a lilyhead? We might have known he couldn't stay clean!"

didn't know." Whitsun stared in fascination at the figure on the bed. "At least I hoped. This is a new intensity for him, at least since last I saw him. I did wonder though. He's a man of many vices."

Glustred grunted. "Yes? What are some of his other ones?"

"A number of things, actually. He had a liking for some of the establishments in Firelight that cater to . . . special tastes. Sometimes he sought out lower parts of the city. I suppose there's nothing for it but to wake him up." Whitsun walked over to the bed and shook its inhabitant roughly by the shoulder.

"Lamonn! Wake up! It's Dasquith!"

The scholar made no response. Whitsun shook him harder. "Come! Time to get up!"

Still nothing. Whitsun examined Lamonn's arm where he had injected the lilyweed, looked at his eyes, and felt for a pulse. He turned to his companion.

"It's no good. He took a heavy dose on top of something

199

else—probably ashermead. If we just wait for him to come out of it, we'll be here until next week sometime."

"Do we really need his help that much?"

"Yes." Whitsun shook his head irritably. "Apart from the fact that he's the only one who probably has much of an idea of the meaning of the inscriptions on these things, I need him to tell me what he did with the ring. I don't want it hanging around where someone else can find it. And if anyone finds out that he knows where it is, they're going to bring him around and pry the information out of him with a blunt boning knife."

"So what do we do?"

"Bring him out of it the hard way." Whitsun sighed and looked around. "Get used to this place, Glustred. We're going to be here the next day or so." He picked up the chamber pot. "Here. Get rid of this thing, or clean it out or something. And tell someone we'll need food and water. Lots of water."

Glustred glared at him, speechless.

"Also, get a glass tube. About eight or twelve inches long. Preferably clean. Go on! What are you waiting for?" Whitsun turned his back on Glustred and began clearing some of the books from the floor.

☞

The learned scholars of Morgrave University seemed disinclined to have anything to do with Lamonn, but Glustred's glowering presence managed to obtain some food and several large buckets of water. Servants brought the supplies to Lamonn's door and left it there, not deigning to enter the rooms. Whitsun poured some of the water into a wooden cup and forced it between the scholar's lips. He bathed the man's head with more of it and spent the rest of the time massaging Lamonn's arm around the place where he'd punctured it. The limb was dotted all over with similar puncture marks that extended all the way up to the shoulder. The skin was dry and papery, and the bones seemed fragile beneath the blue-veined skin.

Lamonn himself made no move, and there was no change in him. His chest rose and fell with each breath, and his expression was one of repose.

Glustred moved into the outer room, which was less close and less depressing than the darkness of the bedchamber. He tried to read a few of the books that were scattered about on the floor or stacked in double and triple layers on the groaning shelves, but they were written in strange and unfamiliar languages. In some the writing seemed to twist and writhe on the page, and Glustred hastily put those books from him before they could enspell him.

He found one book that was mostly pictures, carefully drawn in many colored inks. He sat, turning the pages, examining the pictures, which were marvelous in their detail. In one two armies clashed, and the artist had shone the bright shining spears of the cavalry, the flashing swords of the warriors, and the blood running freely as the two sides struggled for mastery. In another, a tall dark man stirred a smoking cauldron, his lips moving as he chanted a spell, while from behind him the stone walls of the dungeon seemed to loose a thousand demons at his command.

One painting in particular fascinated the big man. It showed a figure in a room crowded with books and papers, hunched over a volume. His face was turned away from the reader, but the artist had depicted his muscular shoulders as well as the streaks of gray running through his thinning dark hair. The viewpoint was over his shoulder, so it was possible to glimpse the book he was reading.

There was something disturbingly familiar in the figure, which Glustred could not put his finger on. He studied it intently—and gasped.

The figure was wearing the same clothes as him, the same tattered jerkin, torn and smelling of smoke and bad wine, the same trousers stained with a hundred spills at the bar. The book the figure was holding . . . Glustred held the page closer to his eyes, straining to see. Surely, surely it was the same volume he himself held. There on the page was the drawing of the man, who in turn was holding an even smaller book. Glustred felt dizzy, as if he were falling forward into the page, into an infinite series of books and readers. He closed his eyes, jerked himself back, and slammed the book shut. At once the silence of the room rushed around him. He tossed the book onto a pile and ceased his examination of the papers.

The hours passed uneasily. At last Whitsun called to Glustred.

"Take over here. Give him more water, as much as you can. And wash him. Keep up the pressure on that arm. If we're lucky, the lilyweed didn't penetrate too deeply. Eventually we can force most of it out."

"And if we're not so lucky?"

"Then he's gone for a while. Since I don't know what else he took with it, it's possible he'll be gone permanently." Whitsun looked about the squalid surroundings. "I wonder how he gets the weed. He must have someone in the library who supplies him. From what he said the last time we were here, he's been doing this for years." He stretched. "I need some rest. Wake me in a couple of hours."

He went into the outer room and curled up, catlike, on the floor between two stacks of leather-bound volumes. In a few minutes, a gentle snore escaped him. Glustred sat for a short time staring at the body of the scholar, then sighed and reached into the bucket for the rag.

The chambers felt as if they were somehow removed from the

rest of the university and indeed from Sharn itself. After the hair-raising chase they had been through to get there, this interval was, in some respects, a welcome change for the big innkeeper. He fed more water between Lamonn's lips and noticed a difference; now the scholar seemed to suck the liquid greedily. Glustred imagined as well that there was a darker color around the area of the arm he and Whitsun had been patiently massaging for many hours. He rubbed the flesh, alternating with holding a cup to Lamonn's mouth. Slowly the seconds ticked by until it seemed as if he had been doing nothing else but rubbing and holding for a long eternity.

After what seemed days, Whitsun stood up and stretched. Going to a side table, he tore off a piece of bread and washed it down with some water.

"How's it coming?" he asked over his shoulder.

"Slowly. But there's an improvement."

Whitsun joined Glustred at Lamonn's bedside and looked closely at the arm. He nodded, satisfied. "Another hour or two and we'll be ready to pull out the drug. Then he just needs to sleep a bit and he'll be back to normal."

"Will he still be addicted?"

"Of course!" Whitsun looked a bit surprised at the question. "I'm not trying to break him of being an addict. I'm trying to stop him from killing himself long enough to answer a couple of questions. After that, I don't care what he does."

For the next two hours they alternated rubbing Lamonn's arm and forcing water into him. He drank readily now, and sweat poured off his face. The spot on his arm grew dark, and some blood oozed through the puncture. Finally Whitsun looked at Glustred.

"We're ready now."

He picked up the glass tube Glustred had obtained, held it against the puncture, and sucked at the other end. Blood spurted into the tube. Whitsun removed his mouth but kept a thumb over the end of the tube. More blood spurted into it until it was full. Whitsun pulled it free of Lamonn's arm, and the blood spilled out in a puddle. Whitsun cursed.

"Give me that empty bucket."

He repeated the actions, but this time he was able to get most of the extracted blood into the bucket instead of on the floor. Glustred watched as his comrade repeated the procedure over and over again. The bucket was a third of the way filled with Lamonn's blood, and the man's face was pale and drawn. Dark circles formed under his eyes.

"You're going to kill him if you go on like that," Glustred observed.

Whitsun shook his head. "We need to get as much of the drug out as possible. There's no other way to do it than to take a lot of blood. Fortunately, we got to him in time so it didn't have a chance to disperse widely in the bloodstream, but he'll be weak as a kitten for a few days. There! That should be enough."

The last of the blood splashed into the bucket. Lamonn's eyes fluttered and his pupils rolled back down to stare wildly about his room.

"Whuh . . . Whuh . . . ?"

"Shut up!" Whitsun told him. "Save your strength. You'll need it. Right now just be quiet."

Lamonn's expression was frightened as he looked at Whitsun and the looming figure of Glustred, but he managed to nod his head and close his eyes. Whitsun wiped the sweat off the scholar's forehead, poured out a cup of water from the clean bucket, and nodded to Glustred.

"You might as well get some rest too. He's not going to be fit to talk about anything for at least three hours."

Glustred went into the outer room and sat down, his back

against a stack of bound manuscripts. He folded his hands in front of him and let his imagination run free in a time when he'd never heard of Ulther Whitsun.

He awoke four hours later with Whitsun's boot prodding him in the ribs.

"Come! Come!" The wait had obviously not improved Whitsun's temper. "Time to wake our friend."

Lamonn was snoring peacefully in his bed. Whitsun reached forward and slapped him hard across the face. The scholar's head jerked, and he came up with a yelp.

"Dasquith!"

"Yes. And not pleased. Not pleased at all."

"But . . . but . . ." The scholar's fingers fumbled with the ragged coverlet. His eyes refused to meet Whitsun's and flickered from side to side, taking in the stacks of books and parchments. "I . . . I was going to sleep. I've been working hard."

Glustred snorted. "You were taking a blow of lilyweed!"

"No! Never! I've not touched weed in months!" A trickle of saliva edged its way down Lamonn's mouth. Whitsun looked at him in disgust then nodded to Glustred.

The big man picked up the scholar by the collar and hauled him from the bed. Lamonn's feet dangled an inch from the ground. He beat feebly on the innkeeper's arms.

"Let me down! I'll scream!"

With his other hand, Glustred reached down just where the man's legs met his torso. He grasped and closed his fingers. Lamonn's moanings died away in an agonized squeal.

"Shut up!" Glustred told him.

"Erp!"

Glustred placed him sitting on the rickety chair in the outer room. Whitsun arranged himself comfortably on a corner of the desk while Glustred stood next to the unfortunate scholar.

"Now, then," Whitsun said. "I don't give a damn about lily-weed or much of anything else in your life, Lamonn. What I do care about is the inscriptions I left with you. I want you to tell me what they say and what they mean. Then I want you to tell me what you did with the ring and how I can get it back. After that, you can go to your gods in any way that best pleases you."

Lamonn's face cleared, and his manner became somewhat less nervous, though his hands and legs still trembled as if he were seized with palsy.

"Good!" he observed. "I'd rather not have it here anyhow."

"Why not?" Whitsun asked.

The scholar ran a lanky hand through his thinning hair. "Well," he replied, "I've been able to translate the inscriptions you gave me. Partially, anyhow. They—"

"Both of them," Whitsun interrupted.

"Both of them. The second one—the one for which I don't have the artifact—was a bit harder than the first. I get the impression that it's older, but I could be wrong about that."

"What do they say?"

Lamonn's manner took on that of a lecturer addressing a group of senior academics.

"For the first inscription, I was able to compare the transcription provided to me against the actual inscription and to deduce certain conclusions from the placement of the markings on the artifact. Such placement in languages has grammatical implications that are not always obvious from mere written text. This is similar to the forms found in language of—"

Whitsun rapped the table sharply, and Lamonn caught himself and began again. "As you might have guessed," he said, "the script is from ancient Xen'drik."

"You mean it's Giant? Or Quori?"

"No." Lamonn shook his head and seemed irritated by the interruption. "There were other people living in Xen'drik in ancient times when the giants ruled and when the quori came from outside. This script was used by a group of elves who were dominated by the giants but were not entirely their slaves—not entirely. They managed to exist in a kind of enclave. Some scholars have theorized that it existed in what today is called the Valley of the Shadows in the south of the continent. Others have placed it even farther to the south among the Scimitar Spires. The point isn't very important. What *is* important is that these elves were very powerful magic users.

"I thought, when you first showed me this writing, that it bore some resemblance to ancient Elven of the kind spoken on Xen'drik. Detailed research and some comparative examination proved this to be the case. There's no question in my mind that this inscription is written in the language of the Xen'drik elves of old.

"Because they were ruled by the giants, the giants had access to much of the elves' magic and used it extensively. But there was some that the elves kept back for themselves. That kind of magic is almost unknown in Khorvaire today. Some have speculated that it might be at the root of the Day of Mourning, but that's mostly loose talk. Personally, I doubt it. Every theoretician has an idea of what caused the Day of Mourning, and I don't see why this magic should be a better explanation than any other."

Whitsun's face was rigid, his brow deeply furrowed. "You got all this just from the inscriptions?" he asked.

"No. Once I understood what language the inscriptions were written in, I examined a number of texts concerning the ancient elves, who lived some sixty or seventy thousand years ago." Lamonn looked around his cluttered room proudly. "I have some resources here that aren't available to the rest of the university—things I've accumulated over a lifetime of study."

Whitsun's mouth quirked sarcastically. "Go on, then."

Lamonn lowered his voice and bent forward. Whitsun did not move, but Glustred leaned toward the speaker to hear better.

"What is fascinating—*fascinating*—about these objects is that they're actually from this ancient elven culture. Up to this point, virtually everything we know about this civilization is third hand. The sources are giantish, mostly. Even our understanding of their language is a matter of deduction, based on giantish writings and a few fragmentary quotations that made their way into giantish chronicles, usually those written thousands of years later. But now we have artifacts with first-hand writing from the elves themselves. Some elf, tens upon tens of thousands of years ago, actually sat inscribing these words on the ring and the other device you've told me about. Think of that! The linguistic implications of this find are staggering."

"Never mind the linguistic implications," Whitsun said. During Lamonn's speech, his feet drummed with impatience against the floor. Now he rose and walked to and fro. "We just want to know why the blasted things are interfering with magic. And what do they *do?* That's the question."

Lamonn nodded. He seemed, somehow, more reluctant to go on and paused for a few minutes. When he began to speak again, his voice sounded cracked and old.

"The ring and the—what is the other thing called? The Orerry of Tal Esk was what you said, wasn't it? The point is, these artifacts are the source of a great magic. They were made by these ancient beings. For countless centuries, they lay beneath the land of Xen'drik. But now they have been brought into the light of day. Therein lies a great danger."

"Danger how?"

"Each one, the ring and the other artifact, was powerful in itself. Together they are almost unstoppable. Though you call the second one an orerry, in fact it would be more accurate to say that only when they act together do they form a true orerry."

Whitsun hooted contemptuously. "If it took you all this time to come to that conclusion," he said, coming off the table corner with a jerk, "I could have saved us all a lot of time and trouble. I've tried these two things together. I've rubbed them against each other, tapped them, banged them. Nothing. So if that's all you've got to tell me—"

Lamonn's voice took on a stern overtone, quite unlike anything he had assumed before, and he drowned out Whitsun's amusement.

"Be silent, Dasquith! You don't know what you are speaking of! The elves knew that the objects they had made were capable of great good or great evil. But to stop them from falling into the wrong hands, they built certain safeguards into them. When they completed them, they kept them widely separate from each other. Each one, when it is taken by a new master, imprints itself upon him. Or her."

Glustred asked, "What do you mean, 'imprints'?"

His voice, coming after so long, startled Lamonn, who jerked around. After a moment he answered.

"The ring and the—well, we'll keep calling it an orerry for now—each can only be used by one person at a time. They cannot be used by the same person; the two must come together and know how to manipulate the magic of the object each holds."

Whitsun's voice was thoughtful. "When Maresun first give me the ring," he said, "I felt a spark, like a sting. And it felt good afterwards. I want to keep touching it."

Lamonn nodded eagerly. "Yes. The ring has imprinted itself upon you. Only you can be affected by its magic now. Only you can control the magic of the ring. But you cannot do so alone."

"Why me? Why not Maresun? Or the person from whom he stole it?"

The scholar shrugged. "Who knows? The inscription does not make that clear. There is more to the magic that is hidden from me, but perhaps it has to do with your innate magical abilities."

Whitsun gave a slight snort.

"In any case, Dasquith, you have now been imprinted with this thing."

"Very well. How long does it last?"

There was a brief silence then the scholar said, "Until you are dead."

A longer silence stretched out for a time. Then Whitsun said, "Anything else?"

"Have you noticed that magic does not seem to work on you?"

"I've seen that it doesn't seem to work normally, at any rate. Every time someone tries a spell on me, something goes wrong with it. And every time I try to use a spell it only works partially. Sometimes not at all."

"That's what I should imagine." Lamonn examined Whitsun carefully. "You're imbued with some of the magic from the ring. It hasn't reached its full fruition yet, and it won't do that unless you collaborate with the person on whom the orerry has imprinted. But it will tend to interfere with any magic around you."

"What happens if the ring itself is destroyed?"

"The gods only know. That would be a highly irresponsible action."

Whitsun nodded. "I'll bear that in mind," he said. "Now, why don't you return my property and we'll leave you in peace to ruin what's left of your mind?"

Lamonn fumbled among the papers on the desk. At last, from a hidden drawer he produced Whitsun's pieces of parchment. He scanned them closely, lips moving in silence.

"There is something here about 'The Chosen One.' But I don't know what that means."

"Is there anything about the Order of the Silver Flame?"

"The Order of the . . ." Lamonn stared at him in amazement. "Haven't you been listening to anything I've said? This ring and its companion precede the Order by thousands of years."

"Why would the Order be interested in them?"

Lamonn drummed his fingers on the table. "I don't know. Perhaps some within the Church are desirous of the power these objects represent. Many people will be looking for these objects, Dasquith, once it becomes known they are in Sharn."

Whitsun reached a hand into the desk drawer and pulled out a bundle. He unwrapped the ring. Glustred, now that he knew its history, looked at it with great interest.

"At least I've got this now," Whitsun observed. "If I get the orerry and keep it away from anyone else, I control the magic, right?"

"Not exactly," the scholar cautioned. "You merely prevent the full magic potential of the two objects from being realized, with whatever consequences that would bring."

Whitsun nodded then glanced at Glustred. "Let's go."

"Where?"

"Well," his companion said, "since I seem to be able to disrupt magic thrown at me, we might as well head back to the Church of the Silver Flame and get our hands on the orerry."

Glustred followed him from the room, muttering, "All very well. But what about magic thrown at *me?*"

None of the library's scholars paid much attention to Glustred and Whitsun, though their rumpled clothing and tired faces might have attracted attention in less well-attired parts of Sharn. They made their way along corridors bustling with gnomes carrying books almost as big as themselves. Whitsun's strides were strong and decisive, and anyone who crossed his path shrank swiftly out of his way. Glustred was content to follow in his companion's footsteps.

They reached the outer doors of the library, vast portals cast in bronze and figured with murals depicting the many triumphs of Brelish armies against their enemies. Glustred stopped a minute to look at it.

"Seems queer to have a library putting up monuments to armies," he observed.

"Not at all." Whitsun stood breathing in the fresh air that blew around them at the top of the broad steps leading down from the library's entrance. "Armies have to fight for something. Words more often than not are what they fight over."

"How's that?"

"Well, treaties are just collections of words, really. And for all the time and energy we spend hammering out the details of this treaty between Breland and Karrnath or that treaty between Breland and the Lhazaar Principalities, all it takes to invalidate those treaties is one strong army in the hands of one determined general."

"So what're you saying?"

"I'm saying, Glustred, that when it really comes down to it, soldiers spend their lives fighting in the muck and mire over words that diplomats in some high tower have concocted. Those same words that seem important enough to spend hours refining and revising can disappear in a moment under the hooves of a charging horse or the wheels of a chariot. Words are the first thing trampled by war. Principles are the second, and courage is the third. After the war is over, the diplomats get together in their halls and go back to writing words on pieces of parchment as if that's somehow going to prevent the next war. Even when everyone knows it isn't. In a way, the library here can be seen as a magnificent monument to the futility of endeavor." Whitsun looked about. "Let's go."

They started down the steps—in fact they were more than halfway down—when from below came a call.

"Whitsun! Ulther Whitsun!"

A figure came flying up the steps, long red hair streaming in the wind. Scholars and students moving sedately up and down the stairs turned to admire the slender body clad in a silky green dress.

"Delru!" Whitsun's voice was surprised and suspicious. "What are you doing here?"

She brushed back an errant strand of hair. "Waiting for you!"

"For me? Since when did you know I was in there?"

She pushed the matter aside with a pretty gesture. "I have many ways of knowing things, many ears throughout this great city. I heard you had disappeared into the great library and I hurried here, but the foolish scholars who guard the door would not let me enter and search for you. I've been out here for two days hoping you would appear."

"Two days?" Whitsun's voice was studied in its disbelief. "Well, here I am. What do you want?"

"I heard of Freylaut's attack upon you." She placed a slender hand on his arm. "Were you hurt? Did he injure you? I'm shocked he should be capable of such a thing!"

Whitsun, without answering, began walking down the steps. Glustred followed, his eyes examining the lines of Delru's hips as they moved beneath the fabric of her dress.

"He's dead, you know," Whitsun flung over his shoulder at the woman.

"Yes. Yes, indeed. An assassin's arrow." Delru's face lengthened in sorrow for a moment. "Nonetheless, there was no reason for him to attack you at our moment of triumph when you had recovered our possession. I cannot imagine what came over him."

Whitsun's lips creased in a smile. "Can't you? I can. I've been in business too long to think that clients always want to pay their bills when a commission's finished."

Delru smiled back. "Of course. That must have been it. Oh, foolish Freylaut! I would gladly have paid double what we agreed to recover my property." She looked at him sideways from her almond-shaped eyes. "You *have* recovered it, have you not?"

Whitsun nodded. "I've recovered it."

She clapped her hands. "I knew it. Where is it?"

Whitsun stopped and turned toward her. "My dear, I hope you don't think my mother raised me to be feeble minded." He raised a hand to still her protest. "I retrieved your item. Your colleague tried to kill me for it, someone sent arrows after my hide, and someone or several someones burned down Glustred's tavern. All to get this interesting object. So before we go any further, you're going to tell me what it is and why it's important to you."

Her mouth drew into a hurt bow. "And if I don't?"

"Then the knowledge of where it is stays here." Whitsun tapped his forehead.

Delru considered for a moment then smiled again. "Very well. Come with me."

She led the way across a courtyard that extended between the central bulk of Dalannan Tower, housing the bulk of the university, and one of the five smaller spires that ringed it and housed the university's thousands of students. Within the courtyard itself, trees offered pleasant shady nooks, most of them filled with drowsy students perusing books or rapt in conversation. The party passed through an arch to the left of the tower, mounted with a wrought-iron gate, and emerged into one of the streets running just outside the university. Behind them was a tall stone wall that marked its boundaries, and above it reared the great form of Dalannan Tower, crowned far above their heads with a statue dedicated to Aureon, god of knowledge.

Delru led the way along the street until they came to a small tavern that opened into the wall itself. A carved legend over the door read The Bookwyrm. It was tiny, but Delru walked as one who knows her way to a table in the back with two chairs. She looked at Whitsun.

"Is there any reason why your large friend need accompany us?"

Glustred started to growl in the back of his throat, but Whitsun nodded. "Very well. Glustred?"

The innkeeper moved to a table closer to the door and ordered an ale from the tall, thin, silent proprietor. He sat sipping his ale, pausing every now and then to glare at the man and woman in the back of the tavern.

Whitsun and Delru sat, heads bent together. The small space did not permit much air between them. They ordered drinks, and Delru said, "Have you no wife, Whitsun?"

"No."

"No lover either? No one to share your bed?"

"No." He looked at her calmly. "What's the artifact? You called it the Orerry of Tal Esk. Is that its true name?"

"Ah!" Her breath caught in her throat. "You have seen it, then?"

"Of course. Is it really called the Orerry of Tal Esk?" His tone was patient, without emotion.

She seemed uncomfortable, moving slightly in her seat. "Yes. I
. . . believe so. Possibly. What does it matter what it is called?"

"Maybe it doesn't. What *is* it?"

She took a dainty sip of wine from the cup the tavern keeper
had placed before her. "A magical device of great power."

"So I gathered. Where's it from?"

"Karrnath. Our wizards manufactured it in the last days of
the War." She half turned and faced him. "I am going to be truthful with you now, Ulther. More truthful than I was when first we
met. You must forgive me for those times."

Whitsun said nothing.

"I had urgent need to recover my property, but I did not fully
trust you. That was wrong. I yielded to the advice of Freylaut
and kept some matters from you. Since he is dead, it no longer
matters."

Whitsun took a sip of his ale, grimaced, and pushed the mug
away from him.

"The inner sphere, the golden sphere, is called the Sphere of
Amanesh. In the waning days of the War, when all seemed lost
and our rulers despaired of victory, the great mages of Karrnath
met in council to determine how they might throw something
into the scales to tip the balance. For long days and weeks they
debated, and many ideas were considered and dismissed. At last
one declared he had thought of a device that would sway the tides
of victory in our favor."

"So? What does it do?"

"The Sphere of Amanesh confers upon its bearer the gift of
sight."

Whitsun laughed. "You're joking. Any hedge wizard in Khorvaire can call up a spell that lets him see things far away."

"No! You must let me finish!" Her face was urgent. Her
green eyes shone and seemed somehow larger, and her lips were

moist. "The sphere is different. It gives not merely sight, but one who wields it can reach from where he sits and pluck from another place or even another time anything he desires. Do you understand, Ulther? Were I to use the sphere, I could reach back thousands of years and thousands of leagues to the age when the giants and quori struggled for dominion over Xen'drik. I could draw into our own time any weapon I desired from that struggle and use it against my foes. All time and all space would be at my command. Now do you understand my urgency and that of Freylaut—however misguided—in seeking out this object once it had been stolen from us?"

Whitsun was silent for a time. Then he spoke. "When you first gave me this job, you said there was some dispute about your right to this thing."

She blushed. "I long craved this object. I recognized that I had not the skill to wield its full powers, but I feared others among our leaders, some with few scruples, would take it and use it to dominate Eberron."

"So you took it for the common good?"

"You might say that." She placed a hand on his. Her flesh was soft and warm. "Ulther, I must—*must*—have this back. So much depends upon it. Do you not see that?" Her eyes were a deep green, the green of the sea as its tides wash against the rocks of a stormy shore.

Whitsun was silent. She stroked his hand.

"What must I give you, Ulther, for you to give me this thing? Must I give you myself?"

Glustred watched them from his table. His empty ale mug clinked on the rough wooden surface.

Whitsun drew back his hand. His voice was cold. "Once I establish a few things, I'm willing to return your property to you, assuming it's rightfully yours. In any case, it will take a few days."

"No!" She shook her head sharply. "We do not have that much time. It must be now. You know where it is! Why will you not give it to me? That was our agreement."

"You voided that agreement when you lied to me."

"I?" She gestured to herself. "When have I lied to you?"

"As far as I can tell, practically from the moment you walked into my room. You're lying now."

She blushed. "But Ulther, as I have told you, I did not lie. I merely kept information from you. I admit that was wrong, but you must see I was swayed by Freylaut and was afraid. And now I swear to you by everything I hold dear and holy I am telling the truth. Can you not find in your heart to forgive me?"

Whitsun shook his head. "I don't care. Lying by omission's as bad as lying by commission. As for the whole bard's tale you just told me, I don't believe a word of it." He rose from the table and tossed a coin onto it in payment for the drinks. "I told you. A few days. You'll have to wait. Though since you're obviously continuing to lie, we'll have to see. In any case, the price is going to go up, so you might spend the time laying your hands on more galifars." He motioned to Glustred. "Let's go."

They had moved a few steps toward the entrance when from behind, Delru said, "Wait!"

Whitsun turned. She was holding a small crossbow. A dart rested on it, pointing directly at him.

"Where—?" Glustred started. Whitsun made a savage gesture with one hand.

"I am sorry, Ulther. But I must have it. I told you. I must." Her voice was apologetic.

"Very well, Delru." Whitsun's hands were facing palms out, slightly away from his sides. "Let's not be hasty. That bolt doesn't look big enough to do much damage."

"True," she returned. "But it is imbued with a poison to which none in Breland knows the antidote. We Karrns have much experience with such things. The poison causes much suffering and pain, and it is invariably fatal. Death comes slowly and relentlessly. You will die, Ulther. I will regret your death, but you will die."

Glustred started to move to one side.

"Halt!" snapped the red-haired woman. "Unless you want to be killed."

Whitsun smiled. "The truth is, Delru, I don't have it."

Her finger tightened on the trigger.

"I don't. Really."

"Turn out your pockets!"

Carefully, Whitsun reached into his jacket and withdrew the small cloth bundle that contained Maresun's ring.

"What is that?"

"This?"

"Unwrap it."

Whitsun's fingers moved around the bundle. The cloth fell to the floor. Delru stared at the ring, and her lips parted slightly. Her breath came between her teeth in a harsh whistle.

The door of the tavern darkened suddenly, and a tall, spare figure entered behind Glustred and Whitsun. His face was split with a scar. Delru's eyes widened and the crossbow wavered.

Whitsun dived to one side, still clutching the ring. As he came up, he crashed into Glustred, who had at the same time moved to get out of range of the crossbow. The force of the impact sent the ring flying from Whitsun's hand, and the assassin neatly plucked it from the air to the accompaniment of the twang of Delru's crossbow.

A small, feathered shaft sprouted from beneath the assassin's armpit. He looked down at it then across at the woman, whose mouth was open in astonishment.

he scar-faced man stared thoughtfully at the crossbow bolt that protruded from his armpit. He looked across at Whitsun and Glustred and smiled tentatively. His hand caressed his wound, almost as if he found it in some way precious. He plucked the bolt out and tossed it on the floor. Then he turned to go, the ring still in his hand.

Whitsun shot up from the ground and ducked instinctively as he heard the sound of another bolt snapped into place in the crossbow. Delru's face was pale, but her hands were steady as she aimed.

"Halt!"

The assassin ignored her and whipped through the door. The bolt from her weapon struck the door jamb, pinning the flying corner of his robe. He plucked it free and was gone.

Delru reached back to pull out another bolt, but a blow from Whitsun's palm knocked her sprawling.

"Stop it, idiot!" He dived through the door, hands raised,

and fell upon thin air. Glustred, who joined him a moment later, gestured at a dark doorway that opened across the street into an unknown byway. Without a word, Whitsun raced toward it.

A cart bungling along the street blocked his way momentarily. Glustred slammed into his back as he halted, and the two went down on the cobblestones in a tangle of twisted limbs.

"Balls!"

Passing students stared at them, and a few pointed, shouting, to the door of the Bookwyrm. Neither pursuer took the slightest notice of them.

Glustred was first on his feet. He raced ahead of Whitsun, who for once was content to follow the innkeeper as he dived into the darkness of the tunnel.

It was close and airless and evidently led them through some place close to a sewer spout. Glustred choked and coughed as they staggered along, cursing and thrashing. They leaped into the open air, fighting for breath, and found themselves in an alley.

"Come!" Whitsun raced along, not bothering to see if his companion was following. Ahead a dim flash of white showed where the assassin's cloak vanished around a corner.

Here the way was no less congested. People rushed hither and yon bearing large bales and crates of goods. Some staggered and fell as Whitsun and Glustred passed through them, cursing and shouting after the fleeing men. Glustred occasionally looked back; Whitsun never did.

Two figures flew at them out of the gloom in a flying tackle that brought them to earth.

"Nah, then!" snarled one of the figures. "Wha's all this?"

The shapes revealed themselves as two men clad in ragged clothes of brown and green. Their hair was long, black, and greasy, and they were so alike they might have been—and probably were—brothers. Both shared long, ratlike features.

Both carried knives. The blades were wavy, and the steel gleamed in the dim lantern light. Whitsun twisted out of his captor's grip and backed against a wall as the man ranged himself in front of him.

"You don't want to do this!"

The countenance before him split in a toothless grin. "Ah think ah do!"

"No, you don't."

"Ah think you needs a lesson. Meesel, ah think ah need to teach thish'ere fellah a lesson. Ah think ah'll . . ."

The speech ended in a yell of agony as Whitsun's boot kicked out. From the tip, the light reflected on a hidden stiletto that pierced his enemy's knee and ripped upward, tearing the muscle and leaving the thief screaming helplessly on the ground.

"Here, now! What—?"

The man attacking Glustred half turned and sprawled flat on his face as the innkeeper's clenched fist came down on top of his head. Whitsun didn't stop to look at him or his companion, who was writhing on the stones. A swift kick to the temple silenced his opponent, and he and Glustred ran on.

The conflict had slowed them, but there was only one path their quarry could have taken. A narrow road ran down between two houses whose stout locked doors proclaimed them impregnable to assault.

At the head of the street, Glustred halted, chest heaving.

"No good. He's gone!"

Whitsun shook his head. "He's been poisoned. He's got to slow down!" He kept running.

Glustred shook his head and followed him. "Balls!"

At the end of the street stood two tall pillars, fashioned of brick and topped with lead gryphons. Their expression was peevish, as if they'd been guarding this road so long they'd grown tired and wanted a change. The pursuers halted and looked up and down the cross street.

"Which way?"

Whitsun bent close to the cobbles, staring at them in concentration.

"This way!"

He set off running again. Glustred cursed and took up the chase. For better, though, this time their path seemed to lead downhill, along a narrow street that twisted and turned. It sprouted markets on either side and an increasingly brisk crowd that shouted and swayed as vendors purveyed their wares.

"Shugga melons! Fresh!"

"Berries! Get your fresh challow berries! Straight from Zilargo!"

Whitsun, slowing to a fast walk, dodged among the various stalls and carts. His eyes searched eagerly.

"What do you see down there?" he asked Glustred.

The innkeeper looked down a long flight of stairs that ended in a steep bridge. "A trap," he answered.

"That's what I thought. Me too."

Whitsun raced down the stairs, Glustred panting after him. Ahead of them, the bridge was a narrow arch, spanning a vast pit of nothingness. On either side, walls fell steeply away, leaving only a few ragged protrusions. Glustred bumped against the rail, and a crumbling piece of mortar fell into the abyss with a whistle.

Halfway across the span, a figure bent and bowed with age or infirmity leaned against the slender rail. Whitsun ran toward him, Glustred pounding along behind.

"Hey! Excuse me! Have you seen—?" He stopped as Whitsun

tackled the old man, pulling him to the ground. "Balls! Don't you have any——?"

Whitsun and the old man rolled together back and forth.

Glustred took a tentative step toward them. "What're you doing?"

"Grab his hand! His hand!"

The old man stretched his hand upward, holding a bundle of rags. Whitsun stretched toward it with his right hand while, with his teeth, he tried to tear the glove from his left hand. Glustred gaped.

"It can't be!"

"Grab it!"

With a supreme effort the old man stood and jerked Whitsun to his feet. He pushed him backward, at the same time diving down the far end of the arch. Whitsun went head over toes across the narrow railing of the bridge.

Glustred jumped and grabbed. His hand clasped Whitsun's right hand. He could feel it beginning to slip.

"Your other hand! Give me your other hand!"

Whitsun swung with his gloved left hand. The leather, already loosened during his struggle with his assailant, flew from it. The glove sailed serenely into the emptiness. Glustred dodged back.

"Not that hand!"

Whitsun's left hand waved wildly. Glustred's hands were around his companion's hand and right wrist.

"Don't touch me! Don't touch me!" Glustred shouted.

"All right!"

Glustred's knees were locked against the metal struts of the rail. They stung as if they were on fire. Whitsun reached up with his left hand and locked his fingers around the edge of the bridge. His companion leaned back and hauled him onto the span.

Whitsun lay on the stones for a moment, chest heaving. Then he jerked to his feet.

"Where'd he go?"

"Who?"

"The scarred man."

"I don't know. Last I saw, you were trying to grab that old man on the bridge."

Whitsun knelt and banged his hands softly against the stones. "You incredible imbecile," he groaned. "That's the man we were chasing."

"What?"

"Yes!"

"But he was . . . he was . . ."

"I know. But he was the one. He had the bundle. I'm sure of it."

Glustred's slower mind had worked through the problem. He was on his feet. "What are you waiting for, then?" He set off down the street, Whitsun in his wake.

＊

The trail of the scarred assassin—now, unaccountably turned old man—led inexorably downward. Glustred stopped trying to keep track of the levels they crossed as they pursued him down stairs and along narrow byways.

"How do you know where we're going?" he asked Whitsun at one point. They had stopped at a busy cross street while Whitsun scanned the crowds that rushed up and down it. Across from them, another road plunged between two towers. The spires were joined, far above their heads, by a bridge, whose gossamer struts glowed golden in the fading rays of sunlight.

Whitsun's eyes moved swiftly back and forth. "This way!" He motioned ahead. They darted across the street, narrowly avoiding the endless stream of carts, horses, and sky carriages that maneuvered along it.

"You never answered me," Glustred pointed out.

Whitsun kept his face to the front. "I have *some* experience following people," he snapped. "Besides . . ."

"What?"

"I can sense the ring." He shook his head angrily. "I know, I know. Don't ask me how. I don't know myself. But I know where it is."

The street they were following narrowed as the buildings on either side drew close to one another. Arches opened to the left and right. Without hesitation, Whitsun hurled himself through the left arch, followed by his companion. They trotted down a winding staircase that circled in a spiral around a deep pit. Winds and vapors rose from the pit and flowed by them and the dozens of other people moving up and down the stairs.

Whitsun led the way, eyes fixed forward. Below them they could now see the distant figure they were pursuing. Several times it seemed as if they were gaining on him only to see him snatched away and reappear hundreds of feet ahead. Glustred, between pants, said something of this to his companion. Whitsun nodded.

"It might have something to do with the magic of what he's carrying. I don't know. It seems to be keeping him from us."

"But it's still drawing you to it," Glustred retorted. His companion made no comment, so he tried again. "You don't suppose he's the one who—what did your friend call it? 'Imprinted'?"

"Not on the ring. Lamonn said I'm the only one who can imprint on it."

"Well, what about the other thing? The orerry?"

"Maybe. But if he's got anything like the power I do—" Whitsun glanced at his left hand, wrapped in a rag he'd snatched from a passing cart—"why doesn't he stop and fight us?"

Glustred shook his head. "Don't know. And where's he going?"

"Oh, that's quite clear. I've known that for a while."

"Where then?"

"Watch. Don't you see where we are?"

Glustred looked around. The architecture in this part of the city was of cleaner lines and more gracious spaces than that below. There was something familiar about a number of the buildings. He squinted as they left the great staircase and started down a broad way lined with stately pillared porticos.

"Oh!"

"Yes."

Ahead of them, their quarry hurried on. Whatever had caused him to age, it did not seem to slow him down, and his feet moved swiftly and easily over the broad flagstones that formed the street here. From a byway ahead of him, there was a tramp of feet, and a company of the Watch rounded the corner. The assassin halted, turned, and fled.

"Hoy!"

The commander raised his hand and hurled a bolt of force after the scarred man. The bolt got halfway to its goal, ricocheted, and struck the entrance to a temple, shattering its great wooden doors. Splinters of wood flew in all directions, some of them shattering windows in nearby buildings, while others impaled a beggar who had been crouched by the side of the temple. His body flew back against a wooden post and hung there, blood dripping from his mouth, his head sagged at an unpleasant angle.

The explosion knocked the pursuers down as well, though they were shielded from the worst effects of the blast by a garbage cart standing in the street. As the dust cleared, Whitsun stood.

"Well," he said to Glustred, half to himself, "at least now we've confirmed that the ring still has power to disrupt magic."

The commander, who'd been knocked down by the force of the blast, along with most of his troop, scrambled to his feet. "Get him!" he roared. Ten men raced after the assassin. The commander looked around, saw Glustred and Whitsun, and his eyes widened.

"Balls!"

Glustred turned and plunged back up the way they'd come, Whitsun behind him. They heard the clatter of feet but no voices hurling spells. Evidently word had spread to the Watch of what happened to those who used magic on Whitsun.

They raced along a street. Whitsun leaped, caught a stone ledge protruding from a building, and pulled himself up.

"Come!"

With effort Glustred followed him. They clambered upward, fingers clawing at broken bits of masonry and protruding iron spikes. Like spiders, they clung to the side of the tower, flattening themselves against it, out of the light of the everbright lanterns. A clatter of boots in the alley below told of the arrival of the Watch. There was a muttered colloquy and shouts from the impatient commander. After a few minutes the boots tramped off, their steps echoing against the narrow walls.

Glustred sighed in relief and started to slide down the wall.

"No!"

Whitsun pulled himself up along the wall. Thirty feet off the ground a narrow ledge wound its way beneath mullioned windows. Whitsun reached this and with some difficulty climbed onto it. He extended his right hand down to steady Glustred. The innkeeper, whose fingers were white with the effort of holding on, took the hand and mounted slowly onto the ledge, one knee at a time. He hastily let go of Whitsun as soon as possible.

"What now?" Glustred asked in a harsh whisper.

Whitsun pointed to their left, where a dim glow came from behind a grimy pane. The two men edged their way to the window, and Whitsun peered around the corner of its stone frame.

"All right," he muttered to his companion. He pushed against the window, then pulled, and the glass swung open. Whitsun eased himself through the window and stood back to allow room for Glustred.

The room in which they found themselves was narrow and dusty, lit by a single guttering torch on the far wall. The space seemed taken up with boxes, and Glustred subjected them to a cursory examination while the smaller man prowled along the wall, seeking a door.

"Curious," he remarked as much to himself as to the innkeeper.

"What?"

Whitsun gestured. The door was marked by a thin, dark line along the wall. There was no sign of a knob or keyhole. Evidently it was meant to be opened only from the outside.

"What do we do now?"

"Well, we can wait for someone to let us out."

Glustred raised a hand to bang on the door and was stopped by Whitsun's finger on his sleeve.

"Stop!"

Whitsun walked over to one of the boxes and examined it closely. He pulled at the lid, then removed the knife from his boot and pried it open. The wooden lid fell back, and Whitsun lowered it to the floor to prevent it from making any noise.

"Look!"

Glustred looked inside the crate.

"Balls!"

Before their eyes, row after row of slender lilyweed stalks lay neatly packed.

"A weed house! Curse it all, we've stumbled into a weed house!" Glustred was already halfway to the window. He opened it, got one leg over the sill, then looked down and slid hastily back into the room. He shut the window with extreme caution and turned to Whitsun.

"A Watch patrol is below. That way's blocked."

Whitsun nodded. "They can't figure out where we went, so they've decided to wait for us. Typical Watch behavior: when you run into an obstacle, stop and stand where you are until it goes away." His eyes were bright with contempt.

"What about if we yell? The Watch would break into the house to get us and find all this." Glustred's gestures took in all the crates lining the room's walls. "We might be able to slip out in the confusion."

"Oh, really, Glustred! Use your intelligence! An operation this big, the Watch must know about it already. The only question is how much of the profits they're skimming as protection." Whitsun looked around. "Well, if we can't go out the window, and we can't get out of the room, we really only have one choice."

"What's that?"

"Stay here."

Whitsun sat down, his back against one of the crates, and stretched his legs in front of him.

Glustred paced the room. "Meanwhile, Scarface is clean away. Can you still sense where the ring is?"

"Yes, though there seems to be something blocking it or interfering with it. I don't understand that. But since he's headed back to this district, it's pretty obvious where he's going."

"To the Church of the Silver Flame, you mean?"

"Yes. Though it's equally clear to me that there's something more to that cathedral than the Silver Flame." Whitsun's face was thoughtful. "It must be—"

The sound of voices and a scrape at the door broke off his voice. He moved quietly to one side of the door. Glustred took up a post on the other.

The door swung open, but no one came through the opening. A moment of heart-stopping silence, then a dry, familiar voice said, "Come out. No point in staying in there."

Neither man moved.

The voice continued, "We can starve you out, you know. No one's coming in to get you, not with that hand of yours, Master Whitsun. But we don't have to come in. You have to come out."

Glustred's face tightened in a mixture of anger and surprise, but Whitsun, whose face showed no emotion, nodded. "Very well," he said.

"Keep your hands up where we can see them." The voice coughed, a deep, wracking sound. "No tricks."

Whitsun went first through the door. Glustred followed, bending his head slightly to pass beneath the frame.

In front of them were ringed half a dozen heavily armed men. Their faces were harsh with menace, and all had crossbows pointed at Whitsun and Glustred. They were pulled back from the door, and their fingers twitched on the triggers.

Behind them stood a figure, bowed and gray-haired, hands shaking.

The assassin.

"How did you know we were there?" Whitsun asked.

Whitsun and Glustred were walking down stairs. Their

hands had been chained behind them by a young man, obviously nervous at having to be so close to Whitsun and his deadly left hand.

The assassin followed the escort. "We control most of the weed houses in this part of the city," he said. "One of the guards saw you go up the wall and through the window. All we had to do was keep a patrol of the Watch under the window and come for you."

" 'We.' Who is 'we' exactly?"

The assassin ignored the question and said something to the leader of the guard in a low voice. The man nodded and vanished down a passageway.

Whitsun addressed himself again to the assassin. "You might at least tell us what's happened to you."

The scar-faced man almost doubled over coughing. "That woman's poison is powerful," he gasped. "I . . . I . . ." His words were lost in coughing. In his right hand he clutched the ring. Whitsun's eyes followed it.

"Why don't we go to a healer?"

The assassin shook his head, unable to speak. He gestured ahead, and Whitsun and Glustred's captors pushed the two men roughly along through a narrow-framed door.

They were in a large room that evidently occupied most or all of two entire floors of the building. They stood on a narrow balcony overlooking a work floor across which scurried dozens of men, elves, dwarves, halflings, orcs, and other less-identifiable creatures. At either end of the room were large double doors guarded by hulking warforged. The room was brightly lit, and the visitors had no trouble seeing what was going on.

It was a lilyweed factory. Crates of the drug were being packed in one part of the room and labeled for shipment. In another area, magical fires glowed as mages transformed the stems of the theska plant to the long, slender brown needles of lilyweed. Others inserted essence of dreamlily into them. These finished needles, in turn, were moved with extreme delicacy—lest they shatter and lose the precious drug they contained—to the packing area. There was little noise from the workers. Idle chatter was clearly not tolerated and was discouraged by several large ogres with whips, who prowled among the workers, poking at those whom they deemed to be working with insufficient speed and dedication.

Whitsun and Glustred took this in as they were led along the balcony, which circled the factory floor. It ended in another double door, which their escort pushed open. They passed through, accompanied by the scar-faced man, who was now staggering as if drunk, bumping into the marble walls of the corridor as they walked. He choked and bent, spitting a stream of phlegm and blood onto the floor. The guards holding the prisoners waited patiently until he had finished.

Even before their eyes, he seemed to be growing older. His hair was now stark white and falling from his head, leaving his scabrous scalp showing through in patches. His hands shook worse than ever, and his face was lined. When he looked at them, they could see his cheeks had sunk, and when he opened his mouth to speak, his teeth were yellow and rotting in his mouth. His eyes rolled in his skull, with great lines and creases beneath them.

"You're dying," Whitsun said, coldly. "Why don't you tell us what's going on? You're going to have us killed as well—you can't let us live after what we saw back there. What possible difference is it going to make if you tell us the truth?"

The man wheezed and choked in a horrid parody of laughter. "You will . . ." he gasped. "You will . . . see . . . truth soon . . . enough."

Glustred, looking about, realized where they were. They had come back into the Church of the Silver Flame from which they'd fled several days earlier. The priests and acolytes seemed to have disappeared. At any rate, there were none to see the strange procession as it wound its way through the maze of corridors, sanctuaries, and halls that made up the cathedral. They slowed and stopped several times as their guide rested. Once he sank to the floor, and the innkeeper thought he had died at last, but he rose after a few minutes and continued, though clearly he was growing weaker by the moment.

"Flame!" Glustred muttered to Whitsun. "What kind of poison did that woman use?"

"Probably something Karrnathi." Whitsun's voice was calm. "During the last part of the War, the other side was developing all sorts of poisons to throw into the battles. I seem to remember hearing something about the battle of Lethoso's Reach in which half the dead were found with yellowing skin and their lungs dissolved into acid."

Glustred grunted. "At least our side never did anything like that."

Whitsun stopped and stared at him then shook his head in disbelief. "You never fail to astonish me, Glustred."

The guard behind him gave him a shove.

"I'm going."

They passed under an arch and down a familiar corridor. The assassin, his breath coming in labored hacks, threw his body against the door.

"Come in!" called a cheerful voice from the other side.

One of the guards opened the door. The assassin half fell through it. The guards shoved Whitsun and Glustred through then withdrew, shutting the door behind them.

The high priest sat in his comfortable chair. A cup of wine

was beside him, and a bright fire burned in the grate. The room was warm, inviting, and smelled of wine and cloves. A few books lay scattered about, ready to pick up again when their owner was so inclined. The furniture was of dark wood, smooth and rich. The firelight played over it all, dancing and reflecting from the mullioned window pane.

The assassin staggered to stand before the high priest. He knelt, head lolling between his knees. His trembling hands held out the ring.

The high priest reached out and took it. He examined it carefully, turning it over in his fat hands, holding it to the light.

The only sound was the assassin's wrenching gasps, attempting to draw air into his tortured lungs.

The high priest smiled. "You have done well, my son," he told the assassin.

The scar-faced man raised his head. His eyes looked into those of his master with liquid love.

The high priest reached beneath his robes and brought out a slender knife. The firelight caught it as he lifted it.

With a single smooth motion, he cut the assassin's throat.

CHAPTER
14

The body of the assassin slid to the marble floor. Blood pooled beneath him. His eyes looked up at his killer. The eyelids fluttered and closed, and his mouth twitched into a thin smile. He gave one more long gasp and was silent.

Neither Whitsun nor Glustred moved. The high priest sank back into his seat and took a long sip from his cup. There was something so cold-blooded in that action that Glustred took a small, involuntary breath. The high priest looked at him, eyes bright, and smiled. Then he reached behind him and pulled a silken cord. High above them a bell sounded sweetly.

The door opened, and several white-robed servants entered. They did not act as if anything were amiss. Instead, two of them grasped the body and bore it from the room. The other, who carried a pitcher of water and a cloth, washed the blood from the floor. When the water in the pitcher was pink and the flagstones were again gleaming, he bowed and withdrew.

The high priest gestured, and the bonds fell from Whitsun

and Glustred's hands. At once Glustred began a cautious, crablike movement, so as to get behind the high priest. The man looked at him and smiled. Glustred's steps slowed, and he halted, moving as if struggling with some unseen force that plucked at his limbs, holding him in place.

"Much better, I think," the priest said amiably. To Whitsun, he said, "Now, master, would you sit down?"

Whitsun sat. Glustred remained where he was, face red from exertion.

"I think some refreshment would be agreeable. Yes? I think so, I think so."

The priest rang the bell again, and the silent attendant, he who had cleaned the blood, appeared.

"Some wine for our guests, Alfrath. And some tea cakes, I think. I enjoy the ones from Aundair, myself. Delightful but *so* difficult to obtain during the War. Now that peace has broken out, I can indulge myself fully in a harmless vice." He patted his stomach and chuckled. His chins jiggled.

Alfrath disappeared, and Whitsun, turning his eyes after him, observed, "Your servants don't seem to talk much."

"Ah, well, Alfrath has been with me for some little time. When he was a young lad, he was of a more talkative disposition."

"What happened?"

"He spoke more than was good for him in front of a noble with whom I was negotiating. It made the negotiations somewhat more difficult. Afterwards, I sent for Alfrath and had his tongue torn out." The fat priest made this statement with no more emotion than if he'd been telling Whitsun of the injury of a favorite pet. "Now his conversation is more agreeable to my ears."

Glustred made a sound that sounded halfway between a laugh and a moan. Whitsun glanced at him. The big man's feet were an inch or so off the floor. His face was contorted, the flesh drawn back over his mouth, revealing his teeth.

Whitsun addressed the high priest. "Not that it makes a lot of difference to me, but you might as well put him down. Torturing him isn't going to affect me one way or another."

"Possibly, but it gives me a certain amount of amusement. However . . ." The priest twisted a negligent hand and Glustred dropped back to the floor, landing on his knees and breathing heavily.

Whitsun continued without paying any attention to him. "Now, suppose you tell me what this is all about."

The priest leaned back in his chair and laughed long and softly. "My dear, dear Whitsun," he said at last, wiping his eyes, "you've no idea what pleasure I take in your manner of putting that question. I should have expected anger, indignation, any number of things but this. A charming way of asking the question."

"Suppose you answer it then."

The priest nodded. He rang the bell again, and another servant appeared. Hallah said something to him in an undertone, and the servant disappeared. Hallah leaned back in his chair and smiled at Whitsun.

"Do you mind talking?"

"Not in the least." Whitsun leaned back as well. "I like to talk."

"Excellent. Never trust a closed-mouth man." Hallah chuckled. His eyes almost disappeared into creases of flesh, and his bushy brows drew together.

The servant returned, silently bearing a salver on which rested the Orerry of Tal Esk. The fat man lifted it, using a clean cloth to hold it, and examined it, letting it catch the light. He set it back on the salver and became more serious. "You have some idea of what you possessed, albeit briefly?"

"I know a bit of their history. From Xen'drik, right?"

"Correct. Relics of the titanic struggle in ages past between the giants and the quori, a war that makes our recent troubles appear no more than a ripple in the great ocean of history." The priest placed the tips of his fingers together. "Had we world enough and time, I should like to tell you of that whole great struggle for mastery of Eberron. It would fascinate you, *fascinate* you."

"Very possibly," Whitsun agreed. "But as we don't, let's keep to the here and now."

"As you say," agreed the priest.

Here Alfrath entered with cakes and cups on a tray. The high priest treated the food as if it were every bit as important as the matter under discussion, spreading a thick layer of butter on top of half of one of the cakes, followed by an equally thick layer of jam. As he chewed, small crumbs dribbled down his chin in a thin stream. He disposed of most of the cakes, though Whitsun ate several with every appearance of relish. He did not attempt to resume their conversation until the last of the cakes had been cleared away and the last cup of wine had been drunk. Glustred remained half insensible on the floor, and no one paid him any attention.

When Alfrath had cleared the plates and departed, Whitsun said, "So."

"So." The priest looked at him through half-closed eyes. "Your friend at Morgrave University told you something of the power of this artifact, did he not?"

"*This* artifact."

"Of course. They are one, though they are, at present, two. At one time, indeed, they were three, but as you see——" Hallah indicated the sphere and the ring that had been joined——"they have been united as they were meant to be. *This* however . . ." He gestured to the ring. "This remains apart, waiting to be reunited with its fellows."

Whitsun raised an eyebrow but made no comment.

"Most of what Scorpeth told you was correct. The devices are, indeed, from Xen'drik, are indeed the product of the giantish-quori struggle, and do, indeed, work together. Your friend was also correct in suggesting that they must imprint upon one person and that person must be the sole controller of the device's magic."

Whitsun nodded. "So what if his information was a lie?"

"Really, my dear Whitsun, it is less a matter of him telling you lies—or incorrect statements, at any rate—than of him simply not giving you the entire truth. That was not malicious on his part. It was merely that he knew only what he could find from the incomplete records of the great library of Morgrave. More can certainly be found in the archives of the Korranberg Library. If Scorpeth had been able to travel there, he might have found a manuscript giving much of the history of these objects. And he is one of the very few people in Khorvaire who would be able to read it."

"What about you?" Whitsun asked. "Have you read it?"

"I, my dear Whitsun? Alas, no. Unlike your friend Scorpeth, the life of the scholar has been denied me. A pity, for I believe that is truly my calling. Perhaps someday I shall retire and spend what remains of my life in study and contemplation of the infinite variety of languages and cultures contained within this world of ours." He took another draught of wine. "No, I have but a second-hand acquaintance with the manuscript from the description of one who read it."

"What happened to him?"

" 'Happened?' Really, my dear Whitsun, you do have a suspicious mind. Why should anything have 'happened' to him?"

Whitsun said nothing, and Hallah gurgled with laughter. "Very well, very well. Yes, he is dead. Alas. A loss to the scholarly community. Truly a great loss. But not before he performed the service I required from him.

"Scorpeth told you what he had discovered in the books he read. But, as you might suspect, the truth is not to be found in books but in the knowledge of those who actually discovered these treasures.

"These devices have been known to mages in Eberron, of course, for many hundreds of years. Some sought them, while others dismissed their existence as a myth.

"Thirty years ago, while the War raged, certain factions at the court of Karrnath determined that there must be some truth to the stories. They sent an expedition, secretly and with great difficulty, deep into the jungles of Xen'drik. The expedition encountered numerous tribes and races living deep within the dark continent. They were harassed by certain elves living there. Those peoples looked with hostility at anyone intruding into their territory. The War had no meaning to them—rumors of it barely reached them. Gold was useless to them, and they did not care for anything the expedition had brought in trade.

"The leaders of the expedition were well aware that if they returned to Karrnath empty-handed, their fate would be highly unpleasant. Karrnath does not care for failure. The explorers therefore persisted, fighting the native races when they had to, attempting to intimidate them through force or magic as was called for."

He paused and took a sip of wine.

"Of course, as time went on, the size of the expedition dwindled. It had begun as almost a hundred men and women. After six months it was cut nearly in half. Another few months passed, and their numbers were now barely a score. Death from disease and the darts of the elves had done for the rest. Some, indeed, proposed to return to Karrnath, saying they might escape the wrath of the rulers by begging the extreme difficulties of the task they had been set. Yet one, more devoted than the others to their quest, urged them onward. He argued that the objects they sought must exist, else there would not be so many stories of them. He believed that if they could discover these wonderful magic artifacts and return with them to Karrnath, the balance of the War would be tipped, and Karrnath would be victorious. Yet persuasive as his arguments were, the others—most of them—rebelled against him and determined to return."

He sipped again.

"One night, while the members of the expedition slept, he arose and went from tent to tent with his knife. When dawn came, only three members of the expedition yet lived—himself and two who were devoted to him, body and soul."

Whitsun stretched out his feet to the fire. "To cut a long story short," he said, "the three of them found the ring and the orerry."

"No, not all three. In any case, you are missing the full story. You must not neglect the tale's atmosphere. The long, painful search. The staggering heat. The eternal sound of insects, enough to drive one mad in such a place." The priest sighed. "I can see you are impatient. Yes, in the end, one found it. But when he did, the leader of the expedition knew that he could never bring it back to Karrnath."

"Why?"

"One night, the young man fell into a fever. His companions, fearing they would become ill as well, fled, leaving him to his lonely death. He lay wrapped in his blanket, while all around him the jungle bent and swayed in its eternal dance. Creatures screamed in the trees, and snakes slithered along the ground and wrapped themselves about his body. Sweat poured like water from his brow. But when the morning came, he still lived. And, though weak, he rose and went without hesitation to the spot where the treasures he sought lay concealed."

"He had a vision?"

"Yes, my dear Whitsun. A vision. One that made his path clear to him. The Karrnathi people had become corrupt. Their leaders were senile and thought only of the War and never of larger questions, of the future. What would the world look like when the War was won and one nation bestrode Khorvaire? How could the fate of such a nation be entrusted to such people? They had been unable to win the great struggle in which the kingdom had been immersed for nearly a century. Surely they were not worthy to decide the greater fate of Karrnath and indeed of all Khorvaire. Surely that fate belonged to the strongest, most successful individual. Surely."

"To himself, in fact," Whitsun interrupted.

"Yes. To he who had proven through his suffering that he was worthy of so great a task." Hallah fell silent for a few minutes, and Whitsun did not break the peace. At last the high priest resumed. "In a few days, the cowards who had fled returned, expecting to find only the body of their leader. Instead they found him recovered from his fever and now in possession of the treasures they sought. They marveled at this, but not for long. For the leader, in his righteousness struck the life from each of them. Then he knew he was right, for their deaths were easy and he felt no hesitation in dispatching them. He left the bodies for the ants and the animals and began his long, slow return to civilization."

The priest rose, stomach wobbling beneath his brocaded robe, and walked over to the window.

"Come here, my dear Whitsun."

Whitsun joined him, and the priest opened the window. They looked out on the plaza before the cathedral's main entrance. Two hundred feet below where they stood, crowds of people surged to and fro, sweeping past one another, roiling and scouring the buildings that lined the square. The high priest watched them in silence for a moment then spoke.

"The world has failed, my dear Whitsun. Those living in it are merely existing upon borrowed time. The gods, if gods there be, must be laughing at us."

"That's a strange observation, coming from a priest," Whitsun said.

"There are priests and there are priests. All religions these days are pointless. All signs indicate a coming cataclysm that will sweep away life from the surface of our world. Great walls of fire crossing the land, while ice rains from the sky. The earth writhing in torment, torn open as volcanic fires spew forth. Comets flashing through the sky and lashing Eberron with their tails. And amid it all, men, elves, dwarves, halflings, every living being in all the world perishing. Then the storm passes, leaving the world wrapped in darkness. Such was the vision granted to the young man in the jungles of Xen'drik."

There was silence for a few minutes. Hallah closed the window and returned to his seat. Whitsun followed.

"It was you," he said finally. "The young man. That was you."

The priest made no response. After a time he spoke again. "When the time of darkness has past, the world will be born again. So it goes, in a great cycle of tens of thousands of years. Always there are the few, the strong, the powerful who recognize what must be done to achieve this. It is a lonely and awful responsibility." He was silent again for a time, then continued. "The young man brought the artifacts out of the jungle and back to his home in Khorvaire. There, he hoped to abide in peace for a time until deciding how best to bring about the truth of his vision. However, that was not to be.

"Upon his return, he was arrested by the White Lions. He was tortured, released, rearrested, and tortured again. He knew that his chance of surviving was small, yet he had survived before.

"The two artifacts, the orrery—only partially complete—and the ring, are one but also two and indeed, as I said, three. Each has power, but together they have a power that none can withstand. But that power can only be wielded by those upon whom they imprint themselves."

Whitsun spoke. "That's not clear to me."

"No. I suppose not." The priest drained his cup. "It would perhaps be surprising if it were. Each artifact, my dear Whitsun, imprints itself upon someone. Your friend at Morgrave told you that, and he was correct. The power to use the artifact then resides in its owner."

"Yes, that's fine. But *you* found the cursed things! Why didn't they imprint on you?"

"That is a mystery." The priest nodded, and his face became lost in thought. He stroked one of his chins while his other hand, unconsciously, rubbed his great belly. "I strove for it. Night after night, I sat and willed the objects to do my bidding. But nothing. Nothing happened. I began to realize that the artifacts themselves somehow choose whom they will imprint upon." He smiled. "You are honored, my dear Whitsun. I don't know what makes you special. One wouldn't think it to look at you."

Whitsum, not in the least insulted, smiled as well. "I suppose not. So who was imprinted by the sphere and the ring that make up the orrery now?"

The priest rang the bell, and Alfrath appeared, accompanied by two other attendants. They refilled the priest's and Whitsun's cups.

"When the two cowards returned and found me, one, Amashti, perhaps guessed more of what I had accomplished than he should have. As I slept, he rifled my belongings and found the golden sphere and the silver ring. Fool! He had no idea of what he was dealing with. The objects drew power from him and united with one another. He sat by the fire, staring at them, marveling at their beauty. That was where I found him the next morning when I awoke.

"He saw my anger, and he tried to defend himself. But the power of the righteous cannot be set aside. I smote him down and, when his companion attempted to come to his aid, I struck him down as well. Thus were they repaid for their betrayal of me."

Hallah's voice had grown deep and laced with fury. Now he looked across at Whitsun, laughed, and relaxed. "As to your question of whom the orerry will imprint on, I don't yet know. Nor do I know if, once it is united with the ring you possessed, the entire object must yet again imprint on someone. That is a matter of great interest to me, of course. So until I find out, I thought it best to keep you here with me. Once we discover the owner of the orerry, matters can proceed. It would appear that you have no power to unite these artifacts. But I was curious to see just what power the ring had given you."

"You were willing to allow me to roam unfettered around the cathedral?"

"Unfettered in some senses, my dear Whitsun, but hardly unwatched. I saw no reason to impede you in your investigation of our headquarters, though you were carefully headed off from anything that might be of greater consequence."

Whitsun nodded. "The doors I couldn't open. The windows I couldn't see through."

"Precisely. You found out exactly as much as we cared for you to know at that point. You see, my dear Whitsun, I wanted to show you, quietly and unobtrusively, the scope of our organization to give you some notion of its size and power. You may think yourself very good at your business, but I assure you we're far better. Your path was predetermined."

"What about Soorlah?"

"My dear Whitsun, I fear that even now you don't fully grasp the extent of our planning and power." The high priest took a generous mouthful of wine. His lips were stained purple. "Everything—*everything*—that has happened to you over the past few days has been controlled by us. Soorlah's treachery was planned as soon as you left your base in Firelight. As for his death . . . well, that perhaps couldn't be helped. In any case, he was a mere halfling. I hope I'm not more prejudiced than the next man, but as far as I can see, the fewer halflings in Khorvaire, the fewer remain to be exterminated in the future. As for the rest, both halflings served their purpose—to guide you to the Church of the Silver Flame and to bring you within our power."

"And Delru Abaressena?"

The high priest, losing his composure for the first time, growled an oath that should be unspoken by any in priestly orders. He took another gulp of wine to calm himself. "The redhaired bitch is an accident!" he said. "She should not be alive!" He recovered his composure and smiled again. "However, that defect will soon be remedied."

"Whom does she represent?"

"It's not important. Really, Whitsun, you don't need to know everything about this business." For the first time, Hallah seemed on the verge of overwhelming anger.

Whitsun made no response. His eyes followed the high priest's every movement, and his brows were drawn down in a hard, black bar.

"Even that poor fellow you killed," Hallah continued, regaining his composure. "The priest you assassinated after knife exercises—"

"Yes, what about him?" Whitsun interrupted. "I didn't mean

to kill him, if that's of any interest to you."

"Quite. Quite." The high priest chuckled again, setting his flesh to wobbling. He reached up and massaged a thick pinch of skin around his neck. "But in so doing, you gave us a good notion of how far the magic of the ring had progressed. Of course, I am always sorry to lose one of my people, but in this case the result was well worth the cost. Tell me, is your touch always lethal now? Always? Yes? Hmph! Most interesting and unexpected. And just with the left hand, I notice."

Whitsun lifted his hand and examined it as if seeing it for the first time. "For all the fact that you found these things," he observed, "you don't seem to know much about them. Magic doesn't work on me. You've seen that yourself. And some of the magic of the ring has flowed into me now. Thanks to this thing—" he gestured to the ring—"I seem to have some powers that even you and your friends ought to be afraid of."

The priest nodded. "Of course. Your left hand certainly deserves closer study."

The movement was very well timed. The priest made no sign and spoke no word. Yet in simultaneous motion the servants struck, gripping Whitsun, pinning his hands to the arms of his chair. One stepped behind him and forced his head back. His neck creaked ominously.

Hallah rose and stood over him. One of the acolytes produced from beneath his robes a glittering knife. He held it high.

The priest nodded. The knife swept down.

Whitsun cried out as his left hand fell to the ground.

It was hours later. The church had been cleared of all but the white-robed servants of the high priest. Their faces were smooth and expressionless, and they moved across the marble floors with noiseless footsteps.

Whitsun opened his eyes. High above him, the ceiling looked down. He moved his legs and arms experimentally then tried to sit up.

A hand pushed him down. He turned toward his left arm and saw the bloody bandage around the stump. Pain surged up the limb and struck at his shoulder and his chest. He gasped for breath. Someone lifted his head so he could sip a cool drink. His mind swirled and drained, and he sank back into a slumber that removed his senses without giving him peace or rest.

Somewhere a hundred miles above him, a gong sounded. It chimed the hours. One. Two. Three. Four. Five. Whitsun waited, but there was nothing else. Around him there was silence. He listened. It sounded good.

He turned on his right side and eased up. His eyes fell on the end of his left arm, and he shuddered. Carefully, he levered himself off the bench, avoiding the use of his injured arm. He looked around. Glustred was gone. The priest's chair was as it had been, but it was unoccupied. He was lying on a low bench to one side of the room. No one else was there.

He sat on the bench and held his head in his hand for a moment. Then he was violently sick. He retched until his stomach was empty then sank back on the bench and fell into a troubled sleep again.

He awoke later. Still alone. Someone had cleaned the stones he had stained with his illness. A bowl of fresh water stood by his chair. He had a raging thirst, but he made no move to drink it. He sat up again and with great effort pushed himself up. Once on his feet he staggered once or twice but at last achieved balance. He took a few tentative steps, shook his head, and tried again. This time he made it halfway to the far wall before he had to stop and rest. After a time he got up and doggedly tried again.

An hour later he was almost steady on his feet. His left arm throbbed, but he planted one foot in front of the other, his lips creased in concentration. The wound had begun bleeding again and had dripped red on the floor, but he held it up, which seemed to stanch or slow the flow of blood. Back and forth he paced, counting the steps under his breath.

After he reached a thousand, he stopped, breathing heavily. He bent his head, exhaled violently three or four times, and straightened.

He walked to the door. His pace was almost normal.

The door was locked. He rattled the handle. Then he began a search of the room.

Twenty minutes later he was ready. He banged on the door.

"Hey! Hey, lizard spit!"

Silence for a few minutes, then the sound of running feet. The lock clicked, and the guard entered.

Whitsun struck with the wooden arm he'd wrenched from the priest's chair. The man's skull rattled, and he staggered. Whitsun drew back his arm and struck again with more force. Something crunched, and the man fell to the ground without a word. Whitsun dragged him a bit of the way back from the door and gave up. He stepped outside, looking around. All was quiet.

He moved down the corridor.

A long, thin man stepped out from a side passage. Whitsun brought around the chair arm. The man tried to block it, but his arm cracked as the wood struck against it. He screamed, a shrill, echoing sound, and fell back against the wall. Whitsun leaped forward and struck again. His stick drew blood from the young man's forehead, and his opponent fell to his knees. Whitsun kicked out, and his boot heel took the man on the tip of the chin. His mouth clicked shut and he fell sideways in a heap.

Whitsun flattened himself against the wall and waited, but there was no response. The scream had evidently gone unheard.

He moved on.

From the far end of the corridor came a cry of pain, echoing faintly from behind a stout wooden door. Whitsun moved closer. The door opened, and he barely had time to flatten himself against the wall.

Another priest emerged, carrying a long, slender knife stained with blood. He was wiping it on a cloth.

Whitsun stepped behind him. With his left arm, he grasped the man about the neck while his right hand snapped on the man's wrist. The struggle was momentary. Whitsun twisted the knife about and jammed it up under the priest's ribs. He pulled it hard to the left, and the priest gave a choking moan, half smothered by Whitsun's left arm. The victim slid down in his killer's arms and lay in a pool of blood on the floor.

Whitsun wiped the knife clean. Then he stripped the body and donned the white robe, now stained with red. He hid the knife beneath his garment and slid through the door.

Twenty minutes later, he stood behind a pillar. From his hiding place, he could see the entrance doors to the temple. He gritted his teeth against the pain in his left arm and began carefully walking toward the doors.

Halfway there, several priests crossed the space. Whitsun bowed to them, keeping his head low. They passed him without showing any sign they had seen him. He continued. The floor before him stretched out for miles. He could barely see the great doors as they gaped before him. They were partially open, but by their side stood two guards.

Whitsun debated with himself how best to approach them.

Any attempt to rush through was impossible; he would be caught and stopped in a moment. And he no longer had the lethal power of his left hand to fight back.

As he cogitated, the sound of singing came from behind. He stood aside as a column of monks, chanting a hymn to the Host, moved through the hall and toward the door. Whitsun joined the tail of the column as it passed him. The monks, still chanting, passed through the door under the watchful eyes of the guards.

A few minutes later, Whitsun, still clad in the monk's robe, ducked into a message shop. The young man behind the counter looked up.

"What—?"

Whitsun's hand gripped his neck and squeezed. Hard. The youth choked, gasped for air, and sagged. Whitsun hurled him behind the counter, strode behind the curtain that concealed the back part of the shop, and began to compose a message.

"Dolurrh take her!" he muttered. "Get this message! Come on!"

Minutes passed. The youth stirred, and Whitsun kicked him in the temple. He stopped moving.

A soft bell indicated an incoming message. Whitsun scanned it quickly, and for the first time in hours, a smile covered his face. He went to the door of the shop and looked out, drawing the monk's hood over his face.

"Now," he growled to himself, "to get my property back!"

Glustred hung from a beam in the ceiling, his arms secured above his head by a rope. He was bare to the waist. His arms ached, and he felt the sting of the cuts the priest's knife had made along his torso. Blood trickled down his legs. His eyes stung, and his head ached. Oddly, it was the headache that bothered him the most. He wished they would stop asking him questions so he could go lie down.

From a great distance, he heard a voice.

"It's no good, sire. The truth spell doesn't seem to have any effect on him. We'll have to go back to the knife."

Hallah, sitting in his chair, chuckled. "I didn't expect the spell would work," he observed. "Because of *this*." He lifted something lying in an earthen bowl beside him, but Glustred couldn't lift his head high enough to see what it was.

"With respect, sire, why'd we try the spell if you knew it wouldn't work?"

"Call it an experiment, Stavrosh. We deprived Whitsun of his hand. I was curious to see how much power lay in him and how much in the hand itself. Now we know."

"So shall I call Merriell back in, sire? To continue his work?"

"No. No, let's find out how far things can be pushed. Have another go at that truth spell. I want to see if the power shows any signs of fading."

Glustred's heart fell. The truth spell had given him the headache in the first place. He didn't know if it was likely to work any better the second time around, but of one thing he was sure.

It was going to make his head feel worse.

The door opened. An acolyte pushed his way through. He was a bit heavy, his robe straining against his stomach, and his feet seeming a bit clumsy beneath his garment.

Glustred looked at him and grinned, drool spilling over the side of his lip. His head felt as if someone were boring into it with an awl. The pain was just above his right temple. He tried to reach up to touch it and realized his arms were bound above his head.

The acolyte was smiling at him. His eye was winking.

Glustred winked back. Then he moaned. His teeth grated together. The pain in his head was much worse.

The fat priest held out the bowl to the acolyte. "Here," he said. "Move to the door with this. I want to see if distance has some effect on the disruptive magic."

The white-robed man took the bowl and looked as if he were going to be sick. He turned, reached into the bowl with cloth-covered fingers, and brought out a severed hand. Fluid still dripped from the wrist, where the shattered bone could be seen protruding from the ragged flesh. The acolyte swung the hand against Stavrosh, who, head bent, was concentrating on his spell. Stavrosh gave a strangled cry, clutched at his neck, and sprawled on the ground. A thin stream of smoke rose from his hair.

The fat priest stared as the acolyte cast back his hood, revealing Whitsun's whitened face. Whitsun stepped forward, brandishing the hand.

"Not a sound," he snarled. "Not a move. Not even a muscle unless I tell you."

His hand was shaking badly, and he did not look at the left hand he held in his right. The high priest sat very still. Only his eyes moved, rolling from side to side, scanning the room.

Finally Whitsun spoke. "Get up."

The high priest rose, rolls of fat wobbling beneath his vestments.

"Cut him down."

Hallah lifted a hand and Whitsun made a sharp gesture toward it with the hand he was holding.

"No magic!"

The priest sighed. From beneath his robe he produced a knife. Whitsun watched him closely as he stepped over to Glustred, reached up with a grunt, and sliced through the rope holding the innkeeper erect.

Glustred slumped on the floor. After a moment, he rose, hands shaking, holding his head. He looked at Hallah and, in a flashing gesture, struck the knife from the man's hand. It spun across the room. Glustred's hand went back for a blow, but Whitsun's voice stopped him.

"No! Bar the door."

Glustred dropped a metal bar into fastenings across the entrance to the room. Whitsun stood next to the priest, the hand poised near his foe's neck.

"Where are the ring and the orerry?"

The priest gestured to a cabinet, six feet tall, as many broad, carven of a single piece of ivory, which stood on one side of the room. Glustred wrenched open the door and plucked out a bundled cloth. He opened it, careful not to touch what was within, and nodded to Whitsun.

"Very well."

The priest said, "The ring is useless now."

Whitsun stared at him. "What are you talking about?"

"I should have thought you would have realized. All the ring's power has now passed into *that*." He pointed to the severed hand that had once belonged on Whitsun's left wrist. "We tested it to be sure. For the past few days, the power has been slowly draining from the ring. I wasn't sure where it was going, but now I know. All of it is in your hand." He summoned a faint chuckle. "Well, of course not *your* hand any longer. Let's say, the hand formerly yours."

Whitsun stared at him. "I don't understand," he said. "Why didn't you just kill me?"

Hallah laughed, and something of his old manner returned. "I don't believe in waste. I can see you still don't entirely understand. The ring and the orerry, as I said, imprint themselves on two individuals. Those imprints remain as long as those two individuals live."

"Exactly. So why not kill me and imprint the ring on somebody else?"

"Because neither I nor you nor anyone has the power to imprint the artifacts. They themselves choose on whom to imprint. True, I could have killed you. But who could say upon whom the ring would next imprint? Or when? It might take centuries, and I don't have centuries. For all that I know, the completely reconstructed orerry, once it is assembled, might imprint on you. The ring, at any rate, seems to like you, if such a thing can be said of an object." He sat. "It seemed more useful to remove the—appendage—in which the power had become concentrated and see what could be done with it. I was not, I confess, entirely sure whether I would still need you. If I had determined you were no longer useful, you may rest assured you would cease to exist."

Whitsun nodded. "Reasonable. What about the orerry—that is to say, the gold sphere and silver ring?"

The priest looked troubled for the first time. "As to that, I'm not sure. I believe, though I may be mistaken, that it has already imprinted. It does not seem to have any reaction to your hand—excuse me, *the* hand. I don't believe it belongs to you any more." He chuckled again.

Whitsun did not join him. "It's *my* hand!" he snapped.

"Now, my dear Whitsun, no more. It serves a higher purpose."

Whitsun sat down on a stool. His body slumped. The force of events seemed to be overtaking him. Glustred, standing behind and a little to the left of the priest reached out and took a firm grip on the side of the high priest's neck. A single twist of his fingers could snap the bones.

"What is that higher purpose?" Whitsun asked. "You were getting ready to tell me before you cut my hand off."

The priest, as much at ease as if he had not had a large man prepared to break his neck, leaned back in his chair and crossed his legs. His voice took on a lecturing tone.

"The recent war proved, if it needed proving, that nations cannot rule themselves. They want someone to rule them. In short, peace requires order. After a hundred years of war, surely that's a reasonable goal."

"Reasonable," conceded Whitsun. "And you think the nation of Karrnath is going to provide peace and order?"

The priest shook his head. "No. Karrnath has shown its leadership is weak. A stronger force is required. A stronger *man* is required."

Whitsun raised an eyebrow. "Let's start from the beginning. I got this thing—" he gestured vaguely toward the ring—"when a thief stumbled into my rooms and gave it to me. Where did he get it?"

"Your friends the shifter and Abaressena told you the truth. He stole it from them."

"Where did they get it?"

"They are, or were, in the case of the shifter, agents of the Karrnathi government. They came here to steal it from me."

"And succeeded?"

The priest inclined his head in agreement. "And succeeded," he agreed. "Much to my shame, I confess. The bitch Abaressena is somewhat more ingenious than I gave her credit for."

"Why send Maresun after them to steal it? Why not just kill them?"

"It didn't seem necessary at the time. I was mistaken in thinking Maresun was sufficient." The high priest leaned back in his chair. Glustred's fingers were still pressed against his neck, but he did not seem to notice. "It may surprise you, my dear Whitsun," he observed, "but I'm really a very humane man. I dislike killing unless it's necessary. In that respect, I suspect you and I are much alike."

Whitsun seemed to be growing weary. He passed a hand over his eyes. "What happened then?"

"Maresun decided to get more than his fee from me. He guessed at the value of what he stole from his target, though he was, of course, ignorant of its true nature."

Whitsun sighed. "His girlfriend wanted more lilyweed, and Norn needed money to pay for it. The things we do for love!" He shook his head. "And he managed to make it back to me to give the ring to me. I wonder why?"

Hallah nodded. "The question, my dear Whitsun, has occurred to me as well. Doesn't it strike you as more than coincidental that Maresun, whom I shouldn't credit with much intelligence, brought the ring to the person upon whom, out of all others in Sharn or Breland or all Khorvaire, it imprinted?"

"Well?"

"You were *meant* for this magic, my dear Whitsun. You have been an instrument in the hands of some higher power."

"The gods, you mean?" Whitsun's tone was scornful.

"If you like. Though personally I prefer to put my faith in men."

"Odd talk for a priest," Glustred said, speaking for the first time, his voice thick. His hand on the side of the high priest's neck was steady as a rock.

"Priest!" His prisoner laughed. "All this, you mean? Oh, this has nothing to do with the idiots of the Silver Flame!"

Whitsun nodded. "What did I tell you?" he asked Glustred.

"So what are you if you aren't that?" the innkeeper demanded.

Slowly the priest turned and stared at him, his blue eyes boring into Glustred's brown ones.

"We are the future."

CHAPTER 15

he future," Glustred said. "The future?" He turned to Whitsun. "Do you understand what he's talking about?"

Whitsun's mouth was opened to reply when a blast sounded from beyond the door. The rumble of falling masonry mingled with shrieks of dying men.

"What the—?" Hallah half turned toward the door.

Whitsun grinned. "You aren't the only one who has a claim on the future, Hallah."

"What are you talking about?"

"I got a message to Delru. As I suspected, she was only too eager to hear from me. What you're hearing are her forces from the government of Karrnath. What she couldn't take by stealth, they're intent on taking by force."

Hallah glared at him. All his good humor had fallen from him like a cloak for which he had no more use. "What have you done?" he screamed.

Whitsun appeared completely calm. "You should know,"

he said. "It's an old adage: It's better to have two enemies than one."

This time it was Glustred who asked, "What are you talking about?"

"One enemy, Glustred, attacks you because he sees only you. But if you have two enemies, it's possible to step out of the way and let them fight each other. That's all I've done."

Glustred seemed lost in working out the implications of this statement. He looked at the door, beyond which came the sound of fighting. Hallah seized the moment to dive away from the big man, his hands moving in an arcane gesture. Lightning crackled from his fingers, twisting in the air toward Glustred. It almost reached his skin then bent toward Whitsun and veered into the severed hand he held above the bowl. There was a flash and a roar. Smoke leaped up in clouds, leaving them all choking, lying on their backs.

Another blast resounded along the corridor outside. Something heavy struck the door with a horrid squelching sound and the crunch of breaking bones. The room quivered.

Glustred crawled across the chamber. The high priest lay against the remains of a broken table. The blast of his magical lightning had destroyed half the room, shattering the window and hurling books and papers from their shelves. Whitsun was sprawled amid the ruins of an armchair. A dark sear mark cut across his face, and blood oozed from an ugly cut on his forehead.

Glustred got slowly to his feet and looked about. Outside he could hear the pounding of footsteps and shouted orders and counter-orders. There came a clash of steel and cries of anger. Another magical roar cut through all sounds, shaking the floor. Glustred rocked but kept his balance this time.

Whitsun stirred and sat up. He rubbed his hand across his

forehead and looked at the resulting blood smear.

"Come!" he told Glustred. He pushed himself up and began to grope among the debris.

Glustred hesitated. "What about him?" he asked, pointing to the high priest, who was emitting soft groans.

Whitsun's reply was lost in a crash as the door flew off its hinges. Two black-clad mages stepped through, hands raised to loose spells on anyone within the chamber. A moment later, another figure was framed in the ruined doorway, red hair cascading over her shoulders.

"Traitor!" she spat. Glustred looked over to see to whom she'd spoken. Hallah was sitting up, his face flecked with blood. One arm hung useless by his side. He rose with an effort. The black-clad mages tensed, and he held out his good hand to show there was nothing in it.

"Ah. Manilla. I wondered if you would come in person or merely send others to do your work."

The woman known to Whitsun as Delru glared at him. "Give me a reason why I shouldn't blast you to ruins here and now."

"Of course. A very good reason. Our friend there is holding it." He gestured to Whitsun, who was standing in a corner of the room. In his grasp was the hand that only a few hours ago had been attached to his left wrist.

There was a grand moment of silence. Whitsun broke it. "Believe it or not, I'm glad to see you," he said to Delru. "I assumed we'd left you behind in the chase after our scar-faced friend. But I guessed that after we'd lost you, you'd return to your quarters. That was why I sent the message there."

The high priest laughed, a high jarring sound amid the chaos. Out in the corridor, shouts and sounds of fighting still echoed, but they were growing fainter, as if the battle were moving to a different part of the cathedral. "You can't leave Manilla behind.

She refuses to be left behind. In fact, the last few people at Rek-kenmark who attempted to leave her behind ended up dead, I believe. Isn't that right my dear? Of course, I don't know if you did it yourself or merely had someone else do it for you. You've always had an aversion to doing your own dirty work."

The red-haired woman's face paled, and one of her mage companions lifted a hand, but she stopped him with a touch on his sleeve. She turned to Whitsun, ignoring everyone else, and smiled.

"I am grateful for your message, Ulther. My people will deal with this traitor and his followers. But now I'm sure you can see, Ulther, that the best thing would be to give me the ring and the Orerry of Tal Esk. Those artifacts belong to me, after all—or, at any rate, to Karrnath, which I represent. We sent this . . . this . . ." Words failed her. She gulped and began again. "We sent *him* to find the artifacts and return them to us. But he proved himself a traitor. He understands nothing about the value of these devices to our kingdom. But you, Ulther, you've been caught in some-thing far beyond your understanding." She came a step closer, her voice low and pleading. "I am begging you, Ulther. You might not believe it, but I want nothing more to happen to you. You have already paid a price. Now give up these things. You needn't have any further trouble about them. And your reward will be very rich indeed."

Hallah laughed again. "You have to be alive, my dear Whit-sun," he said, "to spend a reward. And I can assure you that the instant the artifact leaves you and comes into her possession, you'd better start making out a will. You'd be much better off giving that to me."

Delru snorted. "You'll last no time at all with him, Ulther. Has he told you his plans yet?"

"He said something about being the future."

"The future!" Delru almost shouted the word. "Has he told you what kind of a future he wants? A future in which he and his gang of mindless thugs rule all Khorvaire! A future in which there's no magic but his! A future—"

"Surely," Hallah's voice rose above hers, "that's better than the past you and your kind have been responsible for, Manilla. My dear Whitsun, how can anyone look back over the past century of war and the suffering it has brought to the people of Khorvaire and not believe we deserve something better?"

Whitsun nodded. "Better how?"

"Imagine a world in which there is no more war. In which there is no more struggle of one nation against another for supremacy. Only peace and order. In such a world, events such as the Day of Mourning and the destruction of Cyre will be only a bitter memory. But in the new dawn, when the cleansing fires have swept away all the rubbish deposited by the cataclysms of the past century, a great race will take its rightful place, ruling Eberron in the name of universal harmony. That is what I and my friends promise."

"Yes," said Delru, "but only if everyone agrees to give up every last freedom to you. Only if we agree that you and only you should possess the power of life and death over every last being on Eberron."

The priest's voice rose over hers. "I am the chosen ruler by virtue of my strength, woman! I alone found the artifacts in Xen'drik. I paid for them with my sweat and my blood."

"What about the blood of your companions?" she cried. "What about those whom you murdered to gain the object of your lust?"

"They were weak and foolish! They did not have my great vision. In my suffering, they betrayed me and abandoned me. When they returned, they attempted to betray me again. They showed the stock of Karrnath has become weak. That is why I must be ruthless in weeding out all who fall short of my desires. My followers are poised to sweep all before them. Yes, I will rule—but in the name of mercy and justice, peace and order!"

The woman laughed. "For power, my friend. Always for power."

"And wasn't that what you and the rest of Karrnath fought for in the War? The power to rule? Don't tell me Karrnath's motives in the War were any more high-minded than that. There's no difference between you and me. Merely that you're hypocritical about it."

"Shut up!" Whitsun's voice cut through the argument like the crack of a whip. Delru and the high priest fell silent. Whitsun looked from one to the other. "What happens," he asked, "if I don't choose either one of you? What if I choose to keep the thing to myself?"

Delru spoke first. "You don't know the true power of these artifacts, Ulther. You don't know what they can do together."

The high priest chuckled. "You're a bit behind the times, Manilla. The ring, at least, is no longer of importance. Look at what our friend is holding."

Delru stared at the object Whitsun clutched. Her face turned white. "What . . . is that?" she whispered.

"The power of the ring has passed into the hand of the one to whom it imprinted itself," said the priest. "It's exactly as the ancient tablets in Xen'drik predicted. The ring is no more. A new stage has begun."

Delru shook her head as if to clear it. "It doesn't matter," she said. "The ring belonged to the Karrnath. If the power of the ring has passed into that . . . that . . ." She didn't finished the phrase. "It too belongs to Karrnath."

Hallah's face grew red with rage. His voice rose in timbre. "To Karrnath? To *Karrnath?* I am the one who suffered for the orerry.

I was the one who climbed through the jungles of Xen'drik to claim it. I was the one who starved for weeks, who fought snakes and scorpions. I was the one who killed for it. It belongs to *me* and no one else."

He lifted his hand. One of the mages by Delru's side shouted a word. Fire sprang from his hand, bent, shimmered, and exploded in his face. The remains of his head were torn from his shoulders and thudded against the wall as his body slowly collapsed. The other dark-robed mage began to move both hands in an incantation. Delru grabbed his arms and pulled them down to his side.

"No magic!" she screamed. "You idiot! That *thing*"—pointing to Whitsun's former left hand—"will tear and twist it. No magic unless you want to die."

Hallah had seen in the diversion his opportunity. For one heavy of build he was remarkably swift. A knife glittered in his upraised hand as he took a long stride forward and slashed down.

The mage dodged out of the way, and the blade tore a long cut in his robe. But in escaping the blow, he stumbled and slipped on the floor. The high priest's knife rose and plunged into his neck. The mage wailed, a sound cut off suddenly as the priest jerked the knife, cutting the man's vocal chords and throat. A spout of blood came from the mage as he fell, wriggling, on the floor.

Delru moved behind the priest. Her fingers held two metal rods, between which was strung a fine wire. She threw the garrote around the priest's neck and pulled. He gasped and choked. His hands reached up to claw in vain at his neck. His face darkened, and his eyes bulged. Delru pulled harder, never letting up the pressure.

The silence in the room was absolute save for the final choking of the high priest. His legs beat frantically against the floor.

His body slid to the ground to lie beside his victim, the mage. In death, it seemed somehow fatter and bulkier than it had in life. Delru bent and kept her garrote about his neck for a few moments more, then rose and pulled the wire free. She pushed the body with a shapely foot, plucked the ring from his dead grasp, and turned back to Whitsun and Glustred, who had watched without moving.

"Let us continue our talk. Things have changed, Ulther. Surely you can see that it would be best if you cast your fate with me. Karrnath can be very generous."

Whitsun stared at her, expressionless. "Go on."

"Freylaut is dead, but he was never much more than muscle. I prefer to run with those who show a certain finesse in their work. You and I could be partners, Ulther. We could be a great team." She moved closer.

He held up the hand. "Stop! Stay where you are! I can hear you from there."

"Ulther." Her voice was softer. "I know you think I'm doing this only to get the power you now have in that hand, but there's more to it than that. I've watched you. I've spoken to you. And I like you. I don't know why or how, but I feel safer with you by my side than ever I did with Freylaut." She turned to the recumbent body of the high priest.

"This man and his followers would have brought terror and misery to all Khorvaire. Now I am destroying the last remnants of them." She gestured to the door through which the sounds of battle were steadily diminishing. "Yet there are others who think as he did, who would impose their rule and their power upon Khorvaire to the misery of its people."

"Are you telling me," Whitsun said, "that Karrnath really cares about some little group of fanatics trying to take over Sharn?"

"No. I would be dishonest if I said that. But you must believe me, Ulther, when I tell you that *I* care about that."

Whitsun spoke to Glustred, keeping his eyes on Delru. "Go out there," he said, "and find out what's going on. It sounds as if things are quieting down. Don't start anything and don't get into any fights."

Glustred seemed unhappy at the prospect. "What about you?"

"I'll be fine."

"I mean, why can't you come with me?"

"The lady and I need to finish our business. Really, Glustred, I don't need to hold your hand all the time. Just do what you're told and let the grown-ups finish in private."

Glustred gave him a savage look, picked up the knife from the dead priest, and went out. He was careful never to get between Delru and Whitsun.

Whitsun eased into a chair. His face was pale and bloodless, and the bandage around his left wrist was soaked with crimson, but his voice was strong.

"Why should I join you? I have the hand." His mouth twitched slightly in disgust as he said it. "You have a useless ring—"

"Not useless!" She shook her head, and the red strands shifted across her shoulders in a shimmering wave. "Merely different from what it was before. This fool—" nodding at the dead body of the high priest—"imagined in his petty schemes that he could control everything without the Chosen Ones on whom the artifacts have imprinted. But the Orerry of Tal Esk must be together and must be held by the right people for the artifact to work fully. Now the ring has delivered a great part of its power into your . . . hand, but, I suspect, not everything. I can use the ring to find the rest of the orerry, wherever Hallah hid it." She smiled. "You see, Ulther, alone you cannot win. I have the ring, and I can find the remainder of the orerry. Once I find it, I will find out upon whom it was imprinted. And then, even without your hand, I shall gain great power. Enough for me to find you and take from you that which belongs to me."

"And together?" Whitsun's voice was very quiet.

"Together? Together! Ah!" Her eyes sparkled. "Together, who knows what we might do? We would have all the ancient power of the giants, perhaps, flowing through our fingertips. We could heal all the troubles of the world and could sail together the seas of immortality. In our hands, Ulther, would lie the fate of Eberron, and we could make of it what we choose. Imagine that!"

She reached out a hand to his face. Her blood-red nails gleamed in the light shed in the shattered room by the everbright lanterns.

Whitsun's brows drew together in a supreme effort of concentration. He clutched the hand, which had already begun to wither in his grasp. Blood rushed to his face, and he gasped with the sudden effort.

Delru cried out in pain and dropped the ring. Smoke rose from it, and it glowed a rosy red. The engraved pictographs shimmered in the light, flashed, and vanished. There was a prolonged hiss, as of hot irons plunged into cold water.

A dark spot on the marble floor showed where the ring had been.

Delru stared at it. Sweat beaded on her forehead. "What have you done?" she screamed. "What have you done?"

Whitsun's voice was tired. "Ended this nonsense." He stood up, still holding his left hand. "I'm not interested in grand schemes for remaking the world, Delru. I don't care enough about it to want to save it. All I want is to go through it earning a living and surviving. Most people don't want any more than that."

The red-haired woman stared at him. A knife appeared in her hand.

"Give me that!" she snarled, pointing to the left hand Whitsun held. "Give me that or you die!"

"Help yourself."

Whitsun tossed it at her. She shrank back, but not in time to avoid it. It struck her face in a horrid parody of a slap. She screamed once. The hand fell to the floor.

Nothing happened.

Delru stood poised, staring at it, one hand clutching her throat, the other holding the knife. Slowly she lifted her eyes to stare at Whitsun.

"What have you done?"

Whitsun moved forward and picked up the hand again and examined it. "The power's gone," he told her. "I don't know if I used it up destroying the ring or if when the ring's destroyed the power goes with it. But it's gone. I felt it leave when the ring melted."

Delru sank to her knees and bent her head, weeping. "I cannot go back!" she wailed. "I cannot go back now. I have failed. There is nothing back in Karrnath for me but death." She looked up at Whitsun. "Ulther, please! Let me stay here with you! Please! I beg of you! Together we can find the rest of the orerry. We can make a bargain with Karrnath. Something!"

There was a tramp of booted feet in the corridor outside, and Glustred came through, followed by a troop of the Watch. He said briefly to Whitsun, "They're all dead—all of *his* people." He motioned with his head to the body of the high priest. "Most of the Karrns, too. I think it was a tougher fight than they expected. The Watch have the rest in custody." He looked at Whitsun with something almost approaching admiration. "That was a neat trick—getting out of the way and letting the

Karrns and these people fight it out and destroy each other. I have to remember that one."

Delru moaned, a low animal sound. Tears spilled between the fingers pressed against her eyes.

Glustred spoke in a lower tone to Whitsun. "When they saw which way the fight was going, the Watch decided to change sides and be neutral. At least that's what it looks like to me."

The Watch Captain looked coldly at Whitsun. "Ulther Whitsun, I arrest you—"

"Yes, yes, of course you do!" Whitsun nodded toward Delru. "She's an agent of Karrnath. Better contact someone higher up in the city. They're going to want to arrange a transfer for her back home."

Delru's lips parted. "Ulther," she whispered, "Karrnath does not tolerate failure by its agents."

Whitsun said nothing as the Watch closed around her.

Glustred rapped on the door and waited for the voice on the other side. When it didn't come, he pushed open the door anyway.

Upon his release by the Watch, the innkeeper had made his way back to Firelight and to the brothel run by Thavash. Whitsun seemed to have managed to send some sort of message to the halfling, for Glustred was given shelter and food. His companion appeared two days later in battered condition, having struck some sort of bargain with the halfling thieves who ran the establishment. Whatever the case, they had been well cared for.

Whitsun was seated by the window in a low chair, resting his head on his hand. The window was open, and outside the rain was falling. Water dripped onto the windowsill from a ledge above. It bathed the building's stones in spray that reflected the light from a few stray shafts of sunlight that made their way down to the depths from the sky far above.

"What's doing?" the innkeeper asked.

Whitsun turned toward him. His face was bruised, and there was a half-healed cut along his forehead. Glustred inspected him and announced, "You look terrible."

Whitsun grunted. "The Watch doesn't like people running away from them. They like it even less when their quarry escapes, even if temporarily. They exacted a price for their humiliation, that's all."

"But you showed them what was really going on?"

"As much as they need to know. When they'd had their fun, they let me go."

Glustred dropped into a chair facing Whitsun. "What *did* happen?"

His companion sighed and leaned forward. "Right now there are a lot of people throughout Khorvaire who aren't satisfied with the results of the War. People who think they can fix things. Who think they have a better plan, one that will avoid future wars. Some want to retreat from the world. Others want to expand and dominate it. Our late friend, the high priest, was one of those. He'd gathered a group of followers—I don't know exactly how many, but the Watch seem to think it was about 150—and was breeding his little group in silence."

"Is he really the person who found the artifacts in Xen'drik?"

"I suppose so. The records are none too clear, but it looks like he came here from Karrnath about a year ago, shortly after the end of the War. That would fit in with his story. He really was a priest of the Order of the Silver Flame, given leave by the church in Karrnath to go on this expedition. When he came here, he was able to take over one of their churches. The members of the Order who didn't fall in with his plans were driven out or murdered."

"And then Delru showed up."

"And then Delru showed up," Whitsun said. "From his point of view, that was where everything started to go wrong. They stole the artifacts from the temple, where he was keeping them until he could figure out whom they would imprint on. He sent Maresun after her and Freylaut to steal the things back. But Maresun, as we saw, got greedy in the interests of his girlfriend and tried to sell the artifacts. I think he must have been told to keep them separate. We may never know why he didn't carry them together. In any case, when Hallah saw he was selling one of the things he'd been hired to steal, the high priest assigned one of the church members to take care of things. Maresun made a run, still carrying the ring. He made it as far as me."

"Why you?" Glustred asked.

"Again, I suppose we'll never know. Maresun and I crossed paths a few times. Maybe he thought I'd be able to help him. Maybe he thought I could protect him. Perhaps even the ring itself had something to do with his choice of me. Who knows? Our old friend Scarface got to him before he made it."

"But he got there in time to give you the ring."

"Yes. And the ring imprinted on me. From the high priest's point of view, that made me both valuable and a threat, and he wasn't sure how to reconcile those two things—whether to kill me or keep me." Whitsun stretched. "I owe my life to that hesitation. Even when he'd arranged for the Watch to chase us in the general direction of the temple so he could capture me, he still wasn't quite sure how much power I had. He just knew he couldn't use magic on me, and he wanted to keep me alive until he could discover what would happen if I died. I was lucky, I suppose. I had a little room to maneuver, and I got a message to Delru telling her where the ring was. I gambled that she was desperate enough at that point—with Hallah having both me and the ring—to get her agents together and try a frontal assault."

"You'd think," Glustred said after a short silence, "that the Watch would have been grateful to you. If nothing else, you pulled a group of Karrn agents into the open and got them nicely killed off."

"The Watch, or at least the officers, were being paid off by Hallah. They're none too happy with that source of funds drying up. Now they'll have to find someone else to blackmail."

Glustred looked at the fresh bandage around Whitsun's left wrist. "What are you going to do about that?"

Whitsun held out the stump, considering it. "I could get someone to try a regeneration spell on it, I suppose. That's horribly expensive, but it might work. But there are reasons not to."

"Like what?"

Whitsun bent and unwrapped a cloth at his feet. Glustred stared, revolted. "You're *keeping* that?" he asked. "Why? You told me all the power went out of it when you destroyed the ring."

"That's what I told you," Whitsun said. "Of course, at the time there were a lot of watchful ears about."

"You mean it still has power?" Glustred moved back from it hastily.

"I don't know. Perhaps a different kind of power. Perhaps no power. I'm not sure. There's something there. But I don't think growing another hand would help to find out. For right now, I'm content to be right-handed."

"And the orerry? I mean the other two pieces—the gold sphere and the silver ring?"

Whitsun shook his head. "No sign of them. I went to the temple after I got free of the Watch and made a pretty thorough search of it. Either Hallah hid them effectively or someone else took them. They aren't there. They'll probably turn up sooner or later in the wrong hands. But that's somebody else's problem."

Glustred stood up. Whitsun looked at him in some surprise. "Where are you going?"

"I've been talking with our hosts. There's a tavern a few streets down in need of a proprietor."

Whitsun managed a faint grin. "What happened to the last one?"

"He had an argument with Thavash and walked into a knife. I'm taking his place."

"You want to turn over half your takings to the gang here?"

"Not any worse than the last place." He looked around with a sloppy grin. A few scantily clad women sauntered by the door, hips playing sweet music. "And the scenery's better."

"Hmph!" Whitsun turned away. "Well, at least you know when to keep your mouth shut—usually."

Glustred headed for the door then stopped.

"By the way, what happened to your red-haired friend?"

"The Watch turned her over to someone higher up. She'll be sent back to Karrnath."

"She'll be killed there, won't she?"

Whitsun shrugged. If he felt any emotion at the topic, he gave no sign of it. Glustred watched him for a moment, then echoed his shrug and went out. A while later his voice filtered through the speaking tube. "Visitor. On the way."

The knock on the door was followed by Soonam Mirkor. As usual, the councillor carried with him an air of gravity that seemed to stir the room's stale air. Whitsun rose and gestured to the other chair.

"Councillor."

"Whitsun."

Mirkor sat in silence for a few minutes. Whitsun did not

appear anxious to begin the conversation. At last the councillor observed, "One hears things."

"Does one?"

"One hears rumors, stories . . . nothing definite of course. But one has heard a disturbing story about your involvement with a church. A very powerful church. Even with a government."

Whitsun said nothing.

"One hopes—" Mirkor refused to look at Whitsun and instead addressed his remarks to the far wall of the chamber—"one hopes you were discreet in all your dealings with the authorities."

Whitsun snorted in amusement. "Oh, yes. That was my big goal, Mirkor, to keep the name of House Vadalis clean and out of the eye of the Watch."

There was another silence. Finally Mirkor observed, "It would be most unfortunate if you were not discreet. One could not answer for your safety in the upper city, were that the case."

"Well, you needn't worry. What happened had nothing to do with your House or the piece of business we transacted. Speaking of which, you still owe me money."

"You still owe one papers."

Whitsun reached into a drawer of the table between them and took out a small roll of parchment. Mirkor reached for it, but Whitsun drew it out of his reach.

"Money first."

Mirkor drew forth a small sack that jingled when he placed it on the table. He kept a hand on it.

"Together."

Whitsun put the parchment on the table by the sack. Simultaneously each man transferred his hand to the other's offering. Mirkor glanced at the parchment and appeared satisfied. Whitsun opened the sack, gazed quickly at its contents, and stowed it in a pocket.

Mirkor rose. At the door, he turned. "One should not think many commissions will come your way from the houses of the dragonmarked," he observed. "At least, not for some time. Those from the upper city prefer their tasks to be carried out by someone less notorious."

Whitsun glowered at him as he went out, shutting the door quietly behind him. He was replaced a time later by Thavash. The halfling leader, accompanied by two of his bodyguards, sat down opposite Whitsun.

"You owe."

"What?"

"For Soorlah and Chemsh. You owe me."

"Oh, don't be an idiot, Thavash. Chemsh's death couldn't be helped, and Soorlah was a traitor. I told you all about that." Whitsun closed his eyes.

Thavash glared at him. "You want I should cut off your other hand?"

Whitsun pulled out his left hand, now withered and leathery, from its trappings. The fingers had bent inward, making it look like a claw. "You want to find out if this has magic left in it?"

Thavash sprang up and retreated hastily against the door. His bodyguards looked as if they were trying to go through the wall.

"No need to be hastylike!"

Whitsun grinned. "No need at all." He replaced the mummified hand in its wrappings and looked around. "I need a place to stay for a bit. I think this'll suit me."

"You gotta pay rent!"

"Ten galifars a month."

"Hundred."

"Fifty."

"Seventy."

"Done."

Thavash started to hold out a hand to shake then thought better of it. "Very well, then." He and his cronies went out.

Whitsun leaned back in his chair. His right hand drifted to his side while he cradled the stump of his left across his chest. His eyes closed, and his lips moved soundlessly.

There was a scrabbling sound. The cloth bundle on the floor quivered. From the middle of it, three clawlike fingers poked out. The hand moved slowly across the floor, pulling itself along. Whitsun watched it, brow wrinkled in concentration. He whispered a word of command and it returned to its bed.

Whitsun's lips curved in a small smile.

During the Last War, Gaven was an
adventurer, searching the darkest reaches
of the underworld. But an encounter with
a powerful artifact forever changed him,
breaking his mind and landing him in the
deepest cell of the darkest prison in
all the world.

THE DRACONIC PROPHECIES

BOOK I

When war looms on the horizon, some see it as more
than renewed hostilities between nations. Some see the
fulfillment of an ancient prophecy—one that promises
both the doom and salvation of the world. And Gaven may
be the key to it all.

THE STORM DRAGON

The first EBERRON® hardcover by veteran game designer
and the author of *In the Claws of the Tiger*:

James Wyatt

SEPTEMBER 2007

RaVenLoft
the covenant

RAVENLOFT'S LORDS OF DARKNESS HAVE ALWAYS WAITED FOR THE UNWARY TO FIND THEM.

Six classic tales of horror set in the RAVENLOFT™ world have returned to print in all-new editions.

From the autocratic vampire who wrote the memoirs found in *I, Strahd* to the demon lord and his son whose story is told in *Tapestry of Dark Souls*, some of the finest horror characters created by some of the most influential authors of horror and dark fantasy have found their way to RAVENLOFT, to be trapped there forever.

LaureLL K. HamiLton
Death of a Darklord

CHristie GoLDen
Vampire of the Mists

P.N. eLrod
I, Strahd: The Memoirs of a Vampire

andria cardareLLe
To Sleep With Evil

eLaine BerGstrom
Tapestry of Dark Souls

tanya Huff
Scholar of Decay

October 2007

JEAN RABE

THE STONETELLERS

"Jean Rabe is adept at weaving a web of deceit and lies, mixed with adventure, magic, and mystery."
—sffworld.com on *Betrayal*

Jean Rabe returns to the DRAGONLANCE® world with a tale of slavery, rebellion, and the struggle for freedom.

VOLUME ONE
THE REBELLION

After decades of service, nature has dealt the goblins a stroke of luck. Earthquakes strike the Dark Knights' camp and mines, crippling the Knights and giving the goblins their best chance to escape. But their freedom will not be easy to win.

August 2007

VOLUME TWO
DEATH MARCH

The escaped slaves—led by the hobgoblin Direfang—embark on a journey fraught with danger as they leave Neraka to cross the ocean and enter the Qualinesti Forest, where they believe themselves free. . . .

August 2008

VOLUME THREE
GOBLIN NATION

A goblin nation rises in the old forest, building fortresses and fighting to hold onto their new homeland, while the sorcerers among them search for powerful magic cradled far beneath the trees.

August 2009

A World of Adventure Awaits

The FORGOTTEN REALMS® world is the biggest, most detailed, most vibrant, and most beloved of the DUNGEONS & DRAGONS® campaign settings. Created by best-selling fantasy author Ed Greenwood the FORGOTTEN REALMS setting has grown in almost unimaginable ways since the first line was drawn on the now infamous "Ed's Original Maps."

Still the home of many a group of DUNGEONS & DRAGONS players, the FORGOTTEN REALMS world is brought to life in dozens of novels, including hugely popular best sellers by some of the fantasy genre's most exciting authors. FORGOTTEN REALMS novels are fast, furious, action-packed adventure stories in the grand tradition of sword and sorcery fantasy, but that doesn't mean they're all flash and no substance. There's always something to learn and explore in this richly textured world.

To find out more about the Realms go to www.wizards.com and follow the links from Books to FORGOTTEN REALMS. There you'll find a detailed reader's guide that will tell you where to start if you've never read a FORGOTTEN REALMS novel before, or where to go next if you're a long-time fan!

FORGOTTEN REALMS

THE KNIGHTS OF MYTH DRANNOR

A brand new trilogy by master storyteller

ED GREENWOOD

Join the creator of the FORGOTTEN REALMS® world as he explores
the early adventures of his original and most celebrated
characters from the moment they earn the name "Swords of
Eveningstar" to the day they prove themselves worthy of it.

BOOK I
SWORDS OF EVENINGSTAR

Florin Falconhand has always dreamed of adventure. When he saves the life of
the king of Cormyr, his dream comes true and he earns an adventuring charter for
himself and his friends. Unfortunately for Florin, he has also earned the enmity of
several nobles and the attention of some of Cormyr's most dangerous denizens.
Now available in paperback!

BOOK II
SWORDS OF DRAGONFIRE

Victory never comes without sacrifice. Florin Falconhand and the Swords of
Eveningstar have lost friends in their adventures, but in true heroic fashion, they
press on. Unfortunately, there are those who would see the Swords of Eveningstar
pay for lives lost and damage wrecked, regardless of where the true blame lies.

August 2007

BOOK III
THE SWORD NEVER SLEEPS

Fame has found the Swords of Eveningstar, but with fame comes danger. Nefarious
forces have dark designs on these adventurers who seem to overturn the most clever
of plots. And if the Swords will not be made into their tools, they will be destroyed.

August 2008